CW00428313

DARK AS ANGELS

WE ARE THE ENEMY

DOMINIC ADLER

This is a work of fiction. Names, characters, places, and incidents either are the product of the author's imagination or are used fictitiously. Any resemblance to actual persons, living or dead, events, or locales is entirely coincidental.

Copyright © Dominic Adler 2018

All rights reserved. No part of this book may be reproduced or used in any manner without written permission of the copyright owner except for the use of quotations in a book review.

First Edition published in 2018 by Ambuscade Books

Cover design by BespokeBookCovers.com
Typesetting by Ryan Ashcroft

www.dominicadler.net

All rights reserved

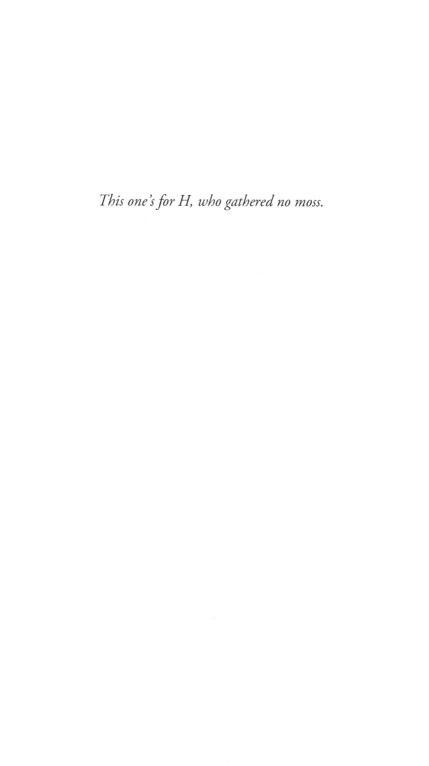

This one's for H, who gathered no moss.

Barbarianism is the natural state of mankind. Civilization is unnatural. It is the whim of circumstance. And barbarianism must ultimately triumph.

\-   Robert E. Howard

In this epoch of cyborgs, hybrids, mutants, chimeras and virtual reality, mankind will only be saved by tradition.

\-   Alexsandr Dugin
    (21st Century Russian ultranationalist)

Archangel(s)
(Disambiguation) (Colloquialism)

One who has undergone a Rudenko-Xiaoping Procedure (RXP) or variant thereof (a Transhuman with genetically-augmented physical and cognitive ability);

and / or (*plural*)

Clique of Transhuman fascists, also known as the *December 13ᵗʰ Group*. Warmongers responsible for the (failed) coup d'état to form a World Government, heralds of The Emergencies.

ONE

The Reconciliation Tribunal had only one window – a wall of armorglass, overlooking a ruined city. The Judge cleared her throat, scratching notes with a gold fountain pen. "Next case?"

Clerk of the Court, funereal in black, bowed. "Yes, Milady. Case 137 of Tranche 11. We adjourned last week. The accused was… unwell."

The Judge glanced at the clock. An hour until lunch. "Quite. Are we ready for closing speeches?"

"Yes, Milady."

Counsel to the Tribunal, bewigged and gowned, stood. "With regards to case 137, My Lady, you will recall the Accused was a low-ranking police auxiliary."

The Defence jumped to her feet. "My Lady, please. He was a sworn Taskforcer. The prosecution uses the term *auxiliary* in a deliberately pejorative manner."

"I'm well aware of the distinction," the Judge replied. "Sit down, Miss Hope."

Counsel nodded his thanks. "The Accused, whatever his status, authorised the deployment of anti-armour rockets on a marketplace crowded with civilians. His intended targets were two UK nationals, Evelyn and Christian Moran. The Crown submits the Morans died for no other reason than their decision to undergo Rudenko-Xiaoping therapy. RXP was, and indeed remains, controversial. But it was not *illegal* at that time. Indeed, it was a proven treatment for many hitherto fatal illnesses.

"Not only were the Morans executed, but an estimated thirty non-combatants lost their lives. In his after-action report, the Accused describes this as *collateral damage, consistent with operational exigencies*. His defence, such as it is, relies on the Morans alleged status as near-invulnerable terrorists."

"Anything else?" said the Judge, eyes on her ledger.

"Indeed, My Lady. We suggest the Morans murder…"

Defence counsel cocked her head. "Do you mean *alleged* Murder?"

"You're both trying my patience," said the Judge.

"Apologies," Counsel smiled. "The Morans *deaths* add weight to allegations that extra-judicial execution of transhumans was a de facto policy during the Emergencies – covertly agreed and targeted by deep-state operators. We've witnessed many examples of such egregious uses of force during these proceedings. I submit a pattern has emerged, strongly suggestive of collusion." Counsel shuffled his papers and sat down.

"Thank you, Mister Lyons," the Judge replied. "Counsel for the Defence?"

The Defence barrister was young, her gown too big. "The *Accused* has a name, Milady – Mister Rufus Duarte Hooker. We've heard how Mister Hooker, who previously served with the army in North Africa, was a squad leader on Police Taskforce 17. On the day of the Morans death, he was in his fifteenth consecutive month of combat duty. The casualty rate across his unit was, at times, sixty-five percent."

The judge pointed at the ruins across the Thames. They once called it Canary Wharf, now a henge of boneyard rubble. "I'm sure it was. Miss Hope are you summing up or offering mitigation?"

"My Lady, I'm merely providing context."

"Context duly noted. Please proceed, Miss Hope."

"We've seen copies of Security Service reports identifying Evelyn and Christian Moran as Archangels. High-value terrorist targets believed to be fleeing to St. Petersburg to join their co-conspirators. Need I remind the Tribunal, the Archangels were architects of the Hate War. The devastation we see from this place is *their* legacy, not Mister Hooker's. Nor, for that matter, any of the other Taskforcers who've found themselves in that dock."

"This is a polemic, Miss Hope, not a defence," the Judge sighed. "You've been warned before."

Hope glowered at Counsel for the Tribunal. "Perhaps, My Lady, as is my learned friend's assertion concerning state-sanctioned murder. Mister Hooker acted on the circumstances as he found them, not via shadowy instructions from above. He has never sought to hide behind any sort of Nuremberg defence. The real reason, that of lawful use of force, is less sensational perhaps…"

"I think I see where you're heading, Miss Hope," the Judge warned. "My advice is *don't*."

Hope curled her lip. "The thrust of the allegations against volunteers like Mister Hooker are a political ruse, and this Tribunal's conduct does nothing to waylay criticism of these proceedings as an exercise in hindsight and, *in extremis*, an attempt to rehabilitate the Archangels. Revisionism concerning the role of Transhumans during the Emergencies may be…"

The Judge's gavel cracked, gunshot loud. The Accused flinched. "Ms. Hope, confine yourself to *evidence.* Not a meta-commentary on politics or, indeed, my Tribunal."

Hope bowed her head. "Of course, My Lady. May I move to the medical reports?"

"As long as you confine yourself to *evidence*, you may."

"The Morans had previously travelled to Russia, to undertake Type Nine RXP therapy. This was an experimental, military-grade augmentation, bestowing extreme physical and cognitive ability. Crucially, it was prohibited for civilian use by international treaty. This belies the Tribunal's assertion the Morans RXP transition to Archangels was for *health* reasons."

"I must object," said Counsel to the Tribunal. "This information is…"

The Judge held up a finger. "You've had your say, Mister Lyons. Let Miss Hope finish."

The Defence nodded. "Thanks to their augmentation, the Morans were superhuman combatants, suffering from the psychiatric side-effects attributed to RXP – Psychopathy.

Sociopathy. Paranoid schizophrenia. As for the tragic events described to the Tribunal, Mister Hooker ordered escalation of force protocols as per his Rules of Engagement. His decision to deploy his unit's rocket system was unfortunate, but *not* disproportionate…"

Counsel for the Tribunal scowled. He whispered to his juniors, tapping notes into a pad. One sniggered. "Thank you, Ms. Hope," said the Judge.

"My Lady, I've yet to finish."

"I'm sure we've heard the gist of it. Before I rise to consider my verdict, does the Accused have anything to add?"

Rufus Hooker stood, head-bowed, mumbling to himself. He was a big man, brawny and dark-skinned, handcuffs glinting at his wrists. He glanced at the Judge with eyes the colour of amber and shrugged. The Judge leant forward. "Mister Hooker? It's your right to offer a few words."

Hooker's fingers gripped the dock. The Judge couldn't know he was on The Estuary, Eddie Webber's corpse bobbing in the Thames. She didn't see the muddy riverbank, carrion birds skirling across coffin-black clouds. Dark towers, like war-scorched titans, loomed from brackish lagoons. The Judge motioned to an usher. "Is the accused unwell again?"

Hooker felt something wet on his chin. Drool or blood. Here or there. Then or now. *350 milligrams every morning, Rufus.* The tactical net squawked contact reports, red-and-green tracer spattering his position. Taskforcers lay in whatever cover they could, weighed down with weapons and equipment. *Kilo One-Seven? They're in the market east of the prison, over.*

Hooker's ears rang, balls shrinking into his body. He

keyed the mic, fingers trembling. "This is Kilo One-Seven Actual. Any call-signs with eyes-on target?"

"One-Seven Actual from One-Nine. They're in a bunker. Marketplace – green aspect. The bastards are fast. Really fast."

Archangels.

Hooker scaled the riverbank, fingers bleeding and raw. He saw the sand-bagged bunker, muzzle flash blossoming from a pillbox. The defences lay on the market's perimeter, built to protect the locals from bandits. "This is One-Seven Actual. Can anyone get over there with a demo charge?"

"Hooker, this is Keegan," replied a gravelly voice. "The female target killed the whole of Blue Team with her bare hands. They had our demo kit. I say Gustaf the target now."

"Negative, too many civilians on the plot," Hooker replied. "Jonas, we got air support?"

"No air on the grid." A woman's voice, matter-of-fact. "Male target leaving bunker now, white aspect. He's got Blue Team's demo pack. Hit him twice – he's moving like nothin' happened. No contact with Grey Team."

Hooker began running towards the marketplace. Lungs burning, armour rubbing like sandpaper. A bullet glanced off his breastplate, hurling him into a tangle of barbed wire.

"Keegan's dead!" shrieked a voice.

"This is Kilo Two-Zero. Red Team down. We're withdrawing to…"

An explosion mushroomed overhead, making Hooker's ears pop as debris pitter-pattered into the river. Razor wire bit into flesh, as if trying to drag him beneath the water. "One-Seven, receiving?" he gasped. "I'm trapped in the wire, riverside market approach."

"I see you, Hooker," said a gravelly voice, London-rough. "Proper fuck-up, ain't it? Superman down there must be laughin.' He's throwin' C4 like fireworks."

"You got the Gustaf, Jase?" Hooker replied.

"Roger that. HE round in the pipe. Ready to go."

"One-Seven, *do it*," Hooker ordered. "Engage with the Gustaf."

"Roger that." A rocket fire-balled into the marketplace, a spray of rubble and body parts spuming skywards. "Archangel down!"

"This is Two-Zero. Female target down on the red aspect. No legs, but the bitch is still alive. She's got Blue Team's machinegun…"

"I can take her with another rocket."

Tearing himself free of the wire, Hooker stumbled towards the market, blood trickling from slash wounds in his legs. The bunker was gone, replaced by a smoking crater, debris falling like fiery confetti. Stalls and shacks smashed like matchwood, charred bodies scattered like dummies. He bawled into his throat mic, tongue thick in his mouth. "Ceasefire! I repeat, ceasefire."

"Fuck this," said One-Seven. "I've got eyes-on the female target. She's got a weapon. Rocket two downrange…"

"I SAID CEASEFIRE." The Gustaf roared, the warhead glancing off concrete, skittering like a smouldering comet. "Ceasefire," Hooker croaked, "Cease…"

"Man, that was *so* fucking Taskforce 17!" said Hughes, Black Team's support gunner. He died a month later, shot by a sniper near Erith. Or was that Baptiste?

"One-Three, we've got multiple civilian casualties," said Two-Zero. "We need medics. Now."

"*Mister Hooker?*" said the Judge. To Hooker's mind, it was just another voice over the radio. "*This is your opportunity to…*"

Hooker snapped to attention, thumb pressed against forefinger along the seam of his trousers. Just like they'd taught him at the depot. "I'm guilty, Your Honour. Lock me up and throw away the key."

TWO

Twelve years later.

Dogs lay in fly-blown shadows, fangs bared. Hooker growled, and they loped away, Leah's voice hissing through his earpiece. "The guard's at the food shack, on the junction with Mare Street. Bushmeat with chilli sauce."

"Rifle optics that good?"

"Yeah."

"Got a clear shot?"

Leah chuckled. She liked sniping. "I can see the small print on the chilli bottle."

"Okay. Tell your man to do this thing." Hooker pulled a coppery tube from his pocket, a mezuzah. The prayer case was pitted and scarred, rimed with verdigris. A grateful rabbi had given it to him a lifetime ago, in the ruins of a synagogue in Spitalfields. They'd all gone now, the Jews, wary of hate and archangels. They knew better than most how this game ended. They packed up and left, to Israel and the Sky-Shield.

Inside the mezuzah was a tightly rolled photograph, waxy and blood-stained. Once upon a time it would have contained a prayer, but Hooker had no need of those. He studied the image, edges blistered and burnt. A little girl, hair in cornrows. Denim dungarees, stained with ice-cream from the aquarium. Pink training shoes, with a tiny Nike swoosh. Beatriz hadn't cried when the Tribunal investigators came for him. Sara told her it was just some men from work. They want to ask daddy a few questions.

Leah's voice was sharp. "My man's flicked the switch. Move it."

Hooker slid the photograph back inside the mezuzah. Checking his wristwatch, he counted slowly under his breath. The target was a ramshackle bar, rotting concrete draped with sun-frazzled vines. Snapping goggles over his eyes, Hooker hammered on the door with a fist. "Eduardo, you in there? It's Rufus."

The voice was deep. "You're early, Hooker. I don't like early."

"Better'n being late, ain't it?"

The rusty metal door swung open, revealing a golem of a man. Bare-chested and muscle-bound, a metal-studded club hanging from his belt. "You know the score – dump your tools," he ordered.

"Well, a cheery good mornin' to you too, Eduardo," Hooker replied, unbuttoning his leather coat. He put his revolver and fighting knife in a metal box and smiled.

Eduardo peered up and down Mare street. Nothing but boarded-up shops and freight container housing. Tumbleweed rolled towards the old Hackney Empire. "Quiet today, ain't it?"

Hooker tapped the dosimeter clipped to his collar. "Cancer weather – you can smell it on the wind. Burns your nose."

Eduardo motioned Hooker to come inside. "Best you step in, but I'm gonna search you again. House rules."

Hooker shrugged. "Your house, your rules."

The giant frisked him, forcing meaty hands into Hooker's armpits, groin and the small of his back. "Comms?" he said, finding the radio in his pocket.

"So what? Never killed a man with a radio," Hooker lied. He'd once dashed a man's brains out with a broken Motorola. Dartford. 2nd Cliffe Woods offensive.

Eduardo raised an eyebrow. "No fob?"

"You said no fobs."

"Good," Eduardo sniffed. "Just make sure the radio's turned off. Boss gets touchy 'bout electrics an' shit like that."

"It's done," Hooker replied, making a show of switching off the handset. He followed Eduardo into a dingy barroom. A cracked mirror ran the length of the counter, a list of services written in lipstick. Blow jobs and vanilla, gang-bangs and anal. Want it rough? That's fifty dollars extra. Want to MAX the ROUGH...?

Sex-workers sat on stools, watching music videos on a flickering omni. Ragged and shackled, chains snaking across a beer-sticky floor. "Who have you come for today?" said a skinny African girl.

"Shut your mouth, 'fore I give you a taste of this," Eduardo growled, tapping the cosh at his belt.

"Beating kids? Shit like that comes back to haunt you," said Hooker. Quietly. Maybe meant to be heard, maybe not.

Eduardo's piggy eyes narrowed. "What the fuck d'you say?"

Hooker shrugged. "I was thinking 'bout karma. Maybe bad things come back to haunt you. It can happen, you know."

Eduardo bristled. "You threatening me?"

"Threaten you, Eduardo?" said Hooker. "Why would I do that?"

Eduardo spat on the floor. "Save your do-gooder shit for the Red Cross, or the Answerers. I don't give a fuck what you think. You try running a shop."

The African girl muttered under her breath. Hooker shot her a not-now look and followed Eduardo. They passed a row of dank booths, filthy mattresses on the floor. The place smelt of cheap perfume, unwashed bodies and spilt seed. A broken sexbot lay in one of the cubicles, eyes fixed on the ceiling as if in surprise. Eduardo pointed down a flight of stairs, red light bleeding from under a door. "Go on down. The man's waitin' for you. Just remember, show some respect."

Hooker rolled his head, loosening neck muscles like a boxer entering the ring. A lithe figure stood in the blood-lit basement, surrounded by crates of stolen gear. Cigarettes and drinking water, instant coffee and toothpaste. Most were marked AID FROM THE UNITED STATES OF AMERICA. "A good mornin' to you, Chief Marku," said

Hooker.

Marku nodded, self-styled bandit king, pocket Mephisto of Old Hackney. The pimp wore a catsuit of black leather, hair an outrageous pompadour. He squinted at Hooker through the sights of an oversized pistol. "They say, Rufus, you were a pig during the Hate War."

Hooker was counting in his head. 62... 61... 60... "I was a Taskforcer. Ain't no secret, Marku."

"A Taskforcer?" Marku replied. "I heard about them. What sort of country puts its soldiers in prison for defending it?"

"This one," Hooker replied. "It's a funny old place."

The pimp's hair glistened with oil. "Then maybe you're a NatSec informer. They say you never really leave the pigs." Marku wrinkled his nose, "I must say, you've that stink."

Hooker smiled. Some of his teeth were yellow, and some where gold. More than a few were missing. "Really, Marku? Callin' a man a grass? That's fightin' talk where I come from. Did you ask me here to fight?"

Marku studied his pistol, too big for his spindly fingers. The weapon was a bulbous-barrelled Walther, extended magazine jutting from the grip. "Perhaps I did, Hooker. This is my turf, I do as I wish."

Hooker had lost his appetite for violence, but the scent of bad blood reminded him why he used to enjoy it. "Then fight or do businesses, Marku. You know what I'm here for. We agreed five-hundred RDs each."

Marku smiled. A man-with-a-gun smile. "Only a half-thou? I think not. Far too generous a price."

"No, you agreed on five-hundred," said Hooker. "A

deal's a deal. You've got a reputation to maintain."

"My reputation says seven-fifty RDs apiece. A new rate, but not unreasonable." Marku licked his top lip, eyes bright. Hooker noticed a film of white powder under the pimp's nose.

Eduardo pulled the club from his belt. "Pay up, Rufus. We know the Americans pay decent money for the meat." The giant stomped to the doorway, whispering to somebody at the top of the stairs in Babble.

Hooker spoke Babble just fine – just pretended he didn't. Timor! Marku's screwing Hooker over. Bring me a gun. Make sure you've got one too...

Marku pointed the gun at Hooker's chest. "Tell me, why do the Americans buy whores from you? Rotten meat? It's like buying corpses. Are you a necrophiliac?"

Hooker shrugged, Marku's features blurred mauve in his goggles. "The Americans at the Red Cross are Evangelical Christians. They believe in God and salvation."

"God? Now, that's funny," the pimp chuckled. His teeth were sheathed in a golden grid, studded with rubies and diamonds. "God turned his back on this world."

"Make you right, but I ain't interested in religion. Just business. They said you were a man of honour among the Clans. They were wrong."

"Watch your mouth," Marku hissed, chest puffed out. A leather-clad cockerel. "Remember, I am a Chieftain."

Hooker made a show of examining the basement, lip curled. "Really? A Chieftain? Of what? A shit-heap?"

Marku snarled, jabbing the pistol into Hooker's forehead. "Your mouth is too big."

Hooker grinned. "Do it, king-of-shit. Explain to your Over-Chief why you're four grand down this week, an' still with extra mouths to feed."

Four seconds…

Marku pushed the gun harder into Hooker's skull. Cold metal on hot skin. The pimp's finger wormed inside the trigger-guard. "You talk shit, Hooker…"

Three

Two…

Clunk.

The room turned black, lights dying. Hooker jinked left, goggles flickering to night vision. Marku's pistol flared white, bullets slicing the air next to Hooker's ear. The ex-Taskforcer balled his fist.

Snick.

The punch-blade in Hooker's glove was razor sharp, protruding from his knuckles like a monster's fang. He struck once, piercing the pimp's throat.

"Marku?" Eduardo's voice, booming in the darkness.

The lights flickered back on, bathing the room red. Marku lay dying, eyes bulging, blood pooling beneath his body. Hooker aimed the pimp's Walther at Eduardo. "Weren't his cleverest moment, was it?"

"What did you do to the lights?" asked Eduardo. He winced when he saw Marku's body. As if the dead pimp were a tricky plumbing problem, or a flat tyre.

"Who knows? Maybe it's magic," Hooker replied. The lights were Leah's idea – she bribed a maintenance engineer to kill the local grid. Or maybe she'd threatened the guy. You could never tell with Leah. "Do the right thing, Eduardo. Or I'll kill you."

The big man picked up the telephone. "Get the merchandise ready. Yes, now!"

A runty kid ushered a gaggle of youths downstairs. Four boys, four girls. They wore stained robes, eyes dark-ringed and arms track-marked. One was the crop-headed African girl who'd badmouthed Eduardo earlier. "My name is Hooker. I'm taking you someplace safe."

Runty kid was a mono-browed thug in a muscle vest. He wore gaudy jewellery, a pistol stuffed in his waistband. He saw Marku's body and scowled. "Să te ia dracu!"

"Don't do it," Hooker warned.

The kid went for his gun.

Hooker fired. The spent cartridge bounced on the floor, making a smoky pirouette. Runty kid lay dead, the top of his head missing. Several of the kids cowered, covered in gore. Eduardo clicked his fingers, as if a djinn might appear. "That was the Over-Chieftain's nephew. You have brought hell upon you, Hooker."

Hooker sucked on a tooth. "D'you want a war, Eduardo? Zone Clans versus PROTEX Companies? Echo-Seven is honour-pledged to me, and they're pledged to a dozen others. You'd get the shit kicked out of you."

The African girl suddenly grabbed the runty kid's pistol. Eduardo raised his club, but she shot him between the eyes. The giant fell to his knees, dead, but the girl kept firing. When the magazine was empty, Hooker prised the weapon from her fingers. "What's your name, girl?"

"Mercy."

From outside came the whip-crack of rifle shots. Mercy ducked behind Hooker. "It's okay," he said. "The shooter's with me. She's taking out the guards."

Leah checked in, voice crackling in Hooker's ear. "Okay, they're down. Where d'you want me?"

"Front door," Hooker replied, stowing Marku's pistol in his pocket. Heading upstairs, he retrieved his weapons and herded the kids outside.

An armoured truck rumbled around the corner, a six-wheeler shrouded in oily smoke. Leah's fingers rested on the steering wheel, face hidden behind a hockey mask. "Get in," she ordered. "There'll be an army of these goat-fuckers here any minute."

"You bet there will," Hooker replied, jerking a thumb at the girl. "Meet Mercy, who just slotted Eduardo of the Pogradec Titans. I did for Marku and one of his boys. Over-Chieftain's nephew, apparently."

Leah shrugged. "Did he try to skank you?"

Hooker nodded.

Leah revved the truck. "They never learn."

They motored along the PROTEX, the protected expressway that soared over the No-Zone. Leah wove through a convoy of lend-lease American plant, the armoured truck belching smoke. The Americans, displaced NordAnglos from the Secession states, swore and shook their fists. A PROTEX guard, sprawled in the back of a gun-heavy technical, recognised Leah and waved. "Where are you taking us?" said Mercy suspiciously. "Another shop?"

Hooker shook his head. "You'll go to the Red Cross station at Essford."

Mercy's lip curled. "Red Cross? Americans? What can they do for us?"

Leah peeled off her mask. Her hair was short and dyed red. "Aid program – they'll check you for STDs, give you meds and test you for HIV. There's rad screening, clean clothes and food. Then you'll go to a Displaced Persons' camp."

"The Red Cross ain't too bad," Hooker agreed. "Better than a shop, anyhow. Just put up with the prayin' and shit and you'll be fine."

"Praying isn't shit. I believe in God," Mercy replied solemnly.

"So, you're ahead of the game," Leah replied. "They'll love you."

The kids conferred among themselves, whispering urgently in Swahili and Pashtun and Urdu. "Five of us will go to your Red Cross," Mercy translated. "Two want work in better shops. And I go my own way."

Hooker pulled a face – only five bounties. It was still a crazy waste of money - the clans trafficked hundreds of kids every week, recycling those who'd run away from the DP camps back to the sex-shops. Yet the American churches still paid. Led by penitent Archangels, they said. Saving the world, soul-by-soul.

"Okay, Mercy, what you gonna do?" said Leah.

"The Harlot sits on a Scarlet Beast, so it says in The Book. It is The End of Days - I make my own way and wait for the Lord." Mercy pulled a wooden cross from her vest and kissed it.

Hooker studied the girl. Fifteen, maybe sixteen. Wiry

and lean, eyes hard. She wiped away lipstick with the back of her hand. Hooker dabbed a smear of Eduardo's blood from her cheek with his sleeve. "Okay, Mercy. Maybe I know someone who'll give you a job," he said.

"I am not fucking anyone," Mercy replied, making a gun of her fingers. "The only time I will go to a shop again is to return pimps to hell."

"I like the kid," said Leah, "and you have to admit, the bible-bashing adds an extra dimension. Give her a gig."

"We ain't got a vacancy," Hooker replied. "Trashmob might have."

Leah made a snaggle-toothed smile. "We'd have a vacancy if you honoured our deal."

Hooker grimaced. Leah never gave up. "Not now, Leah."

Mercy's eyes swept Leah's armour and weapons. "I work harder on my feet than on my back. I know how to use weapons – Glock, HK, Kalashnikov, Hanyang, RPG, M4-series carbine..."

"I saw," Hooker replied. "Leah, we'll go to Essford then Echo-Seven, okay?"

Leah crunched gears. "Essford then Echo-Seven, you got it."

Mercy threaded her way past Hooker, sitting between him and Leah. She touched his cheek, finger tracing welts and scars. "Are you from Africa, Mister Hooker?"

Hooker smiled. "Nah, Woolwich. My dad was from Liberia and my old lady was Moroccan-Portuguese. Mebbe a bit of Irish too."

"Everyone's got some Irish," Leah added. "It's the law."

"I am from Sierra Leone," said Mercy. "Nobody can go back there. Not now."

Leah raised an eyebrow. "I'm from Brighton. It's only sixty miles down the road, an' nobody can go back there either."

"True." Hooker nodded. "Ain't nobody got the monopoly on fucked-up places nowadays."

"Then the Book is right," Mercy replied. "It is The End of Days. This is the New Babylon, and will be destroyed. It is written."

"Why did we rescue her?" Leah smirked.

"The reward," Hooker lied.

Leah stopped on the road to Essford, north of the flood plain called the Goons. Two of the kids, a boy and a girl, jumped down from the truck. With a wave, they scurried into a warren of plastic-roofed shanties. "They will be back in a shop by dark," said Mercy. "They are fools."

Essford Red Cross station lay inside the old Olympic village, where a woman in khakis and face-mask ushered the kids towards a medical tent. She asked no questions of the hard-eyed girl with the rifle, or the careworn giant in the leather coat. "There's your money," she said, handing over a wad of Reconstruction Dollars.

Hooker counted the cash, handing Leah half the plastic banknotes. "Fifty-fifty, right?"

Leah stuffed the money inside her armour. "Generous, seein' how you took the risk on that one."

"You're a better shot with a rifle."

Leah shrugged. "I'm a better shot with everything."

Returning to the truck, they crossed the Thames into Lagoon City. Leah headed for a fortified compound, blast walls and wire, amidst a cluster of burnt-out buildings. The compound's gates were painted with the sigil of the PROTEX Escort Companies, a stylised wheel on a shield. "What is this place?" said Mercy suspiciously.

"The neighbourhood? Kidbrooke, but we call it Echo-Seven," Hooker replied. "Keep your mouth shut, unless someone talks to you first."

The gates opened, a sentry nodding when he saw Leah's wagon. She parked next to a row of gun-studded technicals and climbed out of the cab. A wiry man in fatigues smoked a roll-up, watching a mechanic tinker with an engine. "Yo, Trashmob," said Leah.

"Yo yourself, Martinez," Trashmob replied, gifting her a lazy salute. "You been fuckin' with those No-Zone Albanians again?"

"I think they were Romanians. Word travels fast."

"Romanians, Albanians, whatever. Anyhow, their radio discipline is shit." Trashmob was scrawny and bearded, hair greying at the temples. He wore a pistol on a webbing belt, a knife tucked in his boot. "Rufus, when you gonna give up this good deed bullshit? It's a waste of talent and money."

Hooker shook his head. "Not again, Trash. Got some karma to claw back, ain't I?"

Trashmob kicked an armoured car's tyre. "Think of the coin you'd make. This private detective stuff is bullshit."

Hooker shook his head. "The PROTEX? Been there, done that. I'm too old for convoy work." Hooker ushered the girl forward. "But Mercy here? I make her a prospect." Mercy climbed down from the truck, ragged and barefoot.

"I got socks older'n her," Trashmob sniffed.

"Just watched her melt six bullets into a man's head," Hooker replied. "Looks like she ain't no stranger to the work."

Trashmob summoned Mercy forward, the girl sweeping him with heavy-lidded eyes. "She's got attitude," he said. "Think she can take orders?"

"I'm vouching for her," Hooker replied, arms crossed.

"Me too," said Leah, resting a hand on Mercy's shoulder. "Give the kid a break."

"Fucking hell, what's happened to you two?" Trashmob replied. He began rolling another cigarette, a lop-sided smile on his face, "Mercy, see that shack over there? Go and ask for a guy called Three-Guns. Tell him Trashmob sent you. He'll find some armour for your bones."

Mercy smiled, revealing a row of gappy white teeth. "Then I have work?"

Trashmob lit a cigarette. "You'll ride shotgun on the London-to-Dover run, which is a fucking nightmare. On probation, just to see how you get on. Okay?"

Mercy nodded. "Do I pay for food, like in the shop?"

"No, food is part of the deal. You get a clean bed and fresh water. Nobody'll lay a finger on you. If they try, tell me and I'll break the fucker's legs. Pay is twenty RDs a week, rising to thirty when you're confirmed. Then you'll also get a share of squadron war-spoils."

"Spoils?" said the girl. "Like, ruins?"

Trashmob laughed. "Loot. Plunder. Y'know? When the Bloc or scavengers attack us, or bandits? We kill the fuckers. Then we take their stuff. Gold, weapons, ammo, tech, petrol.

It's how you'll earn most of your pay."

"This sounds like Freetown," said Mercy, offering her hand. "I will take your job, Mister Trashmob."

"It's Captain Trashmob to you," he replied, taking it.

"God bless you, Captain Trashmob. He will have mercy on your soul, and pluck you from Hell come Judgement Day."

Trashmob laughed. "I'm glad some fucker will."

Hooker pulled Marku's gun from his pocket. "Mercy, you take this – Walther Type-28 personal defence weapon. Thirty-round magazine. Solar-charged optics. Keep a blade for back-up. Always. Understand?"

"I understand, Mister Hooker." Mercy stood on tip-toes and kissed him on the cheek. Handling the gun like a pro, she padded towards a sand-bagged bunker.

"Ain't nuthin' like that moment you give a kid her first proper assault weapon," Leah dead-panned.

"I got me a warm fuzzy too," Trashmob chuckled. "Another thing, Rufus. There's a message for you. Came over the Darkwire, 'bout an hour back."

Hooker frowned. "From who?"

Trashmob pulled a scrap of paper from his pocket, squinting as he read. "It's from Gordy Rice, requesting an audience up in The Smoke. Urgent. There's a Green Zone pass waiting for you at the North Greenwich gate. You've gone up in the world."

Hooker shrugged. "Gordy? He'll want dark work doing."

Leah slapped Hooker's back. "That means coin, right?

What you waitin' for?"

THREE

Leah drove to the border with the Green Zone, bullet-pocked signs warning of mines and unexploded ordnance. She shook her head at a pack of sharp-eyed scavengers, perched on the roof of a burnt-out supermarket. The younger ones threw bricks at the truck. "They need a softer target," she said.

"True," Hooker replied. "I reckon we're safe from rocks."

"Or mebbe they need an airstrike?"

Hooker shrugged. "We tried it back in the day. Did six years in prison for that kinda shit."

They neared the city, twenty-metre blast walls protecting the cloudscrapers beyond. Towering over it all was a screen, a two-kilometre expanse of cobalt omniglass. The BluSky, projecting a high-definition summer day. Images of butterflies and bees fluttered across it, puffy clouds limned with golden sunlight. "Why don't they call it the Blue Zone?" said Leah.

"Fuck knows. And when's the last time you saw a bee?" Hooker replied.

The truck jolted, a wheel rolling in and out of a pothole. Leah cursed. "Yeah, why spend money on clean water or electricity, when you can put up a giant omni and show endangered species instead? Makes perfect sense."

"It just sits there, taking the piss," said Hooker darkly.

"Yeah, like, this is what it's like over in Wessex, you sad No-Zone motherfuckers," Leah replied. "Why don't we shoot it with an RPG?"

"Waste of a good rocket."

Everyone hated the BluSky.

They reached a bunker, guarded by black-armoured tacticals. Hooker unloaded his pump-gun and lowered his goggles. "I'll Darkwire you soon as I'm done. Wait here, okay?"

"Got it," Leah replied, stopping the truck by the roadside. "I'll refuel the wagon."

A shanty hugged the Green Zone checkpoint. Beggars and refugees loitered by tavernas, looking to cadge a few RDs or an evernet tab. Aid workers, pimps, mercenaries and mafioso sipped nettle-vodka mojitos, puffing on skanj pipes. Two Clan pimps, bedecked in gold, recognised Hooker and muttered curses. The hem of Hooker's coat blew open in the breeze, displaying gun and blade, and he made a *come-and-get-me* smile. The pimps looked away, knowing the she-demon sniper might be covering his every move.

Inside the dome, Hooker passed scanners and sniffer

dogs, picking up a pass from a uniformed clerk. Beyond lay a jetty, a tactical directing him to an open-topped river launch. The other passengers were Lagoon City dwellers, lucky enough to have a Green-Zone job. "Here you go, mate," said a skinny man in overalls, shuffling along a bench to make room for Hooker. He nodded his thanks and handed out cigarettes. Hooker didn't smoke anymore, but tobacco was the surest way for an investigator to make friends. There was always useful gossip on the Green Zone launch.

They chugged upstream, the launch churning muddy water. In the BluSky's glow, they passed Canary Wharf, American diggers clearing rubble inside a geodesic dome. Commuters gossiped about the war in Kent, which was being won, and the war in Scotland which wasn't. Across the sea, the Irish were at each other's throats (*no change there*, said a haggard Ulsterman). An African woman with a sing-song voice clutched a bible. "The news from Italy is grave. The Crimson Brigade marches from Sicily, where an unholy alliance of Arabs and Reds threatens the Vatican's gates! The Holy Seer itself might fall."

People muttered and nodded. A few crossed themselves, as religion had made a comeback of late. Archangels (it was always Archangels) were behind it all, they said, weaving their web. The true power behind every throne, in America and Muscovy both. NATO's threadbare armies were in retreat, running out of men and supplies, the once-mighty French and German governments reduced to cowering behind castle walls.

And they spoke of Wessex, as Hooker knew they would. Land of plenty, of milk and honey - faraway Wessex, beyond the Heathrow Gate. Peace and jobs and unlimited evernet access. "They say London will be like Wessex," said a high-cheeked Somali nurse, a Koran clutched to her bosom. The little group nodded and hummed and hawed, and hoped it would be so.

They reached St. Paul's Cathedral, the launch bobbing on the wakes of larger vessels – merchant dhows and NatSec patrol boats, commuter launches and barges moving tonnes rubble. Hooker gave the last of his cigarettes to the river pilot and jumped ashore, mingling with the worshippers crowding the Cathedral's steps. The faithful waved banners, demanding a Crusade to liberate Rome from the heathens. All the while, a wild-eyed man thrashed himself with a flail.

Ducking into the maze of streets off Ludgate Hill, Hooker saw his ride idling by a tram stop. An old electric truck, WESSEX QUALITY PROVISIONS emblazoned in Olde English script. He slid inside, amidst apples and potatoes and sacks of flour. The driver, a wizened man smoking a pipe, accelerated away. "More dark work, Rufus?" he said over his shoulder.

Hooker helped himself to an apple. "Reckon so, Arthur," he replied, stuffing his pockets with fruit. Leah loved apples.

"NatSec's watching Gordy's office," said Arthur, peering nervously in the wing mirror.

Hooker chewed the apple core, spitting pips. "Ain't they always?"

"Mebbe, but Gordy's twitchier than usual. It ain't just the usual watchers. He reckons this is the heavy squad. OCS, mebbe?"

"Gordy's paranoid," said Hooker.

Arthur laughed. "It ain't paranoia if you really are being spied on."

Hooker ate another apple. He doubted the Office of Counter-Subversion had officers to waste, not with civil wars being fought on two fronts. And although Gordy was a greedy bastard, he wasn't a subversive.

The truck whined as it traversed Smithfield Market, farmers herding muddy cattle along Snow Hill. The van finally glided down a ramp, emerging in a subterranean carpark. "There you go," said Arthur. "Now stop stealing all the fucking apples."

Hooker took a lift down to Gordy's lair. Low-ceilinged and gloomily lit, decorated with pictures of faraway places in happier times. Hooker picked pieces of apple from between his teeth. "Hello Gordy," he said. "You called?"

Gordon Rice was sixtyish, with a gnarly, seen-it-all face. Hair the colour of ash, oiled and slicked to his skull. His suit was black, in the Nehru style. "Take a seat, Rufus. This is Miss Hyatt."

Hooker studied the woman. Thirties. Business suit. Honey-blonde hair and a wisp of makeup. Wide-spaced eyes, bluer than the BluSky. An expensive face, surgeon-perfect. "Rufus Hooker," he said, dumping his kit on the floor. "Missing Persons Investigator."

"Vassa Hyatt," the woman replied, voice as firm as her handshake.

Gordy sipped coffee from a thin china cup, giving nothing away. "Vassa represents a high-value client. Sensitive, matter, Rufus. Need my best man on it, so of course I called you."

"You mean deniable, right?" Hooker shrugged, flipping open a dog-eared notebook.

"My employer's daughter's missing," Hyatt replied. "And, yes, we require an element of discretion."

"Let's find her then," said Hooker, licking the end of a pencil. "Let's start with the basics – name and circs of disappearance? I'll also be wanting comms data, recent images and a DNA sample."

Hyatt's smile was as tight as the skin across her face. "In a moment, Mister Hooker."

"A *moment*? The first couple of hours are critical."

Gordy handed Hooker a pad. "You need to sign a non-disclosure agreement."

Hooker confirmed his digital signature with a thumb print. They loved shit like that in the Green Zone, even though Hooker was unlicensed and on the Sanctioned Persons Index. "What's the score? Has the girl got a No-Zone boyfriend? Cotics habit?"

Hyatt wrinkled her nose. "Mister Hooker, Gordy says you're the best off-the-books investigator available. He says there's nobody more familiar with the No-Zone and Lagoon City."

"Yeah, I know my way 'round the Goons."

Hyatt steepled her fingers. "How?"

Hooker raised an eyebrow. "You're telling me you haven't seen my file? You've got government written all over you."

"Files usually tell half-a-story, and I'm not from the Government," Hyatt replied. "I'd prefer to hear your version."

"Okay. I grew up in southeast London, before The

Emergencies. I fought there, after I came back from Libya. Reckon I'll prob'ly die there too."

"You were in the army? That's not in your file."

"Files get lost," Hooker shrugged. "I was in the Military Police. Nothin' special – I directed convoys and guarded prisoners-of-war. I was wounded in Tangiers, then went back to civvy street. I joined the Taskforces after they declared The Emergencies."

"He was a team leader on *my* Taskforce," said Gordy, as if that explained everything. "Taskforce-17."

Hooker never took his eyes off Hyatt. "What Gordy doesn't mention is most of TF-17 are dead. Quite a few died in prison, after the Government shafted us."

Vassa Hyatt nodded. "Yes, Taskforce-17 creates reputational issues for us…"

Gordy opened his mouth, but shut it when he saw the look on Hooker's face. "I was paroled from prison, Miss Hyatt. That's the point, right? I did my time, paid my debt…"

Hyatt smiled. "Weren't most of you given early release? A political decision, red meat for the National Alliance?"

Hooker's lip curled. "Are you saying locking us up for doing our duty *wasn't* political? The Archangels weren't National Alliance, so I remember. They were Coalition all the way…"

Gordy cleared his throat. "Why are we wasting time with politics, Vassa? This is about the girl, and you're forgetting where we're operating on this piece of work. There are a dozen blue-chip security outfits in London, but none of 'em have Rufus Hooker on the books. Most would like to, but he's contracted to *me*."

Vassa Hyatt looked the older man up and down. "Of course, Gordy. Mister Hooker, what do you know of Damon Rhys?"

Hooker shrugged. "Damon Rhys? Minister for Reconstruction. Peacemaker of The Emergencies. All things to all people - soft on Reds *and* Archangels."

"Ah, a political expert," Hyatt replied. "I'd suggest posterity will remember Damon kindly, not least for masterminding the Wessex Accords."

"Wessex – where archangels call the shots?" said Hooker. "If archangels are involved, I'll stick to the No-Zone."

"People want security. Running water. Evernet access. And if the price is coexistence with a handful of supremely gifted transhumans?"

Hooker grimaced. "We blew up our own cities to stop those freaks. RXP makes 'em crazy, it's a scientific fact. Now they get to give the orders?"

Hyatt crossed and uncrossed her legs. "Not all archangels were part of the December 13th clique. And your views on RXP are hopelessly outdated. Instances of psychopathy are almost unheard of with the newer iterations of the procedure."

Hooker grimaced. "We never learn, do we, Miss Hyatt. What's your role in all this?"

Hyatt's smile was thin. "I'm Mister Rhys' security advisor. His *private* security advisor."

"Let's talk about the girl," Gordy interrupted, tapping his watch. "Vassa, what's the latest information?"

"Lottie, Damon Rhys's daughter, was kidnapped yesterday afternoon," Hyatt replied, tapping on her pad. "Delicate ceasefire negotiations with the Black Bloc are due, and Mister Rhys is leading the Coalition delegation."

"So the kidnap ain't a coincidence?" said Hooker, taking another bite from an apple. "Besides, you can't negotiate with the Black Bloc. They're fanatics."

"I've some sympathy with that point of view," Hyatt replied. "However, Damon thinks otherwise. He's established a dialogue with the Bloc's leadership in Kent."

"Here's the ransom demand," said Gordy, offering his pad. "It's the bloody Crimson."

Minister Damon Rhys.

A heroic Special Action Group of the Crimson has taken Charlotte. Do not squander precious time attempting to find her. You will announce a press conference within 48 hours. We demand that you ***REDACTED*** Comply and your daughter will be returned unharmed. Failure will result in her public execution, broadcast via LibNet, Evernet, Darkwire, Net4.0 and similar platforms.

¡Ya basta!

By order of the Command Committee of The Crimson Brigade

Hooker shook his head. "Crimson Brigade? They're worse than the Bloc. You've been given proof of life?"

"We received a timed image of Lottie an hour ago,"

Hyatt replied. "My technical people were unable to scrape location data from it."

"Keep demanding images," Hooker replied. "They might make a mistake, give us something to work on."

"I'm asking for them hourly," said Hyatt, frowning. "In any case, MI5's assessment is Lottie's most likely to have been taken to the No-Zone or the Goons. My own analyst has done probability modelling – he thinks MI5 are onto something. I happen to agree – it's easier for a Crimson Brigade cell to operate there."

"That makes sense," Hooker agreed. "Look, Miss Hyatt, here's my advice if you want to go and play in the Goons – you need a NatSec PersonHunt syndicate, a technical support group, a battalion of tacticals and an Apex Team. Maybe military too, 'cuz they've got the best SIGINT and aerial recce."

Hyatt sighed. "You're not the first *man* who invited me to suck that egg today, Hooker. Besides, it's imperative we find Lottie without any NatSec involvement."

Hooker tried not to look surprised. A government minister, concealing a kidnap from the authorities? *Green-Zoners. Always plotting.*

"We only need a location for the girl," said Gordy, leaning back in his chair. Hooker thought his smile was oily, the one he made when a job was raking in coin. "We've got contractors on standby. The very best, Tier One fighters. Americans and Israelis."

Hooker shook his head. "For all we know, the girl's already in Kent. It's a warzone there, so you're gonna need more than mercenaries, no matter how gnarly."

"Your opinion is duly noted," Hyatt replied, smoothing her skirt across her knees. "However, it's non-negotiable. The National Security Constabulary are to have no involvement in, or knowledge of, this operation."

Hooker sipped from a glass of ice water. "Why?"

"Politics of course, what else?" said Hyatt. "Many are bitterly opposed to compromise with the Black Bloc - especially NatSec. If we tell them, they might well frustrate any rescue attempt."

"Frustrate?"

"They might even let the girl die, so Damon Rhys would cancel negotiations. Or perhaps you consider NatSec above that?"

Hooker knew a few NatSec cops. "No, that's exactly what they'd do."

"Not to mention the Crimson Brigade," Gordy added. "They're dead-set against negotiations with any government. They want the Bloc to keep fighting 'til the bitter end."

Hooker gathered his stuff. "Thanks for the offer, but this job's got aggravation written all over it. I owe Damon Rhys nothing. On the other hand, he owes me six years of my life back."

Hyatt smiled, revealing perfect teeth. Wessex teeth. "We don't have a time machine, Mister Hooker, but I guarantee you'll receive an official pardon. I understand your rancour, but if you find Lottie any convictions from the Reconciliation Tribunals will be expunged. You'll also be removed from the Sanctioned Persons Index."

"How much money we lookin' at?" said Hooker, thinking of Leah. The girl was coin-operated.

Hyatt examined a fingernail. "The bounty for locating Charlotte Rhys? Two million guineas, just for confirming Lottie Rhys's location."

"Think about it, Rufus," said Gordy. "Get off the SPI. I know you need to visit Wessex, that you've..."

Hooker touched the mezuzah. Beatriz. There were ghosts to be confronted in the land of milk and honey, but not for those on the Sanctioned Persons Index.

Vassa Hyatt put a hand on Hooker's. It was cold. "Damon Rhys has a daughter too. I know the circumstances are very different, but find Lottie and you'll get to visit yours."

"Leave it," Hooker growled.

Gordy locked eyes with Hooker. "It's a good offer, Rufus."

Hooker stood. "I'll see what I can do."

Gordy tapped a file on his desk. An old-fashioned folder, stuffed with papers. Impossible to hack. "Lottie's best friend is a girl called Evie Kendrick. I'd start there. She lives in Barnes with her mother."

"Was Evie the last person who saw Lottie?" said Hooker.

"We don't know," said Hyatt. "Lottie's been secretive recently."

"I'd start with the Kendrick girl," said Gordy. "I've got a daughter the same age."

Hooker nodded. The old detective could sniff a lead like a shark. "I'll get over there," he replied. "I'm gonna need assets an' such."

Hyatt rolled her eyes. "Money?"

"Yeah, but gold – not RDs. Information ain't free,

especially if you need it quick."

"Of course," Hyatt replied, unzipping her bag. She put a neoprene pouch on the table and tapped it. "You'll find a handsome sum in there, in Wessex Guineas. There's also a sterile Darkwire fob, contact me using nothing else."

Hooker took the pouch and nodded. It was agreeably heavy. "You'll provide two security contractor's licences, along with open-carry firearms permits for me and my business partner. Gordy has her details. Plus, a vehicle. None of that Green-Zoner 'lectric shit, either. Get me something very fast. Something that can shovel."

Hyatt tapped the fob melded onto her wrist. "It's done. Tell your partner to present herself at the North Greenwich gate within the hour. She's to contact the duty clerk and ask for *Miss Haversham.*"

"I'll get started," said Hooker.

Hyatt offered her hand, but he'd already gone.

FOUR

Lighting a Marlboro Red, Paolo Falcone parsed the terrain like a soldier. He stood atop a tower, the Goons lay before him like a staff college diorama – water features and building lines, trees and obstacles. To the west graffiti-covered housing fringed the marshes, interspersed by bomb-sites and bisected by the PROTEX. Beyond lay London, marked by the BluSky's neon glare. *Most likely route of any security force assault, straight along their main supply route.*

To the north was the ever-swollen Thames, bleeding into a network of fetid inlets. Then the No-Zones, stretching all the way to Essex and the Sharia Reservations. *Possible route for amphibious forces or recon elements.*

South and east? The battle-scarred conurbations beyond were Black Bloc territory, bullet-riddled signs promising minefields, snipers and drones. *Not an obvious direction from which to launch an attack – even more reason to keep an eye on it.*

Paolo had no reason to believe he was compromised. But Africa had taught him whatever could go wrong usually did. It was best to have a plan. Stubbing out his cigarette and lighting another, he descended the stairs. Two squatters greeted him, a stringy, spaced-out girl and a pasty-faced boy. They wore multi-coloured rags and rubber sandals. "*Ciao,*" said Paolo easily. "How goes it?"

"The Bloc will topple London," the boy declared, his accent German. "The *intifada* is close. Can you hear it?"

"The sweetest sound," said the girl, hugging herself. She took a draw on a pencil-thin joint and passed it to the boy.

Paolo heard the distant thump of artillery, math swarming his brain. 120mm mortar line, six tubes. High Explosive rounds. Range fifteen-aught-six kilometres, south-south-east. "The Bloc over-extend themselves," he said. The Bloc are dolts. They need the Crimson Brigade. Instead, they plot Class betrayal and parley with fascists.

The girl gazed through a window, watching a finger of smoke point skywards. "It's difficult for them, Paolo. The fascists bomb every day."

"Don't worry, Anna," the boy replied, swigging from a bottle of grog. "Black banners will fly over London before the year is through."

Paolo nodded, even though the kid was a fool. As a Colonel in the Crimson Brigade's Special Action Group, Paolo had read intelligence reports from agents in Wessex. They said the regime was confident of peace with the Black Bloc, a plot hatched by Archangels. The transhuman fascists were in the ascendant, first in America and now Britain. Several had tried to join the Crimson, declaring themselves part of the struggle. Of course, they wanted to be in charge. Paolo himself was chosen to poison their food and burn their bodies with acid.

On the next floor down, men worked on defensive positions. The Goons were dangerous – the local people were feral scum, given to theft and casual violence. Sweating, labourers busied themselves with sandbags and crates packed with rubble. "*Salut*, Paolo," said a camouflage-clad Frenchman. "Hey, do you have any cigarettes?"

Paolo passed the Frenchman a soft-pack. "Me? Cigarettes? You're the master of rhetoric, Michel. Here's some vintage Marlboro Red. Coffin nail of the true connoisseur."

"Merci!"

More anarchists of the *Commune International* greeted Paolo as he walked its passageways and corridors, humming with music and chatter. The squat stank of skanj, chilli candles and unwashed bodies. He stopped to hand out cigarettes, slap backs and share gossip.

No, Paolo, we've seen no pigs, not for days. We've heard there are food riots north of the river, and the No-Zone Clans are giving them trouble. Yes, we've heard it - the Bloc's mortar fire gets closer every day…

Paolo took a wheezing elevator to a murky sub-basement. Pulling on a pair of gloves he slid open a cobwebby ceiling panel, camouflaged with grease and muck. Inside was sixty kilos of nano-anonymised plastic explosive with acetone peroxide detonators. Sealed in tough plastic, dry and stable.

Seals intact? Check.

Detonators dry? Double-check.

Then check again. Paolo realised his work made him obsessive-compulsive, but it was better than being dead. Or, even worse, failing.

Inspection complete, Paolo headed for the Commune's courtyard. He paused to smear rad cream into his cheeks, still sore from maxillofacial surgery. The agent had undergone three identity-change procedures in five years, and had no wish to undertake a fourth. The courtyard, encircled by a high earthwork palisade, doubled as a marketplace. Squatters traded with locals from the neighbouring estates, materialistic peasants who made Paolo's temple throb. They were modern-day *Kulaks*, ripe for slaughter, wilfully defying any notion of class-consciousness, reliant on aid provided by the London fascists.

"Fuck off," a kid laughed, pushing his friend into a table selling bric-a-brac. Stuff fell everywhere, and they laughed. Nearby, a girl urgently fellated a pimply boy in full view. The crowd cheered, fob-streaming and showering them with hooch. Other men fidgeted with their flies and waited their turn.

Paolo glowered. Beyond Lagoon City, in the No-Zones and Free Medway, scavengers and refugees eked a desperate living. One of disease, sex-slavery, poverty and occasional cannibalism. Pushing his way through the crowd, he returned to the apartment. He stopped, as he always did, to look and listen. Beyond the door, he heard raised voices. Sliding his pistol free, he gazed into a retinal scanner and crept inside. The noise came from one of the bedrooms. Inside, the girl lay rolled into a ball, arms across her belly. Her naked thighs were mottled purple, hair stiff with blood. A big man stood scowling and buckling his belt. Paolo's voice was soft. "Did you rape her, Abid?"

Abid shrugged, eyes fixed on the floor.

"No…" said the girl.

"He couldn't get it up?" Paolo offered.

The girl nodded.

Abid, broad-shouldered and seven feet tall, sneered. Neck muscles tensed like cables. "I do my job, Paolo. The bitch tried to escape. I teach her a lesson."

"Try it again and I swear to god I'll shoot you dead," Paolo replied in fluent Arabic. "You'll die in disgrace, not as a *shahid*. You were chosen specifically for this mission because your commanders assured me you were competent and disciplined. Don't make me doubt them again."

The giant's eyes narrowed. Until the girl arrived, he'd been an obedient and discreet operative. Since yesterday afternoon? Like a dog on heat. "I understand," he said slowly.

Paolo crouched and passed the girl a bottle of water. "Lottie, how did you make Abid mad?"

The girl sneered. "I found a nail under the skirting board. I tried to stab him in the eye."

Paolo liked Lottie Rhys. In other circumstances, he'd have recruited the girl for operations. He thought Bourgeois women made the best revolutionaries, like the Ivy-League bluestocking he'd spun into a suicide operative. He'd watched through binoculars as her truck-bomb crashed into NATO's Milan headquarters. She was smiling when she detonated the device.

"Next time," Abid hissed at the girl in English. Avoiding Paolo's eye, he stomped away.

Lottie studied the dusty floor, spotted with tears. The girl's hair was blonde, the fringe covering her eyes. Fine-featured, Paolo thought, like all the elite's children. Maybe she'd had plastic surgery as a child. He heard that was popular in Wessex. He closed the door behind him and followed Abid into the corridor. "Where's Rourke?"

"She went for food," the Yemeni replied. "Woman's work."

It was these attitudes, thought Paolo, that led to the Global Jihad Brigade's terminal decline. They'd offered nothing but death, enslavement and clitoridectomies. "You've set everything up as I asked?"

The Yemeni nodded as they entered the apartment's main bedroom. The walls were covered with thick black plastic. Positioned in front of a wide-angled camera was a chopping block, a sword embedded in the wood. A tulwar, worthy of a Saudi executioner. Tacked to the wall was a banner, a black hammer and sickle on a crimson field. Paolo tugged the sword free and examined the blade. "From now on, only Rourke deals with the girl when I'm not here. Do you understand?"

"As you wish, Paolo."

"It is. Now go."

After the Yemeni had left, Paolo went to the tiny kitchen and poured a glass of water. He heard footsteps, the flip-flop of rubber on linoleum. "Paolo, are you there?" said Rourke, a bag of groceries clutched to her chest. She had tumbleweed hair, her body hidden beneath a shapeless black dress. Her accent was of Belfast, softened by English years. She read Paolo's face. "Is there a problem?"

"Abid tried to have his way with the girl."

Rourke grimaced. Apart from her eyes, the colour of cornflowers, she was unremarkable-looking. An advantage in her trade. "Last thing we need is for the other side to find evidence of rape after they recover the body. The Committee would have us all shot."

"I agree, standards are important," Paolo replied. Rourke might be occasionally belligerent, but she understood the optics.

"I'll have a quiet word with the big fella," Rourke replied, all hearty Irish *colleen*. "He listens to me, even if he does call me *Kaffir*."

"As long as the savage does his job," Paolo half-whispered.

Rourke pulled a face. "Leave Abid to me, okay?" she said, unpacking groceries. Ramen noodles, stock-cubes and sad-looking vegetables. "By the way, my man loaded the dead-letter drop."

"He delivered as promised?"

Rourke rested her backside against the sink and studied her cigarette. "Yes and no. He says he'll definitely get a location for Rhys's meeting with the Bloc. Problem is, he's insisting on telling me in person. No Darkwire."

"Why? Darkwire is un-hackable."

"They said that about the Enigma machine," Rourke replied.

Paolo shook his head. "A facile comparison."

Rourke was tight-lipped about her agents. Her network

was years in cultivation, like a bonsai forest, and just as delicate. "Let's say my man works in a specialist technical field. He's paranoid about his comms being intercepted."

Paolo had a finely attuned nose for bullshit, especially where informants were concerned. "He's angling for more money?"

Rourke nodded slowly. "Aye, he is."

"I'm more concerned he's setting us up. Maybe NatSec turned him, or MI5?"

Rourke made a *pffft* noise. "It's always at the back of my mind. But not this one. I've been running him three years without a hitch. I've got sub-sources reporting on him, the Centre cleared him twice. He's a good agent."

"How much?"

Rourke shrugged. "An extra fifty grand. US, not Reconstruction Dollars. It's not the amount, it's the principle. I'm running him, he isn't running *me*."

"Kill him after the operation's finished," Paolo suggested. "Principles can wait where this piece of work is concerned."

The Irishwoman put the kettle on. She kept her precious tea caddy next to it, the only luxury she'd brought to the squat. "Killing him is tempting, it'd certainly tidy up some loose ends. But it makes more sense to keep him in place. You don't get many agents with his level of access. The window of opportunity into Rhys's household comms node is very brief."

Paolo nodded. Rourke was the human assets specialist, whereas his talents veered more towards the more… *kinetic.* He allowed himself a smile. "Perhaps I could meet him. Would he benefit from a motivational chat?"

"You know, I'd like to see that," Rourke cackled.

Paolo checked his watch. "Schedule?"

"I'm looking to have a location for the Black Bloc delegation meeting by twenty-hundred. My source tells me they use a place on the border with Croydonia for meetings. Border security is shite down there, it's where most of the cotics come through from Kent."

"Fine. I need to check the lock-up anyway. I'll get your money."

Rourke fussed over tea-making, splashing milk and spooning sugar. Paolo despised the stuff, but Rourke drained cup after cup. "I always thought the operation too complex," she said. "Sequencing Rhys's press conference, *then* ambushing the peace delegation."

Paolo pulled up a chair. "The circumstances behind MADRIGAL demand it."

Rourke sipped tea, grimaced and added more sugar. "Tell me about MADRIGAL." Rourke put her hand on Paolo's, the Irishwoman's fingers spidery against his skin.

"You know it's a compartmentalised operation," Paolo replied, trying not to flinch.

"Of course," said Rourke, "but…"

"My orders are unambiguous. Just remember, people aren't interested in propaganda and fake news. They want cast-iron proof, from the guilty man's lips. Then there's the matter of operational security."

Rourke studied her teacup, stained and chipped. "You can't tell *me*? That's bollix."

Reaching into his pocket, Paolo placed three tubes on

the table. Silver with protective caps, labelled in Mandarin. "These are brainstem injectors. You know what they do?"

Rourke's finger hovered over the injectors. "Of course. Do they really work?"

"Yes. Once the girl is dead and Abid has eliminated the traitors, you'll receive one. You can upload the information directly into your brain. Apart from me, only the Chairperson of the Command Committee herself has seen it."

Rourke nodded, eyes locked hungrily onto the injectors. "Then I suppose that will have to do."

Don't be so fucking impertinent. You're a low-level agent handler. "Have patience," Paolo replied. "The mission first, comrade. Always the mission first."

FIVE

Hooker and Leah stood on St. Paul's Quay, their shadows cast before them, cloudscrapers crowding the cathedral's fire-blackened dome. Demonstrators and flagellants stood in the shade, singing hymns or torturing themselves. "Nice wheels," said Leah, biting into an apple. "None of that 'lectric shit."

Hooker ran a hand along the G-Wagen's armoured flank. A matte grey urban ops model, equipped with roll-bars, ram, armorglass windows and riot-mesh. "We had these on the Taskforces," he said. "Until the other side got advanced RPGs, that is."

Leah shrugged, kicking a tyre. "As long as it starts when I hit the ignition, we're good."

"Where did you learn to drive?"

"Brighton."

"On the beach?" said Hooker.

"Nah, through the rubble. We had an old Land Rover on the Bloc. Nicked it from the army." Leah was comfortable talking about her time as an insurgent. And if she ever resented Hooker for serving on the other side, she never showed it.

An electric car sputtered to a halt, engine whining. Gordy stepped out, face oily with rad cream under a wide-brimmed hat. "Martinez, I had problems with your security clearance. You wouldn't believe the strings I had to pull."

Leah stowed her weapons in the back of the Merc. "I got my de-radicalisation ticket five years ago. What's the issue?"

"You're still on the NatSec intel system," Gordy shrugged.

"Who ain't?" Leah shrugged, running a finger across the old man's cheek. She licked rad cream and smiled. "Hmmm, strawberry. Tell your NatSec source I've killed more Bloc than any toy soldier in *your* private army."

"True," Hooker agreed. "Woman's got an unhealthy taste for it."

Gordy grimaced. "It's not about how many you've killed, Leah. It's about processes."

Leah shrugged. "I fucking hate processes."

"That's why you live in a No-Zone hovel. Just keep your bloody head down and don't give NatSec the excuse to revoke your permit. It won't take long for them to realise you two are cutting about the Green Zone."

Leah strapped on the contractor's armband. "Wow Gordy, open-carry permits? What's the budget on this job?"

Gordy flashed his crocodile's smile. "Welcome to the big league, Martinez. You're going up in the world."

Leah looked around, lip curled. "You can keep it. I prefer it outside the walls."

Gordy muttered something and shook his head. "Rufus, what do you think?"

Hooker was still admiring the Mercedes. A man could lock himself inside and be safe from the world. "I think we need comms data for Lottie Rhys and Evie Kendrick. Any news?"

"Check your Darkwire," Gordy replied. "A load of stuff just dropped in there. Hyatt didn't waste any time."

"I'll be in touch," said Hooker.

"Make sure you are. I'll need updating on the hour." The old detective got in his car and buzzed away.

Leah climbed inside the Merc and studied the controls. "I like this," she said, hitting the ignition and following the navigation system towards the Government Zone. A procession marched by, banners warning of The End of Days. Nobody laughed at them anymore. "Now, what's this job all about?" she asked. "Why's Gordy so pleased with himself?"

"This job's got politics wrapped around it, and Gordy loves that shit. Makes him feel important."

"Politics?"

"A minister's daughter, gone MISPER. Female. Pureblood Green-Zoner." Hooker told Leah about the missing girl, and Hyatt's offer.

"That ain't a MISPER, Hooker. That's a kidnap."

"True, but at least it ain't a rescue," Hooker replied. "That's usually the tricky part."

The Green-Zone streets were crowded with bicycles, tuk-tuks, electric cars and tipper trucks. Horses and dogs. Building sites, workers in hard hats laying bricks and pouring foamcrete. Street food vendors and corner shops. People not wearing armour, or trapping vermin for food. A snake of schoolkids wove through the crowd, escorted by teachers wearing orange tabards. "Man, this place does my head in," said Leah.

Hooker watched the kids, clutching his mezuzah tight. Dammit, he could *smell* his daughter – milkshake and soap, biscuit crumbs on her dungarees…

"You okay?" asked Leah.

"Yeah, just thinking."

"What about?"

Hooker turned in his seat. "Look, if Trashmob ain't interested in selling Echo-Seven, I'll talk to Gordy about investing in you. Mebbe he'd fund you to set up a company."

Leah pulled a face. "Gordy? There'd be strings."

"Do you want your own outfit or not?"

Leah nodded. "Sure, but on my terms. I want PROTEX runs up to the fracking zone, not the shitty Medway gauntlet."

Hooker rubbed his face. He hadn't slept for a while. "You ain't got any terms unless you've got coin. Gordy ain't that bad, having shares in a PROTEX company gives him another pie to stick his fingers in."

"Exactly. Green Zone fingers."

"You need to brush that chip off your shoulder," Hooker replied. "They'll win the war one day. They've got the money and they're patient."

Leah's face was hard. "And they've got the fucking

Archangels on their side, right?"

Hooker sighed. "Like I said, the Green Zone is coming our way, whether we like it or not. Make your dough while you can."

"Oh, I will," Leah replied. "What 'bout you?"

"I'm going to Wessex."

"Your daughter?"

"Sorry Leah, not now," said Hooker, immediately feeling bad about being crotchety.

"Ain't no sweat, Rufus," Leah replied. "Maybe one day."

"Maybe."

Leah laughed. "Definitely."

"Why?"

"I'm your only friend. Depressing, ain't it?" said Leah. They both laughed, Leah punching Hooker's shoulder. Talk of owning her own company always cheered her up. "Now, we goin' straight to the Kendrick girl's place?"

Hooker checked the fob Hyatt's had given him, data streaming across the Darkwire. "Tempting, but there's too much stuff here."

"Good stuff?"

"Possibly, and we'll kick ourselves if we miss it. Barnes ain't far from Bleep's place, and we're gonna need a 'mancer on a job like this."

Leah's lip curled. "Bleep? I hate that freak. Can't you find someone else?"

"He's the best in London. I'm sure you can be civil for half an hour," Hooker replied doubtfully. He fired up his fob. "Bleep?"

"You owe me two grand," spat a reedy Northern voice.

"'Cuz right now you're in my Folio of Utter Shit. It's a lengthy tome I'll grant you, but still…"

"I've got coin. I'm on my way to pay you."

"They've let *you* back in the Green Zone?"

"Yeah, I'm nearby. I'm pushed for time. Can we come over?"

"If '*we*' means you're bringing that Bloc *chica* with the long legs, then you may."

"Funny you should mention it, I'm with Leah now. She's looking forward to seein' you too, Bleep." Hooker winked. Leah pulled a face, opened the window and spat out of it.

"I imagine you've dark work in mind," said Bleep. "So, payment up front, an exciting new policy from Bleepmeister Industries."

Hooker's boot nudged the bag of guineas in the foot-well. "Ain't a problem, not on this gig."

"Then it might be an agreeable afternoon after all," Bleep replied. "Anything I can be getting on with?"

"I'm Darkwiring you data."

"It's coming through now. Do you need anything in particular?"

"Everything. Soon as you can."

"Well, as long as your money's good, so am I," said Bleep.

Hooker ended the call. "Wandsworth it is," he said, tapping the navigation screen.

Leah hit the accelerator, the treacly brown Thames flashing by. "Why is Hyatt insisting on no cops?"

"Does it matter? I thought you'd agree with that idea."

"I do, but I'm not a member of the Wessex *Übermensch*, am I?"

"Damon Rhys is leading ceasefire negotiations with the Bloc," Hooker replied. "NatSec won't want a ceasefire, not when they think they're winning. The Crimson Brigade don't want a ceasefire either. They took Rhys's daughter 'cuz for some reason it'll wreck the peace talks."

"The Bloc are nutters, but the Crimson Brigade?" said Leah, undertaking a convoy of aid lorries. "There were a few in Brighton, shit-stirring and trying to turn the place into another Free Medway."

"What happened?"

Leah laughed. "They realised Nu-Brightonians were beyond Party discipline, so they fucked off back to Russia or Italy, or wherever it is they come from. Then NatSec moved in and torched the place." The razing of the briefly-lived Nu-Brightonian Republic was a political litmus test – National Alliance types toasted the event, the Coalition mourned it.

"That's when you ended up in the No-Zone?"

Leah shrugged. "Via Croydonia. One night was enough."

They crossed the PROTEX at Battersea Marshes. The chimneys of the famous power station, now submerged, pointed out of the murk like mighty gun barrels. Then Wandsworth, where Bleep lived in a maze of peeling prefabs. The infomancer answered the door, powered wheelchair squeaking. "Ah, my favourite War Criminal, and the cutest mercenary babe in the No-Zone."

"*Babe*?" said Leah, pulling a face.

"It's an old-fashioned term, pre-War level-three

microaggression. It generally means *nubile and sexually appealing*."

"Fuck off, Bleep."

Bleep cocked his head. "I find your contempt… exciting."

"Shut up Bleep, there's work to do," said Hooker, stepping inside the hovel. Portraits of Bleep's Holy Trinity lined the wall – Turing, Hawking and Musk.

Leah shook her head. "You're still bolting on false body-parts like a wannabe archangel?"

"Archangel? Please. My augmentations are all *biomechanical.* None of that gene-splicing shite for me." One of Bleep's arms and both legs had been replaced with pinky-grey resin prosthetics. A data socket protruded from behind an ear, his face a patchwork of scar tissue. His left eye was a multi-faceted piece of machinery, resembling a bug.

Leah tapped his arm. "Who pays for all this shit?"

"I'm a veteran, am I not? Our glorious government looks after its injured warriors." A photo taped to a monitor showed a younger, less mechanical Bleep standing in a desert wearing combat gear. "Unless you're Hooker, of course."

Hooker saw the photo and smiled. "You know we met at the military hospital in Tangiers?"

"No, you never said. You were injured too?" asked Leah.

"Nothin' serious," he replied. "Shrapnel wound. Bleep, on the other hand…"

Bleep looked at his legs and laughed. "I'm a fiery phoenix, rising from the ashes."

"Is this a new rig?" Hooker pointed at the gleaming array of computers crowding Bleep's hovel, trunked cables lining the walls. Servers hummed, surrounded by a henge of frost-furred cooling towers.

"This? Just a little something I prepared earlier." Bleep replied, trundling towards the machines, "this baby's equipped with Quantum Two-Twenty processor spurs and Xenon liquid-state drives. Sublimia omniscreens and Tsinghua Everest-Nine chill-towers."

"How d'you afford all this stuff?" said Leah.

Bleep gestured around the dingy room. "What I don't spend on interiors, I squander on technology."

Hooker ran a finger along a tower, frost tingling the tip. "You've got the data I sent?"

"Of course," Bleep replied, fingers dancing across a keyboard. Columns of digits swirled across the omnis, swaying like shoals of digital fish. "I'd say this comes from Gordy Rice's best blagger. Minty-fresh from the service provider. *Very* comprehensive."

Leah's face glittered in the data-flow, zeroes and ones flashing across her cheek. "Have you worked out who the target is?"

Bleep nodded. "Of course. A cutie called Charlotte Elizabeth Rhys."

"Cutie?"

"Come on, that was only a level-four microaggression," Bleep grinned. "Charlotte, known to family and friends as Lottie. Nineteen years old next month, evernets using a GCHQ-encrypted feed registered to a dryer-than-dry Holland Park address. She's Damon Rhys's daughter, of course. Straight 'A' student, enjoyed a starry gap year in Washington DC working for the New Democrats. Soon she'll be off to

Oxford to read Politics, Philosophy, Probability Mechanics and Ethics."

Hooker clapped a hand on the infomancer's shoulder. "Which is all crap I don't need to know. Come on, Bleep, *where is she?*"

The infomancer sighed. "Can you tell me why she's missing? It might help."

Hooker didn't have time to lie. "The girl's been kidnapped by terrorists. The family don't want any police involved."

"Terrorists?" Bleep rolled the word around his mouth, grinning. "Which flavour? Woad-painted Celt Ultras? Derrida-quoting Bloc nihilists? Hyperventilating Caliphate medievalists? I must say, you two must be going up in the world."

"Crimson Brigade," Hooker replied.

Bleep's face was grey. "Oh fuck."

A face appeared on the screen. "That's her?" asked Leah.

"This is indeed the fragrant Charlotte Rhys. I found it on a Wessex lifestyle site – *London's most Eligible Debutants.*"

"Debutant?"

"Not a microaggression," Bleep replied. "Dunno why."

Lottie Rhys. Golden hair, bee-stung lips and a button nose. The spray of freckles across her face might've been painted on individually. She posed on a beach in a wetsuit, a surfboard tucked under her arm, a Jack Russell capering at her feet. Bleep summoned more images. Lottie in a dark business suit, attending a fundraiser for No-Zone orphans. Lottie at the Lord-Protector's ball, dressed in taffeta and lace. Lottie in a wood-panelled officers' mess, posing with a lusty row of red-jacketed soldiers. The infomancer chuckled. "There used to be a writer called Jane Austen. Her stories described the social mores of Georgian England. I'm convinced whoever's in charge of Wessex thinks they're instruction manuals."

"I'd love to go there," Leah replied, baring crooked teeth. "With a flamethrower."

Bleep swept chat logs with a finger, blinking his metallic eye and enlarging the text. "Here we go... the last twenty-four hours in the life of Lottie Rhys. Last person to fob her was a girl called Evie. Standard-issue rich-kid. Plastic revolutionary too, if her LibNet browsing history is anything to go by."

"Evie Kendrick. Lottie Rhys's best friend," said Hooker, pulling up a garden chair.

Bleep swept a data-suite from Evie's fob records. "Evie's been using LibNet to access Medway content, naughty girl. Amateur hour encryption... ah, here we go. Silly bitch, she only went and joined the F4P a few months ago..."

"*Front for Progress*?" said Leah, studying the chat logs, "that's a Bloc sock puppet."

Hooker studied the picture of Evie – a whip-thin girl with hooded eyes and a strong nose. "How'd she get into that I wonder?"

"There's a TIM profiling code embedded in the cache," said Bleep. "Targeted Ideological Marketing, they call it. Propaganda in old money."

"Ain't propaganda if it's true," Leah shrugged.

"*Truth?* Bah! That's a social construct, ain't it?" Bleep chuckled. He skimmed through images from Free Medway. Drone strikes on favelas. Tacticals posing with corpses. "She's watched hours of this stuff."

"Was it sent unsolicited?" said Leah.

"Initially, yes," Bleep replied. "Although it's been altered to look like Evie started it. Look at this – encrypted message logs, embedded inside video files." He jabbed a finger at the omni, digits swirling as Bleep's decryption tools unpacked the data.

This is a message in a bottle, cast into the sea. I beg you - if you receive this share it via LibNet or Darknet. The Government will not show it, their network blocking software deletes our messages. Please, If you can spare a minute, reply. To hear another voice, from someone who cares, means as much as food and clean water. Drones try to pinpoint our location, so they can bomb us. This is happening only 30 miles from London. 30 miles from YOU. The killing must stop - we must reunite our land, with justice for all, not just the few.

Clara of Free Medway

"Let's see what Clara sent young Evie, shall we?" said Bleep, opening another file. "Some misery porn for Green Zoners, I'll wager."

A video camera panned across rubble, a jet flashing across the top of the screen. Explosions shook the ground, the cameraman stumbling into a rubble-strewn street littered with bodies. Then, a voice – *This is Chatham, 18th February. Those are RAF jets. These are civilians. When will it stop? Who will help us?*

"The Bloc place antiaircraft in civilian areas," Leah shrugged. "Funny they don't mention that."

"Try explaining that to a Green Zone teenager," said Hooker. "We can cut it anyway we like. The bottom line is we're bombing our own people down there."

Leah ended the video. "Civil wars are never civil."

"Medway? Nobody has to live there," said Bleep. "They ain't *my* people. If the Bloc win, that means the Crimson wins."

"Fucking hearts of gold, you two. Forget I mentioned it," Hooker replied. "What did Evie do when she got this stuff?"

Bleep blinked, and an email appeared onscreen. "Looks like she fell for the pitch. Look at her reply."

Dear Clara. My name is Evie. I live in the Green Zone and I will share your video.

"Clara comes back a whole seven minutes later, via encrypted Darknet."

Thank you, Evie. This means more than you can imagine. I will send you my next video, if you will share that too. With love and respect, Clara x

Bleep looked up from the omni and reached for a can of energy drink. "I've seen this grooming model before. Evie will receive more replies from 'Clara,' who'll eventually persuade her to join F4P. Then she'll be introduced to a political mentor to *help her discover the direction her activism might take.*"

"They mean a Commissar?" said Leah.

Bleep nodded. "Although I think *handler's* a better description. Here…"

You should meet my friend Roisin, Lottie. Roisin works in the Green Zone occasionally. She can help you understand more and show how you can help bring peace. She's such a good listener, and has done so much with her life…

"I'll wager a hundred guineas 'Roisin' knew Evie was one of Lottie Rhys's closest friends."

"So, Evie's been spun into a sub-source? To provide access to Lottie?" said Hooker, tapping open more messages.

"It looks that way," Bleep replied. "It's consistent with Bloc and Crimson recruitment models."

"Leah, we need to go," said Hooker. "Right now."

"Why?" said Bleep. "I'm not finished."

Hooker shrugged on his coat. "If Roisin's sophisticated enough to get at Lottie Rhys, she'd know any half-decent 'mancer would have found this stuff by now. But she's gone ahead and taken the girl anyway."

"Why?" said Bleep.

Hooker headed for the door. "My guess? The kidnappers are working to a deadline."

"Like they don't care if they get caught?" Leah replied. "They're just going to kill her anyway?"

"I've got a bad feeling. We need to identify Roisin, and

soon."

"I'm on it Rufus," Bleep replied, hunching over his screen. "I'll keep churning zeroes-and-ones."

Hooker slapped a bag of guineas on Bleep's desk. "There's what I owe you with a cherry on top. We're off to check Evie Kendrick's place."

"Barnes?" said Bleep, opening the bag and grinning. "Very posh. Hardcore Green Zone real estate, lots of security. It'll be buttoned-down tight."

Leah shrugged. "If they know what's good for 'em, they'll un-button themselves."

Bleep chuckled, making a strange gurgling noise in his throat. "I forgot how much you like Green Zoners."

Leah finished the rest of the infomancer's energy drink. "I fucking hate 'em."

"In which case, maybe I'll hack their CCTV," Bleep cackled, sniffing the empty can. "This I'd love to see."

SIX

Paolo crossed the lagoon bridge, eyes hidden behind sunglasses. Beyond lay the Thames, a ziggurat island rising from the water. Built from cargo crates, it served as a monastery for the order of monks who called themselves Answerers. A robed figure saw Paolo and waved cheerily. Paolo found himself waving back. Finishing his cigarette, he walked to the Crosland Estate.

The lock-up was in a back-alley, adjacent a long-abandoned industrial estate. Paolo crossed a litter-strewn plaza, all boarded-up shops and burnt-out cars. Lagoon kids lounged on garden furniture, smoking skanj and tipping hooch into their gap-toothed mouths. A girl, face dotted with light-studs, danced to electronic music. A youth saw Paolo and grunted in the guttural language they called 'Tois. "*Who youk be middy?*" he said.

Paolo pulled a guinea from his pocket and flicked it at the kid. He spoke English in reply. "*Ciao.* Have you seen any police patrols today?"

The kid caught the coin one-handed and tested it with his teeth. Smiling, he switched to English. "Nah not today, gaffer. Munis come sometimes, but we only see tacticals if there's proper trouble."

Paolo nodded. The Municipal police were little more than underfunded street wardens who posed little threat. Tacticals, on the other hand, were from the National Security Constabulary. Well-armed, lavishly-resourced and ruthless.

"Ain't scared o' no muni-pigs, ain't scared o' no tacticals," another kid announced, swaying in a plastic hammock.

"Will you make some noise if you see any?" said Paolo. "I'd appreciate it."

A grin split the kid in the hammock's face. "Oh yeah, Mister. We'll make you a proper racket if we see d'pigs."

"Good."

"I've peeped on you 'round the Commune," said a girl, ratty eyes roaming the plaza. "They say you're from It'lee."

"*It-aly.* Yes, I am."

The girl nodded, "There's like a big fightin' gun-a-war there, right?"

"There is. Actually, it's not much different from the one fifteen miles that way," Paolo replied, pointing south.

"That's diff'rent. That's against the Bloc, innit? Reds wanna take our stuff and give it someone else. Make us all the same an' shit."

"Yeah," said another. "Dirty-fucking-Reds."

Paolo sighed. No wonder the anarchists were unable to mobilize these dolts. He handed the girl a Marlboro Red. "Here, try one of these. It's what they smoke in Italy."

"Gaffer, I like dat," the girl grinned, spluttering at the strength of the cigarette. The other youths cackled along, asking for a drag.

Paolo left the plaza, ducked into an alleyway and waited. Nobody followed. He opened a garage door and locked himself inside, leaving a tin of nails against the door jam. The lock-up contained an electric-hybrid pickup truck, liveried with the logo of a Green-Zone courier service. Pulling on surgical gloves, he scanned the interior, prising open panels where he'd conceal plastic explosives. The voids beneath the seats were already seeded with nuts and bolts. When Abid detonated the device, it would make a storm of shrapnel.

The roof-space concealed another hide. Paolo pulled out shrink-wrapped packets of US Dollars, enough to sate Rourke's agent's greed. He tucked the cash in a fabric belt, fastened tight around his stomach. How he missed the days of cryptocurrencies, when he could do business by pressing a screen.

It was cool inside the lock-up, Paolo enjoying the aroma of engine oil and tobacco and coffee. Honest smells, not like the Crosland's stink. Trash and fried food, sweat and cheap body spray. Inside an ammunition box, Paolo kept a tiny coffee machine. It chugged and hissed as he prepared *espresso,* sipped from a china cup. Time for another cigarette and coffee, he decided, up on the roof. Watching the river, Paolo enjoyed the Bourgeois pleasure of *Arabica,* watching dhows bobbing on the chocolate-brown Thames. Gulls haunted the river traffic, clouds bubbling overhead, Stamp music on the wind. Draining his cup and stubbing out a cigarette, Paolo dropped back inside, locked the ceiling hatch and checked it twice.

Then, a rattling noise. *Nails on concrete.*

Three kids studied the van, sniffing the air like rats. One had a pair of bolt croppers in his hands and a gun in his belt. The others looked curiously over his shoulder. One held a wooden truncheon, the other a butcher's knife. "The van?" said the kid with the knife. "How much is it worth?"

"Leave," Paolo said quietly. "This won't end well if you don't."

The kid snatched at the revolver in his belt. "Fuck off, gaffer. You got stuff in 'ere worth somefin' aintya? What is it? Booze or 'cotics?"

Paolo drew his Heckler-Koch 35 – an ugly weapon, snub-barrelled and bulbous. His optical implant pulsed, slaved to the weapon's targeting mechanism. He laser-painted the youths with the blink of an eye, suppressed nano-munitions hissing across the garage. The kids fell, bodies peppered with bullet wounds. Paolo calmly covered the dead with a tarpaulin, pausing only to shoot one boy who still breathed. Locking the door behind him, he walked quickly away.

From the plaza, Paolo heard the indignant, high-pitched whine of Tois and Babble. Three horsemen clip-clopped along the street, municipal cops wearing bright orange jackets. A gaggle of youths made a human barrier in front of the horses, yelling for them to go away. Paolo's audio implant, lodged in the flesh behind his ear, amplified the conversation. "Move," ordered one of the munis. "Unless you want a hoof-mark on your head."

"You can't come 'fru 'ere wivaht no warrant," one of the kids screeched, hopping from foot to foot. "I know me rights, fuckin' Gavvas!"

"You fuckers are takin' liberties, I'm gonna get a lawyer!"

"I said move!" The muni ordered, pulling a shock-gun from his belt. Bluish sparks crackled at the weapon's tip, making the kids cringe.

"Anyhow, you're goin' the wrong way," said the girl who'd Paolo given a cigarette. "I saw a moody-lookin' cutter goin' to the lock-ups 'round back."

"Thassrite," said another, "a proper cutter too. Wiv gold an' evryfink. I reckon he's got stolen shit in there. Or mebbe he's a Red!"

"Now, why 'fess to that?" the muni scoffed, horse neighing. "I know all the cutters 'round here. Who is it? Marsden Delafinch? Royale Hussain?"

"I'm tellin' so you'll leave us alone!" the girl wheedled, turning the words into a crude rap. "*Why hassle a brudder, when you could pinch a cutter?*"

The second muni drew a long baton. "Right, form a line. ID cards ready, you know the score. Papers and pockets."

With the smash of breaking glass, petrol bombs whistled across the plaza. Kids laughed, Molotovs toppling from overhead gantries. Horses whinnied and reared, hooves scattering Goon kids like skittles. A muni flinched, a chunk of concrete bouncing off his crash helmet. Youths surged forward, drawing hammers and knives. The girl giggled, dancing like a dervish while nodes screeched electronic wails from the balconies, missiles falling like hail.

Paolo recognised the music. Not Stamp, with its synthesized bass. The was called *Rage*, berserker screaming, like a wounded beast.

The war drums of the Goons.

The munis fired shock guns, flurries of darts trailing blue fire. Two of the youths shook like landed fish, only to be replaced by more. Sticking close to the building line, Paolo skirted the plaza. The kids ignored him, busy pulling a muni from horseback and boot-stomping his face. More weapons appeared, clutched in grimy fists. Bicycle chains and friction-lock batons, knuckle-dusters and single-shot pistols.

The remaining munis cantered towards the river, shouting into their radios. The crowd surged towards them, yelling and shouting. The horsemen drew carbines from their saddles and opened fire, a bullet hitting the dancing girl in her throat. She spun, a spray of blood making a red crescent on hot concrete. The mob howled, machetes and axes flashing. Gunshots cracked. A horse tumbled, a bloody gash in its flank. The crowd began to chant.

SHANK THE PIGGGSSSS UPPPP!!! SHANK THE GAVVAS!!!

Paolo crossed the bridge, back towards the Commune. Violence in the Goons was like wildfire, a match dropped in a summer-parched forest.

"You there, stop!" ordered a reedy voice. Another muni, shock-gun ready. He was no more than twenty, chin peppered with spots. He shakily dismounted a yellow motor scooter.

"Papa-seven-oh-five," he said into his radio. "Male suspect apprehended."

Paolo raised his hands. "Your colleagues are under attack. They're in serious trouble."

"Don't answer me b-back," the muni stuttered, eyes darting over Paolo's shoulder. His radio crackled, the dispatcher's voice sharp. *Negative, get to the plaza! Urgent assistance, Papa seven-oh-five.*

"Copy that," the muni replied. Turning to Paolo, he tugged a pair of gel-kuffs from his belt. "I'll come back for you."

Papa seven-oh-five, NatSec units ARE running to this call. ALL Papa-Seven units make their way to Kenneth Livingstone Plaza.

The muni pointed his shock gun at Paolo, gel-kuffs in his free hand. "Ball your fists and push them into the kuffs," he ordered.

Paolo chopped the muni's neck with the blade of his hand, a textbook brachial-strike. The cop, eyes bulging, slumped to the ground. Ignoring the voices crackling from the radio, Paolo ratcheted the muni's head like a bottle-top, snapping his neck. He pushed the body in the lagoon, the orange-jacketed corpse disappearing into the brackish murk. The scooter followed.

A riot. Four dead cops. Don't run.

Paolo crossed flyblown plazas and crumbling boulevards, mazes of low-rise housing and early 21st Century tower blocks. A police carrier trundled around a corner, prompting a ragged volley of gunfire from balconies and walkways. The windscreen splintered, bullets punching ragged holes in the carrier's flimsy chassis. Paolo once wondered why the munis drove vehicles liveried in non-tactical orange and yellow. Then someone told him senior officers thought bright colours were *reassuring*. Paolo shook his head. *Reassuringly easy to hit.*

Paolo pulled up his collar. He tasted something on the air. Felt it in his bones. The gathering storm of violence, hungry for blood. A storm that would boil and rage into something else.

War.

SEVEN

Leah and Hooker drove through billowing clouds of yellowish smog. The autonomous steering kicked in, and Leah relaxed. Hooker checked his dosimeter. "Air quality ain't good, but ambient rads are okay."

Leah's smog mask hung around her neck. "You worry 'bout that stuff too much."

Hooker tapped her mask. "You don't worry 'bout it enough."

"And so, equilibrium is achieved."

Barnes was a gated settlement, protected by blast walls and armorglass. Nestled on a defensive peninsula, security guards watched from a copse of artificial trees. Leah stopped the Mercedes at a checkpoint. "Seems like a lot of graft, radicalising Evie Kendrick. Why didn't they just target Lottie from day one?"

A masked guard wearing a hazmat cape ran a mirror under the 4x4. Hooker readied his ID. "My take? Lottie Rhys lives in a fortified mansion in Holland Park with GCHQ-secured Evernet. Her father has a NatSec close protection detail and cronies like Vassa Hyatt to vet newcomers. It would be easier to lure Lottie *out* of that bubble, rather than trying to get inside."

"Yeah, makes sense," Leah replied. "The Crimson are a patient bunch, I'll give 'em that."

The guard was a ferrety-looking man, a machine pistol across his chest. "Welcome to Barnes. What's the purpose of your visit today?" he asked politely, pulling down his mask.

"I'm Hooker. Miss Martinez and I are accredited security contractors," he replied, tapping his armband. "We need to speak with a client on the hurry-up. It's a sensitive matter."

"Which residence?" the guard replied, pulling a pad from his pocket.

"Sorry, client confidentiality," Hooker replied smoothly. "PaxData code restriction. If I told you, I'd be breaching professional confidence. As you can see, we're NatSec cleared."

The guard pointed at the ballistic bag on the back seat. "I'll have to check with my manager. Anyhow, no firearms inside the perimeter. Not even peace-bonded. You can book 'em in with us."

Leah drummed her fingers on the steering wheel. "For fuck's sake. I've got six guineas for you not to give a shit. We ain't here for trouble. You'd know all 'bout it if we were."

"She's from out of town," added Hooker politely.

"I s'pose they do stuff different out there," the guard

replied, running a scanner across Hooker's armband. It trilled happily. "That's fine sir. I wouldn't want to cause any problems for a resident of ours, after all. When you're done, make sure it's via the north gate. I'll clear your vehicle to leave the village."

"I appreciate that." Leah leant over and pushed the guineas in the guard's pocket. More than two month's pay for a working stiff. "Make sure the CCTV's wiped after we've gone. Understand? Technical failure, software glitch... the usual."

"You got it, lady." The guard replied, nodding at the gatehouse. A barrier slid open. "On behalf of Sierra5 Security, enjoy your day in Barnes."

The Kendrick residence was an Edwardian villa, overlooking a manicured village green. Nannies, dressed in pinafores and respirators, wheeled bubble-prams through the smog. Leah nodded at the henge of grimy cloudscrapers encircling the peninsula, shimmering in the BluSky's sickly glow. "I dunno why the rich still live in London. Why not Wessex? It's meant to be perfect, ain't it?"

"Politics," Hooker replied. "Living here shows faith in the Reconstruction. They go back to Wessex at the weekends."

"*Weekends?*"

"Yeah, they only work five days, and take two off. Saturday and Sunday. They call it the weekend."

Leah rolled her eyes. "Lazy fuckers. Let's go and burgle some shit." She parked the Merc on the Kendrick's driveway, next to a vintage Tesla.

"Check this out. Bleep made it for me." Hooker pulled

a grey plastic box from a pocket. He flicked a switch and it warbled happily, an old-fashioned LED screen flickering with alphanumeric sequences.

"Very retro," said Leah. "Brute-force hack?"

"Bleep says its heuristic, whatever that means," Hooker replied. The device began making scratchy noises, a light on its fascia glowing green. "Okay, CCTV off, locks disengaged."

The front door opened into a spacious hallway. Rain capes hung from a hook, two pairs of galoshes on the floor. A poster celebrating a long-ago Olympics had pride of place, pre-Emergency London bathed in golden light. The smell of scented chilli candles pricked their noses. "I hate chilli candles," Hooker grumbled, poking around a side table with gloved fingers. "They make me sneeze."

"They're good for your breathing," said Leah.

"The only place you put chilli is in a curry," Hooker replied, drawing his revolver. "I could murder a curry."

They entered a reception room, painted in white-and-grey checks. "I wouldn't talk about murder," said Leah. The body of a woman lay on the floor, arms akimbo.

"They're definitely in a hurry," said Hooker. "They just capped her in the face." The front of the victim's skull had been blown away, a spume of gore congealing on the carpet.

Leah nodded. "Not very subtle."

"At least two large calibre rounds," Hooker added. "Noisy. A .44 or something similar, I reckon."

Snapping on surgical gloves, Leah rolled the body. "Evie's mother?"

"Reckon so. Evie's prob'ly dead too," Hooker replied, studying the rings on the dead woman's fingers. "Why keep her alive once they'd taken Lottie?"

"Now you're thinking like the Crimson," said Leah, patting down the corpse's pockets. "Nothing much here. No ID or fob."

Upstairs they found Evie's room, white-painted with stripped wooden floors. A vase of black roses withered artfully on a dressing table, next to a tray of cosmetics. "Where do teenage girls hide stuff?" said Hooker.

"At their friend's houses," Leah replied, rifling through a dresser. She made a pile of makeup and jewellery on the bed. "This must be three grands' worth of slap here."

Hooker opened a wardrobe crowded with ballgowns. Velvet and fur and lace, beaded with pearls and gemstones. "I guess Evie was doing the whole Wessex party circuit too."

Leah slid open a drawer and upended it on the bed. Taped underneath was a notebook. "What have we here? Bad poetry. Student politics. Poor-little-rich-girl bullshit about how much she hates her mother. *That's okay, love, you got her killed.*"

"Anything else?"

Leah pulled a slip of paper from the book. "A clue, I reckon. A flyer for an F4P meeting in Camden."

LONDON (NORTH) FRONT 4 PROGRESS RESISTANCE & ASSISTANCE FOR THE BORDERLANDS
Contact Leveller Luke for details - Fob A.00.33-987@14449

"I'll send Gordy the code," said Hooker, pulling his fob from a pocket. "What does *Leveller* mean?"

Leah rolled her eyes. "I can tell you were a pig. The

Levellers were political radicals in the 1600's."

Hooker chuckled. "How d'you know this stuff?"

"Mandatory political education in Nu-Brightonia," Leah shrugged. "Why'd you think I legged it?"

"To avoid being bombed?"

"Well, obviously. But political history lectures and veganism were nearly as bad."

Hooker studied the leaflet. "Leveller Luke doesn't sound very hard-core. I mean, he's put a fob code on a *flyer*."

Leah took the piece of paper and stuffed it in her pocket. "F4P meetings ain't meant to be hard-core, just a recruitment tool. That's how they did it in Brighton, before the Republic. One minute you're making sparkly protest banners, the next you're in the woods setting command wires."

Hooker nodded. He supposed some of the kids he'd killed during the war, starry-eyed revolutionaries, were no different. "Luke might know who 'Roisin' is."

Leah nodded. "I make you right."

Hooker's fob buzzed, Gordy's code flashing on-screen. "Rufus? That fob code is attributed to a Luke Vincent McCaffrey. He's thirty-five years old, only one conviction for fly-posting. Fronts up F4P's London North branch. Beyond that, he's got no obvious security traces to Black Bloc or Crimson Brigade."

"That was the fastest subscriber's check ever, Gordy," Hooker replied. "How the other half live."

"Big fish, big hooks. I'll fob you McCaffrey's address. Looks like it's in Holloway – I know how much you love it up North," Gordy chuckled.

"I'll make sure I've got my passport," Hooker replied, pulling a map from his pocket. "We'll head over there now."

"Have you got anything else? Vassa's fobbing me every five minutes asking for updates."

"Only a theory – Evie Kendrick was radicalised on Libnet, possibly by a Crimson Brigade agent. We think they used Evie to get to Lottie Rhys. Mind you, it happened right under Hyatt's nose." Hooker told Gordy about the videos from Free Medway, and Evie's would-be mentor, Roisin.

"Roisin? What does she have to do with Lottie Rhys?" asked Gordy.

"We're still working on it," Hooker replied. "There's nothing to suggest Lottie's interested in radical politics, is there?"

"I'm sure Vassa would've mentioned something," Gordy replied. "Mind you, it's not unusual for rich kids to get into that sort of thing, is it?"

"Most of 'em draw the line at murder – Evie's mother was executed," Hooker continued. "Several bullets in the face with a .44, which doesn't suggest a domestic Green Zone burglary. I'm assuming Evie's dead too. Tell Hyatt – she can get her hands dirty and call it in."

"Okay, just get out of there Rufus. Find this Luke McCaffrey and squeeze his nuts. We've got thirty-three hours left."

They left the Kendrick residence and drove north. Leah shook her head. "Given how easy it was to bribe the guards, I guess asking for CCTV covering the house would be a waste of time?"

Hooker was half-listening to a news station, reporters

discussing rioting in the Goons. "Asking for CCTV would draw even more attention to ourselves, and the murderer probably used a doppler to change their appearance. We'd be convenient suspects if this thing goes bent."

"That crossed my mind," said Leah.

"Hyatt's too smooth," Hooker replied. "I don't trust her."

They crossed Hammersmith Bridge, neat Regency houses replaced by plastic-roofed favelas. They passed horse-drawn wagons and shoals of muddy cyclists, watched by a gas-masked huddle of *Hammer Brethren*, a local street league. They wore Kevlar breastplates, helmets painted in blue-and-white piebald. Each carried a long truncheon, knives and axes on their belts. Leah pulled a face. "Those knuckle-draggers wouldn't last ten minutes outside the wall."

"True, but the Government likes 'em well enough," Hooker replied. "They keep people in line and don't cost a penny."

"*Ride the crocodile long enough*," Leah said, mimicking the voice of an Oriental mystic, "*eventually it will gobble you up*. Why trust law and order to an army of brain-dead fascists?"

Hooker caught a Leaguer's eye. "Like I said, they're cheap. I remember when this lot started, during the Hate War. They were worse back then."

Leah eyeballed one of the street leaguers. "You don't talk about those days much. Is it true you got a medal?"

"Yeah."

"What for?"

"Killin' people mostly," Hooker replied. "Then they put me in prison."

"Trashmob mentioned it. What exactly did you do?"

Hooker shrugged. "You don't know?"

"I'm your mate, not a stalker. You think I've got time to sit up and evernet you?"

"My unit got involved in a firefight with two archangels. We killed 'em."

Leah's face hardened. "So? They probably deserved it."

"The thirty civilians who died in the process didn't."

Leah spat out of the window. "They kill more civvies in Medway every week."

Hooker's voice hardened. "Things were different back then – after the Hate War everyone wanted to make amends. The politicians offered Taskforcers up as sacrifices, a way of saying sorry." Hooker tucked the mezuzah in his pocket, "I'm starting to think the Government wants Archangels back. I think they'll try to rewrite the history of what really happened."

Leah shook her head. "You're kidding me?"

"It's already happening – look at Wessex. Hyatt said they need transhumans for the Reconstruction."

"The people won't stand for it."

Hooker made a sour face. "The people don't give a shit, long as someone makes the air clean and gives 'em three square meals a day."

"You cheery fucker," said Leah.

Hooker's fob buzzed again. "Gordy's come through with Luke McCaffrey's address. Put your foot down."

"Roger that," Leah replied. "Sooner we can get this

thing done, the sooner I can get back to the No-Zone."

Hooker laughed. "You really do prefer it out there, don't you?"

Leah watched the street leaguers disappear in the rear-view mirror. "Yeah. I really do."

EIGHT

NatSec arrived in the Goons, tacticals spilling from the bellies of personnel carriers. They formed up in neat ranks, armed with rifles and shotguns, radios crackling orders. Riot squads arrived, equipped with armorglass shields, all backed up by cavalry and dogs.

Paolo watched locals hurrying by, pushing barrows piled with bricks and petrol bombs. Up on the balconies, men handed out rifles and crossbows, older Goon-dwellers who remembered the Hate War. Paolo had drunk beer with such men. He knew they'd nothing to lose, and a burning hatred of the police. Yesterday's Taskforcers were today's NatSec. *Same bastards, different uniforms.*

A group of robed figures appeared from an alleyway. "Good afternoon," said a little monk, an Asian man with a wispy beard. He wore an ankle-length robe, a startled-looking hen tucked under his arm. On his feet were sandals fashioned from truck tyres. "I'm Brother Ranjit."

"A good afternoon to you too, Brother," Paolo replied. "Not a good day for a walk, I fear."

"We heard gunfire," said Brother Ranjit. "Lots of it."

Paolo nodded. "You should go to your monastery. It's safer."

The little monk bridled, but said nothing. However, the biggest monk murmured his agreement. A huge man, big as Abid, with the mottled, warped flesh of a burns victim. Paolo had seen him before. The local youths were terrified of his monstrous face and silvery eye implants. He stood at the back of the group like a shepherd, quarterstaff ready.

"Yes, of course you're right," Ranjit replied. "Would you like eggs? We've some spare."

Paolo shook his head. "No time for fragile things today, my friend."

"Of course. Well, we must get back," said Ranjit. The little group melted away, towards the lagoon bridge. The monk with the silver eyes went last, scanning arcs like a soldier.

Paolo walked briskly through a plaza, trash blowing on the wind. He felt the cops before he saw them. "You, in the suit!" bellowed a tactical, three chevrons on her breastplate. Two others broke the building line, carbines ready. They were followed by a six-strong phalanx in riot gear, shields ready.

"Am I glad to see you guys," said Paolo, feigning desperation. "I'm lost."

The sergeant looked him up and down. "You a Green-

Zoner?"

Paolo nodded. He had a resident's permit for an apartment in Southwark, back-stopped by one of Sorcha's agents. "I'm a wholesaler. I was checking stock out here today, of all days."

"You stick out like a donkey's bollock," the sergeant replied. "I'm amazed you ain't been mugged yet."

"My bodyguard went missing, but I know what you mean. Although some of the people here aren't that bad."

The sergeant gave Paolo the look cops reserve for lunatics. "You'll find out how bad they can be, if you don't fuck off sharpish. There's a squad of Munis two blocks up, evacuating all non-residents. Turn right at the next junction and keep going, you'll see their vehicle."

"Thank you, sergeant," Paolo replied. "I really appreciate it."

The tactical studied him closely, taking in his suit and leather shoes. "Wholesaling, you say?"

"Yes, I rent a warehouse nearby." He eyed the sergeant's body-cam, hoping his doppler was working. It would scramble the camera's electronics, rendering him invisible.

"Only reason I ask is sometimes Green-Zoners come out here to score cotics," the sergeant replied. "My men will ID and search you, to be on the safe side. Then I'd get back to the city if I were you."

"Search me?" Paolo felt his pistol, hard against his ribcage. The money belt was damp against his belly. "Is that necessary, sergeant?"

The sergeant shrugged. "Rules are rules. The Goons are on security lock-down. Section Twelve of the Emergency Act is in effect, so papers and pockets. You know the drill."

"Sarge, the blimp's finished mapping the rooftops," one of the riflemen reported. "We're clear to move."

A dirigible passed overhead, a black torpedo bristling with aerials. The sergeant nodded. "Okay, get ready. Roth search this man…"

Paolo shot the sergeant in the throat. Using her body as a shield, his HK35 whispered, nano-munitions slicing through armour. Two more tacticals fell. The riot officers drew their pistols and locked shields, making a wall of armorglass and steel. Bullets chased Paolo, thudding into the dead sergeant, buying him time to roll behind a dumpster. Boots crunched on concrete as the phalanx advanced, Paolo sliding a grenade onto the HK's muzzle. Beyond the dumpster, a voice spoke into a radio. Calm but urgent. "Contact Message. Helios Alpha, this is Helios Six-Zero. We've got three officers down…"

Paolo fired without breaking cover. Trajectory math scrolling across his eye implant, the grenade making a fiery parabola as it sailed into the phalanx. Tacticals scattered, armour melting and trailing smoke. Reloading the HK, the Crimson Brigade agent sprayed flechette into the survivors. Armoured bodies lay in the street like decommissioned robots, ragged figures cheering from the balconies above.

"Six-Zero? This is Helios Alpha," came a voice from a radio. "All Helios callsigns to Six-Zero's last location."

Down to his last magazine, Paolo tugged the dead sergeant's pistol from her holster. Pocketing the weapon, he ran deeper into the estate. The riot was a wildfire beast now, a thing of smoke and blood. Chaotic and surreal, Paolo thought, beauty in its defiance. Men hurled petrol bombs and bricks, hooch-drunk kids dancing like whirligigs. All were masked, armed with axes and staves. They stormed a shield wall, retreating when the tacticals returned fire with choke-gas. Peppery smoke drifted through the streets, loudhailers barking orders to disperse.

Suddenly rifles barked from upper-floor balconies, bullets bouncing off armorglass. NatSec marksmen returned fire and a dozen rioters fell, bloody wounds blossoming across bellies and chests. With a roar, the crowd surged, a wounded beast, smashing angrily into the line of riot cops. Someone barked an order and the shield wall opened, like a monster's jaws, armoured carriers and cavalry storming through the gap. NatSec vehicles crashed into the horde, sending up great clouds of exhaust smoke, rioters disappearing beneath their wheels. Police horses reared, steel-shod hooves smashing skulls. Tacticals with shock guns appeared, sparkling darts hitting any rioter still on their feet. An inspector barked orders and the shield wall reformed, tacticals cracking skulls as they advanced.

Paolo hid in a doorway. Pulling an autojet from his belt, he punched a needle into his thigh. Then, euphoria. The injector flooded his veins with respirocites, a billion microscopic nanobots. Feeling power surge through his body, he scrambled up a wall like an ape. His fingers sank into concrete like crampons, and he soon reached a balcony. "Fuck," said a tattooed pensioner, sipping beer while he watched the rioting below, "you're like Superman, aintya?"

"More of a Joker, I think," said Paolo.

"Where you headin'?"

Paolo pointed towards the Thames. "The Commune International."

"Makes sense – you sound foreign," the old geezer replied, taking in Paolo's suit.

Below the balcony, tacticals advanced, followed by their carriers. As a junction was taken, a new squad emerged from the vehicles to relieve the first. "They must have killed dozens," said Paolo.

"It's a shame, I'll grant you, but some of these kids are askin' for it," the old man shrugged. "Way I see it? They need to teach these little shits how to behave. Like the Taskforcers did, back in the old days. Then there's no need to shoot 'em in the first place."

"You really think that?"

"Why wouldn't I? At least the squatters at the Commune have some manners. Nobody needs to give them a battering, do they?"

He has a point.

Paolo pointed at the estates, an urban sprawl encrusting the entire estuary. "Look at the size of this place. They could kill hundreds of rioters and it wouldn't matter. Won't the people revolt against the police?"

"Nah," the old man replied. "They're rioting for fun. Besides, if it gets worse they'll bring up the heavy squad from Kent. Strike Cadres, they call 'em. Those bastards don't fuck around, just get the flamethrowers out." He grinned, miming with shaky hands and made a *whooshing* noise.

Paolo nodded. "I must go. What's the quickest way back?"

The geezer ducked, a bullet ricocheting off a wall. "Fuck

me, that was close. Take the lift to the basement, if it's working. There's a fire door leading into a long ol' alley. Follow that all the way, you'll see the corner of the park. Then you're home and dry."

Paolo thanked the old man. A few moments later he was in the alleyway, snaking between rows of low-rise housing units. The Crimson Brigade agent ran at incredible speed, arteries flooded with oxygen. He remembered the quartermaster in Bari issuing him the autojet. "This stuff will turn you into an archangel. But only for fifteen minutes. After that? You'll have the worst hangover ever. So be careful, Colonel."

Paolo crossed an apron of scraggly parkland, lying in the Commune's shadow. In the near-distance, a line of orange-jacketed munis patrolled the perimeter. They couldn't get inside the Commune proper, as the anarchists had erected a network of defences – palisades and berms, big as the barrier that once protected Berlin from fascists.

Easily scaling a tree, Paolo leapt from trunk to trunk, the munis no more than a hundred metres distant. A branch snapped like a gunshot. A muni's head turned in his direction when Paolo heard something below.

A thud.

The stolen gun had fallen from his pocket, the one taken from the dead tactical. Munis began shouting, pointing at the figure in the trees. Cursing, Paolo made for the palisade. A gaggle of rifle-toting anarchists stood guard, waving at the mysterious Italian who lived at the top of the tower. The black-marketeer, generous with gossip and vintage cigarettes. Paolo scaled the wall easily. "Nice moves," said a sentry, "but you could have come in through the gate."

"Lock the gates," Paolo replied. "There's rioting, and its coming this way." At the lobby his head swam, the respirocite waning. Praying the lifts were working, he staggered inside. Finally, he returned to the apartment at the top of the tower.

Rourke sat on the sofa, legs tucked beneath her, sipping tea. She studied Paolo for a moment, cigarette smouldering in her thin-lipped mouth. "You look terrible."

"There's a riot out there," Paolo replied.

"It's the Goons. That's what they do."

Paolo unlimbered his shoulder holster. The HK clattered on the cheap plastic table, heavy and black.

"That's been fired," said Rourke, levelling a finger at the weapon's carbon-blackened muzzle.

"I had to defend myself. Where's Abid?"

Rourke raised her voice. "Abid, can you come through please?"

The giant entered the tiny living area, head bowed. He wore the grey and brown uniform of a courier company, fabric straining against muscle. "I am sorry about what happened with the girl earlier, Colonel Paolo," he mumbled.

Paolo slumped onto the sofa, accepting Rourke's cigarette. "Your apology is gratefully accepted, Abid. If my words were harsh earlier, it's because your role's too important to be compromised. That includes how you're perceived *after* your martyrdom. Do you understand?"

Abid nodded slowly, eyes downcast. "Yes, Colonel Paolo."

Rourke smiled a *well-that's-alright-then* smile and

gestured at the omni. Drone footage of rioting streamed across the newscasts. "This is inconvenient, Paolo. I've got to meet my source, and Abid needs to collect the van. With that going on outside?"

Paolo lit the cigarette with a shaky hand. A roll-up. *Uh.* "The worse the rioting gets, more security forces get sucked onto the estate. That means less on the periphery, where you're heading. You'll be okay."

Rourke finished her tea and stood up, knees creaking. Her eyes, watery blue, gave nothing away. "I need to get my arse in gear. If Abid doesn't know where he's taking the bomb, then none of this makes any difference."

Abid nodded. "Rourke is right."

"Then I'll parley with General Ignacio," said Paolo. "He leads the Black Rifles on the fifteenth floor."

"Those crazy Spaniards?" said Rourke. "The Black Rifles are trouble, Paolo. They're too unpredictable."

Paolo made a thin smile. "I doubt we've much choice. The Spaniards will take dark work for gold, and I know they've contacts on the Crosland Estate. I'll ask them to smuggle Abid to the vehicle, and you to your agent."

"Optimistic bugger, ain't you?" Rourke replied, turning her attention to the omni. It showed a trashy news channel, two orange-faced newscasters fizzing with excitement.

"We've received reports from the notorious Crosland Estate in Lagoon City - NatSec sources report NINE tactical officers have been ruthlessly gunned down by terrorists."

"A significant escalation of what initially appeared to be a

typical Lagoon City fracas. Do you have any updates?"

"Yes, Oscar. And, incredibly, the suspect is a lone male. Eyewitnesses say he was armed with high-technology weaponry and explosives."

"A Black Bloc agitator, perhaps? From Free Medway?"

"It certainly fits the profile. There's a police news conference at fifteen-thirty. The Home Secretary, Tobias Castle, has announced full National Security Constabulary and military support to suppress the rioting."

"That's reassuring, although many have concerns about the so-called Commune International? The local Municipal Police have been criticized for tolerating the presence of anarchists in the Goons for so long."

"The Munis have long-complained of a lack of resources. But if there is a link, Oscar, and my sources suggest there might, NatSec's hand will be forced. Dead tacticals on our streets? A nest of potential terrorists on London's doorstep? There's only one way that story ends…"

"Agreed! Viewers might need to hunker down, order pizza and stay tuned. This is going to be a night of epic action out in the Goons. We'll have the freshest coverage, expert commentary and live VR drone-feeds! Be part of the action, only here on…"

Rourke's raised an eyebrow. *"Lone male suspect. Advanced weaponry. Takes out multiple cops on his own.* Now, who the feck might that be?"

Paolo glanced at the HK35 on the table. "Abid, would you mind fixing me something to eat please? I'll be in my room."

Abid nodded and headed to the kitchen. "Yes, Colonel

Paolo."

Rourke crossed her arms. "Seriously, Paolo, I need to get out of here and meet my man. I'll hold you to your word about the Spaniards."

Paolo dusted off his jacket. "Of course, Sorcha."

The Irishwoman's smile was thin. "Otherwise, I'm sure the Command Committee will be wanting to know why this job went tit's up. Why we risked our entire London network…"

Paolo's lip curled. "Threaten me again, *Comrade,* and we'll see who is more favoured. If you handled your agents more efficiently, we'd already know where the conference was being held."

"Really?" Rourke snapped, hands-on-hips. "You'll have to do better than that, big man. My network's never been found wanting. Who else could penetrate the Rhys family security bubble?"

Paolo unzipped the belt he wore against his skin, tossing packets of dollars on the table. "This is for your source, who has *yet to be found wanting*. I'm going to eat. Afterwards I'll make arrangements for us to complete our mission."

"Best you do, my love," Rourke replied. "I've been in this godforsaken city for five bloody years. I'll not let this fuck-up make it six."

Paolo left the room, legs rubbery from the respirocite come-down. He kneaded his face. It felt clammy. Like dead fish. He sat on his bed, shaking, and began cleaning weapons.

NINE

Luke McCaffrey's address was on the fifteenth floor of a municipal cloudscraper, the summit obscured by smog. Hooker and Leah parked outside, masked pedestrians navigating rubble-strewn streets. "North London," said Hooker sourly. "Don't like it up 'ere. Never did."

Leah slid out of the driver's seat. "North. South. Everything looks the same. Rubble. Big buildings. Smog. More rubble."

"Yeah, but you're from Brighton."

"I suppose a sea view makes the rubble look easier on the eye."

The cloudscraper's lobby smelt of boiled vegetables. Hooker found the entry-phone and pressed a buzzer marked *710*. No answer.

"Over there," said Leah, pointing at a woman sitting

behind a desk. A sign said DUTY CARETAKER. She studied a book of Sudoku puzzles, chewing on the end of a pencil. A fire bucket leaked sand by her foot.

"I'm looking for McCaffrey. Apartment 710," said Hooker. "He ain't answering his doorbell."

"Go and knock on his door then," the caretaker replied, not looking up from her puzzles. Neatly laid out on the desk were a fob, a packet of cigarettes and a dosimeter.

"Lift's broken," Hooker replied. "You see him today?"

"Can't say I have." The caretaker replied, putting down her book and studying Hooker carefully. She took in the revolver on his belt, "anyhow, it's only fifteen floors. You look like a fit enough fella."

Hooker folded his arms. "I'm in a hurry."

"And you are?"

Leah tapped her armband. "Licenced security contractors."

The caretaker patted her pockets and found a lighter. She lit a menthol cigarette and sighed. "McCaffrey, you say? You know how many people live here?"

Leah flipped a golden guinea on the desk. "*Leveller Luke*? Come on sister. I bet you call the filth every time he sets foot out of the building."

The caretaker scowled. "I ain't no grass. Fucking dross like you, comin' to the city with your guns and fancy dress. Why don't you fuck off back to the No-Zone?"

Leah slapped two more coins on the table. "I will, but not before I stick that book up your fat, lazy arse."

The caretaker pocketed the guineas. "He left 'bout an hour back. I reckon he'll be at the old library, just off Kentish

Town Road. Near the motor-mart."

"Thanks," Leah replied, plucking the pencil from the caretaker's desk. She scribbled the missing answer to caretaker's Sudoku puzzle. "There you go."

"Bitch."

A shrug. "It's been said before."

They drove to Kentish Town. The library was a crumbling building of yellowish London brick, windows shuttered. Leah reversed into a parking space. "What a dump. I didn't realise how much of the Green Zone is still in ruins."

Hooker pointed at diggers scooping debris into a row of metal skips. "This area got it bad – suitcase nuke went off in Highgate. The Global Jihad Brigade claimed that one. Just shy of six thousand dead and ten years of cancer weather."

"Luckily it was only a suitcase nuke," Leah replied. "Hooker, you okay?"

Hooker peered into the rear-view mirror, lip curled. "See the grey panel van? On the nearside junction behind us."

"Yeah, I see it. Problem?"

"It's the only vehicle 'round here not covered in dents. I smell NatSec."

"Reckon they're onto us?"

"Dunno, they might. Then again, it might be routine surveillance on McCaffrey." They got out of the 4x4 and walked to the library. Hooker pulled a gadget covered in gummy tape from a pocket and stuck it into the doorframe as he entered – a motion-sensitive camera, the kind hunters used. Hooker activated the device, an image of the street appearing inside his goggles.

The library was a place of grimy walls and stained

wooden floors. No books, only empty shelves. The place smelt of damp and old polish, corkboards displaying yellowing posters for coffee mornings, children's play-groups and the local Women's Institute.

WE'RE IN A JAM SO MAKE SOME! PRESERVE AND SURVIVE!

Leah laughed. "That's funny - they've got time to make jam?"

"I like jam," Hooker replied. "Reminds me of when I was a kid. Toast and jam, with butter."

Leah smiled. "Butter? Can't remember the last time I tasted butter."

A skinny man approached, stooped and sandy-haired. Hooker saw the sleeves of his sweater were frayed from being chewed. "Can I help?" he said, arranging folding chairs into neat rows. "The rooms already booked for a meeting."

"You're Luke McCaffrey?" said Hooker.

The man studied their contractor's armbands and weapons. "Yes, I'm McCaffrey. What do you want?"

"My name's Rufus Hooker. This is Leah Martinez. We're looking for Evie Kendrick and Charlotte Rhys."

"Oh," said McCaffrey, taking a sideways look at the fire door. "May I ask why?"

Hooker raised an eyebrow. "'Cuz we are."

"Has a crime been committed? Aren't you supposed to caution me or something?"

"That would suggest we suspected you of something," said Hooker. "Feelin' guilty, Luke?"

"The girls have gone missing," said Leah, pulling up a chair. She adjusted her gun-belt and sat down, armour creaking. "We know they came to meetings here. Yesterday, for example."

McCaffrey pulled at the hem of his moth-eaten sweater, voice rising an octave. "Says who? Besides, a lot of people come to our meetings. I couldn't possibly know them all."

Hooker sighed. "The Reconstruction Minister's daughter turns up in this toilet, all the way from Holland Park, and you don't know 'bout it?"

"Stop taking the piss," Leah added. "We know they met a woman called Roisin. Who's she?"

McCaffrey opened a box and pulled out a sheaf of leaflets. They showed cartoons of tacticals bayonetting civilians. He began placing them on chairs. "May I ask who you work for?"

"Someone with an interest in the girls' welfare," Hooker replied. "No Government, no NatSec and no drama. We just want to find the girls, make sure they're safe and get paid for our trouble."

"That didn't answer my question," McCaffrey replied.

"Why does it matter?" said Leah. "Or don't you care two girls are missing?"

"Of course I care," McCaffrey bristled. A leaflet floated to the floor, a picture of a fighter jet with swastikas scrawled on the wings. "Actually, what I *care* about are the atrocities taking place in Free Medway…"

Hooker nodded. "Ever been down there?"

McCaffrey looked at his feet. "I've seen the videos."

"I've grafted down in Medway," Hooker replied. "The Black Bloc ain't the freedom fighters you make 'em out to be. Just like the Government ain't the good guys they make themselves out to be."

"My politics aren't the issue, are they? In any case, I doubt if I can help," McCaffrey replied. "I remember Evie, but nothing much about the other girl. She only came to yesterday's meeting, I think."

Leah punched McCaffrey in the belly. He doubled up, chin bouncing off her knee. "Bong! Wrong answer, *Leveller* Luke."

Hooker shook his head. "Forgive my partner. She's still learning the basics of conducting investigations in a Green Zone environment."

McCaffrey sat on the floor, nose bloodied. "You're as bad as NatSec, aren't you?"

"Maybe. Then again, we're nowhere near as bad as your friends in the Bloc," said Leah, studying her knuckles. "Or the Crimson Brigade."

Hooker shot Leah a look. *Don't give too much away.* "Luke? Tell us about Roisin and the girls."

"Okay, someone called Roisin does come here now and then," McCaffrey replied, eyeing Leah's gauntleted fists. "I think she travels up from Croydonia on the tram. I assume she's sympathetic to the Bloc, she has that way about her. I leave her alone. *My* politics are non-violent."

Leah stood over the activist. "You still let the Bloc sneak around, looking for fresh meat?"

McCaffrey got to his feet, jutting his chin. "Every struggle needs foot-soldiers."

Leah laughed. "Always the same, ain't it? Wankers like you, sittin' in meetings. Drinking tea and talking about Gramsci. People like me? We take the kickings in the back of a riot van."

McCaffrey cocked his head. "You were Bloc?"

"Trust me, if you'd joined you'd hate 'em too. I was there when they razed Nu-Brightonia, after the Crimson legged it."

"I want you both to leave," said McCaffrey. "Go now. Please."

"Or what?" Leah replied, "gonna call NatSec?"

Hooker pulled out his notebook. "I ain't going anywhere, son. Tell me about Roisin. I need a description. Does she have a vehicle? A fob code?"

McCaffrey fell into a chair, staring blankly at the floor. "I'd say she was thirty-five, maybe older, with an Irish accent. Black hair, squinty blue eyes. She mentioned she was a nurse once, I don't know what sort. I've never had a fob code for her – she didn't offer, and I didn't ask."

Hooker scratched at his notebook with a pencil stub. "What's her surname?"

McCaffrey shrugged, "that isn't how it works."

Hooker rested a hand on McCaffrey's shoulder and gently squeezed. The activist flinched. "You're a poor liar. I need something I can work with. *Think*."

McCaffrey rubbed his brow, as if trying to squeeze a thought out. "I know it sounds silly, but Roisin has a thing about *tea*. Old-fashioned tea. She drinks it all the time, even brings a flask to meetings. It smells awful, like perfume. Apparently, you can only get it on the black market."

"Okay, Luke, that's better than nothing," Hooker replied. "Which black market?"

"I asked her about the tea once, and she laughed. She

told me she ended up in the Goons once looking for a particular type…"

An image flickered in Hooker's peripheral vision, the hunter's camera flickering to life. Dark-clothed figures hurried across the street. "NatSec – Leah, get him out of here."

Leah grabbed McCaffrey's arm. "Move," she ordered, dragging him towards the fire exit.

Hooker faced the door, hands on head. Three plainclothes agents burst into the hall, pistols ready. They were followed by a hard-faced woman wearing a raincoat, three chevrons on the badge clipped to her collar. "Well, fuck my old boots, it's Rufus Hooker," she declared. "Where's Luke McCaffrey?"

"Hanne Tollen," Hooker replied easily. "You're a sergeant now? How long did that take, twenty years?"

"What can I say? I'm on the fast-track," The NatSec officer replied. She turned to her men, "search the place and warn Traynor out back. The girl and the suspect are somewhere 'round here. They're armed, remember."

"We've got contractor's licences and firearms permits," Hooker replied.

"Don't mean shit, Rufus. Not where you're concerned," said Tollen.

Hooker kept his hands where the cop could see them. "You were a good operator. How d'you end up festering in the back of an obbo van?"

Tollen scowled, making the scar on her cheek twitch. "Like I said, my career's on fire. At least I ain't down in Medway. Now, who gave you a gig in the Green Zone?"

Hooker chuckled. "Like I'm gonna tell NatSec."

"Gordy Rice?" Tollen tapped her ID badge with a gloved finger. "Let me remind you of the Contract Security Outsourcing Act – Section Four, Paragraph Two, sub-section C: *independent security contractors will, at all times, cooperate fully with sworn law enforcement. Failure to do so may lead to withdrawal of accreditation.*"

Hooker shook his head. "*Rules*, Tollen? You've changed."

"Stop fucking about, Rufus. You've compromised my operation."

A thick-set agent returned, glaring sulkily at Hooker. "Traynor's gone missing, sarge. He ain't answering his fob."

"Go and find him then, fuck-nuts," Tollen hissed.

"Yes, sarge."

"Hooker, you're pinched," said Tollen. "Section Twelve. I'm taking you in for questioning."

"Ain't my fault you lost your officer," Hooker replied.

Tollen's eyes darted around the room. "Tell me, why is Luke McCaffrey of interest to *you?* You're all about missing persons, right? This is political work."

Hooker rubbed his chin. "D'you remember that night in Gravesend? Drinking hooch and watching artillery fallin' on Tilbury? Sorta romantic, weren't it?"

"Rufus, if you think I'm kidding…"

Hooker smiled. "You were different then, Hanne. Full of the joys of spring."

Tollen jabbed Hooker's neck with a finger. "Ow," he winced.

"I'm gonna throw you in a containment cell, then you

can go back to the Isle of Man. I heard it's rough over there, lots of *mano-a-mano* action."

"Okay, you got me. I've got a lead. Luke McCaffrey's a witness in a people-trafficking case," Hooker lied. "Green-Zone meat for No-Zone shops. You know the drill."

"Bullshit." Tollen keyed her fob, "Nash, Gregory, get in here. Bring the gel-kuffs."

The fob crackled. "Sarge, Traynor's kuffed to the toilet."

"Stay there Hooker," Tollen ordered. "Try to leave and I'll have you shot."

Hooker smiled at the NatSec sergeant. "I reckon your day just got even worse."

Tollen turned on her heel, angry eyes fixed on Hooker's. "What?"

Hooker tapped his goggles. "Someone just stole your shiny new obbo van."

TEN

"What an eejit this Peeler is," said Rourke, eyes fixed on the omni. "Would you look at this ludicrous peacock of a man?"

Paolo swung his feet on the table and lit a cigarette. "He's the NatSec chief? Probably a uniform fetishist with an inadequacy complex. Let's see what the dolt has to say."

The Chief Constable of the National Security Constabulary was taking questions. He glowered from a lectern, face blotched by radiation burns. He wore a smart black tunic and cap, the Emergencies Medal at his throat. "Seventeen officers were murdered today," he growled. "I've got a further fifty-eight injured. Furthermore, we have evidence linking this outrage to the so-called *Commune International*."

"What would you say to the Communards, Chief Constable?" asked a journalist.

"*Communards*? You mean squatters? Anyone illegally occupying municipal premises adjacent the Crosland Estate has twenty-four hours to surrender," the Chief Constable replied, flipping open a gold pocket watch. "As of *now*."

"And if they refuse?" asked the woman from the BBC.

"I shall initiate measures under Section Twelve of the Emergencies Act. NatSec has ample resources. Our tactical options are many, our resolve absolute."

"Can you elaborate, Chief Constable?"

"I'll level the Commune," the policeman replied, eyes gleaming. "The Government has authorised military support. If necessary, Multi-Launch Rocket Systems will be deployed."

"Artillery?" Rourke snorted. She returned to the kettle, humming as she rifled in a cupboard. "Ah, Earl Grey. He abolished slavery, don't you know? This is an ethical cuppa, and no mistake. You know how much I pay those wee bastards for Earl Grey?"

"Who'd have thought there'd be more profit smuggling tea than ammunition?" Paolo replied, switching off the omni. The mysteries of Capitalism never failed to amaze him.

"I've not many teabags left."

Paolo studied his cigarette. "Your source *dried up*, eh?"

"I'm not big on euphemism, Colonel. You know I had to kill her," Rourke replied. "No more Marlboro for you, either."

Paolo nodded. "I need to smoke less. You did what was necessary, like the Kendrick girl and her mother."

"I've never particularly enjoyed wet-work," said Rourke. "What do you think about his threat to bring in the big guns?"

"A hollow threat, I suspect. Although the Chief Constable reminds me of a general I once met."

Rourke sipped her tea. "A general?"

Paolo nodded. "Generals love firepower. I find these things usually boil down to firepower. I was standing next to Colonel-General Kutuzov when he ordered the nuclear strike on Hamburg. I'll never forget the look on his face when he realised the warheads were sabotaged and targeting systems hacked."

"By Archangels?"

"Yes. They wanted a wholly conventional war. The Archangels were whispering in the ears of the Russians and the Americans and the Chinese. Simultaneously. The nuclear weapons capability of all three, completely compromised."

"It doesn't make sense," Rourke replied, shaking her head. "They let India and Pakistan nuke each other..."

"That was only a matter of time anyway," Paolo snorted. "Besides, the Archangels were slaves to a warped logic, way beyond our understanding. RXP opens your mind, in ways cattle like us can only dream of. That's their excuse, anyway."

"What happened to General Kutuzov?" asked Rourke.

"Executed for incompetence. He wasn't the only one – the Kremlin claimed the whole thing was an attempted coup by rogue military elements."

Rourke began rolling a cigarette. "Were you with the Crimson then?"

"No," Paolo shrugged, studying the omni covering Lottie Rhys. The girl sat with her back to the wall, next to a boarded-up window. She stared at the camera, red-eyed and snot-nosed. "Although, ironically, our interests were aligned. I spent a lot of time tracking archangels."

Rourke looked like she wanted to ask more, but instead she brushed cigarette ash from her skirt. "Any news from the Spaniards?"

Paolo glanced at his watch. "It's in hand."

"I'm sorry we had cross words earlier," said Rourke, fussing over the kettle. "I'm sure you know what it's like, when a job hits a bump in the road."

No, I don't. This level of incompetence seems to be your hallmark. "Of course, Sorcha. Think nothing of it. I'll be back soon."

Paolo took the lift down to the Spaniards' lair. He knocked on the steel door, a CCTV camera whirring towards him. A dark-skinned man dressed in camouflage appeared, a Kalashnikov in his hands. "*Qué deseas?*" he said.

"The General's expecting me," Paolo replied in the same language.

"Ah, the Italian. *Ciao,* Mister Paolo."

Ignacio of the Black Rifles lounged on an inflatable airbed. He was a sun-bronzed Adonis, with a broad, handsome face, muscles peppered with scars. Other warriors sat nearby, along with a gaggle of half-dressed concubines. "Ah, my good friend Comrade Paolo! Would you like a drink?"

"Thank you, General Ignacio. Coffee. Arabica, if you have it."

Ignacio barked orders at a flunky. He cradled a bottle of beer in one hand, a reefer in the other. "How the fuck did this riot happen?" he said, waving at an omni. The Chief

Constable was still taking questions, sneering at journalists and promising war.

"I've no idea." Paolo replied.

His mission briefing had included a profile of the Spaniard – the General was a career anarchist, revelling in the contradiction. He'd commanded the Black Rifles in North Africa. *Los Fusiles Oscuros,* a notorious brigade of mercenary freebooters. They'd fought for any number of revolutionary groups in developing countries, from Angola to Zimbabwe. Their price was always the same – whores and booze, glory and gold.

Ignacio popped the cap from another beer. "I'm tempted to negotiate with the pigs, but we have a certain reputation to consider."

"Better to fight another day, perhaps," Paolo replied. He knew the Black Rifles had stretched their luck by coming to London. Trouble followed them like fleas on a dog. A year from now? Perhaps things would be different. The Crimson would need men like Ignacio, come the Revolution. Men happy to form firing squads and hang class-traitors from lampposts.

The General wiped beer from his beard. "Another day indeed, but you know how it goes Paolo. British pigs aren't like the Germans or Spanish, even those black-uniformed NatSec bastards. They will not use artillery, that is bullshit. Yes, I think we can have a fight to satisfy our honour, *then* talk."

Paolo's take on the situation was different – the Commune was a convenient scapegoat for London's intractable political crises. Destroying it would be like lancing a boil. He thought Ignacio an idiot. "A wise compromise, General."

Ignacio took a hit from his reefer and smiled. "I'm glad you agree."

"I have two people I need to move out of the Commune," Paolo explained. "Are you able to get them to the west side of the estate, near the PROTEX ramp?"

Ignacio glanced at his men, who looked back and shrugged. Eyebrows were raised. Paolo wondered if they made decisions via some sort of fell Iberian telepathy. "Yes, that's possible," said Ignacio.

"It's very risky," said one of the Spaniards, a pot-bellied man, bare-chested under his long leather coat. "There's a war going on outside, Paolo."

"But not impossible," said the General.

Paolo raised an eyebrow. "How would you get them out?"

Ignacio pulled himself to his feet, kicking the airbed away. "Ah, Paolo. Always asking questions. I simply confirmed we could do it. The rest is my business."

"Very well, General. Now, as a goodwill gesture, here are fifty-thousand RDs. A tribute to your cause." Paolo pulled off his money belt and tossed it to Ignacio. *Your cause being your continued wealth.*

"I knew I liked you," Ignacio chuckled. He took the belt and unzipped it, "I'm sure I don't need to count it."

"Of course not. Perhaps you can feign preliminary negotiations with the police? Buy more time?"

"Yes," said Ignacio, "an excellent idea. In fact, I was about to suggest it myself."

"Ignacio!" said a woman dressed in black, carbine across her chest. "The omni."

A newscaster looked solemnly to camera. *"Police sources reveal damning evidence has come to light, strongly suggesting anarchist involvement in the murder of tactical officers in Lagoon City…"*

"What have you heard, Anjelica?"

"A stolen handgun, belonging to a murdered NatSec officer, was retrieved from the near the Commune International. NatSec is giving a press conference at the top of the hour, pending forensic tests…"

"The pigs planted a fucking gun!" Ignacio bawled, hurling a beer bottle at the omni. A flunky passed him another. "This is exactly the sort of shit you'd expect them to do."

"Absolutely, General." Paolo replied, stony-faced. "The fascists will use any ruse to justify their aggression. There are bigger webs being spun, I'm sure. Perhaps they plan a new offensive in Free Medway, and this is chaff to distract attention?"

The camouflaged sentry strode into the room, Kalashnikov ready. "Tacticals arrive in force, General. Assault teams of *Federales.*"

Ignacio staggered, beer sploshing on his boots. "Open the armoury. Issue weapons. Send word to our friends on the west side to attack the pigs, draw them away."

"Yes, my General," the sentry replied.

"Get the secondary generators working," Ignacio ordered, "and get our fucking Darkwire access back. I need the surveillance cameras online."

Paolo accepted a dainty cup of coffee and took a sip. It was excellent, as was the little cookie balanced on the saucer. "And what of our deal, general?"

Ignacio puffed out his chest, eyes fixed on the dollars scattered on the table. "It shall be honoured, of course. I will send men to your apartment soon."

Paolo left the Spaniards, pausing in a corridor to look out of the window. Outside, NatSec carriers manoeuvred near the palisade, tacticals forming shield walls. With them were squads of officers with ladders and door-breaching equipment. The Spanish would need to mobilise quickly, or be overwhelmed. Heading to the basement, Paolo retrieved the explosives for Abid to place in the van.

He began the slog to the apartment, a heavy kitbag slung across his back. He found the front door ajar. Abid sat on the couch, a bloody cloth held to his face. Rourke was next to him, head in his hands. "What happened?"

Rourke's voice was thick with anger. "The girl attacked Abid again."

A piece of sharp wood jutted from the Yemeni's cheek. His eyes shone dully, blood rolling down slab-flat cheeks.

Paolo balled his fists. In any other circumstance he'd have shot Abid in the head. "I suggest you explain yourself."

Abid seemed to grow as he threw back his shoulders, voice a snarl. "The girl ran past me, into the room. She saw her fate – the sword, and went crazy."

"Why, Abid? Why were you with her?"

The Yemeni towered over Paolo. He plucked the piece of wood from his face, blood stippling the floor. "Tomorrow I will be martyred, God willing. I have not been with a woman for two years. If I want that girl, who is going to die anyway, then I will have her."

"How many fucking *virgins* are you people meant to have waiting up there?" Paolo sneered.

Abid bared his teeth. "Mock my faith again, *Kaffur*, and I will kill you."

"Paolo, would you put the gun down please?" said Rourke.

Paolo didn't even realise he'd pulled the HK35. His thumb slid to the safety. *Snick.* "This is *my* operation. I am in command. That girl is precious, for reasons you cannot possibly understand."

"You tell us nothing," Abid shrugged. "I *die* for nothing?"

"My word isn't good enough?"

"You insult me, Colonel."

"You insult yourself and your superiors. Focus on the mission, and there'll be no insults on either side."

The Yemeni glowered, indifferent to the blood dripping from his chin. "I do not understand? Why protect the girl?"

"The Crimson Brigade does not tolerate rape. It's non-negotiable, Abid."

The Yemeni met Rourke's eye. She nodded slowly, smiling. "You know he's right, Abid. What would God want you to do?"

"Very well," Abid replied. "I will speak of it no more."

"Good," said Paolo. "The Spaniards will escort you both to the west side of the estate. The explosives are in this bag, Abid. Sorcha, you'll be given an escort to your rendezvous. Fob both Abid and I when your agent provides the location of Rhys's press conference. Is the encryption node working?"

Rourke checked the metal sphere sitting on the table. "The node's ready. We can Lib-net the execution without being traced."

"Abid, do you understand?"

"Yes, Paolo."

Paolo unlocked the door to Lottie's room. The girl lay in the corner, cord lashed around her ankles and wrists. She sobbed, body shaking. He peeled the blindfold from her eyes. "Lottie, listen to me."

"Bastard," she sobbed, face bruised. Sheened with blood and saliva. "You know, don't you? You know I'm…"

"Shush, child," said Paolo, pulling his fob from his pocket. "The sword you saw? It's a ruse to scare your father. D'you understand?"

"Who are you calling?" said Lottie, looking at the fob.

"Vassa Hyatt, of course. Trust me, Lottie, when I say you can get out of this situation alive…"

ELEVEN

Tollen jabbed her pistol into Hooker's chest. "Call your skanky friend. Tell her I want my fucking van back."

Hooker brushed the gun away, eyebrow raised. "Put a weapon within reaching distance of me again, and you'll most likely get shot."

"Always the tough guy, Hooker."

"Give it a rest, Hanne. If you pull the trigger, she'll come for you."

"Who?"

"Leah Martinez. Grew up in the refugee camps, used to fight for the Bloc in Brighton. Your worst nightmare, if she takes a dislike to you."

Tollen's men returned to the hall, one with a badly-bruised face. "I'm gonna kill the runty bitch," he said, fists balled.

Tollen shook her head. "I doubt it, Traynor. You let the *runt* get the van keys, didn't you?"

"She surprised me," Traynor protested. "She was fast."

Hooker pulled up his goggles. "A quiet word, please, Sergeant Tollen?"

Tollen walked across the hall, boots scattering McCaffrey's leaflets. "Best you make it quick, Hooker."

"I know what NatSec are like when it comes to fuck-ups," Hooker whispered. "You're in the shit, and you know it. Just gimme twenty minutes with Luke McCaffrey and I'll get your van back."

Tollen glanced at her hapless officers. "Those clowns wouldn't have lasted ten minutes on the Taskforces. Yeah, they're always dropping me in the shit, but that doesn't mean I'm gonna trust you."

"I promise you can take me in if I don't keep my side of the bargain. I'll lose my contracting permit, and my fee for the job I'm on."

Tollen's lip curled. "Bullshit, Rufus. You'll be back in the No-Zone by then."

Hooker drew close, breath hot on the cop's ear. "During the Tribunals, did I ever mention your name? You went a bit... *feral*, I remember. I might have got a couple of years off my sentence if I'd served you up."

Tollen went to say something. Hooker's finger brushed her lips. "It's history," he said gently. "Ancient history. In fact, I'm forgetting it as we speak."

Tollen's skin was the colour of chalk. "We did what we had to do, right?"

"Only you know the answer to that."

Tollen holstered her gun. "Okay, Rufus, in exactly forty-five minutes I'll have my vehicle back undamaged. Understand?"

"It's a deal. Now, what's the deal with McCaffrey? Were you gonna pinch him?"

Tollen shrugged, "yeah, just routine detention and questioning. Keeps the Red bastards on their toes."

"Hiding in vans? Bit old school, ain't it?"

"You can't put a drone on every bloody meeting" Tollen shrugged. "Resources get sent down to Medway, or up to Scotland. Not to the Green-Zone. Or even the No-Zone for that matter."

"There's rioting there today."

"What's new? If it was going that bent, I'd have heard by now. They'd put us back in uniform and give us shields."

NatSec aren't looking for Lottie Rayne. Not Yet. "Gimme your code," said Hooker, "you'll get your van back."

Tollen scowled. "What about McCaffrey?"

"I ain't got much love for Reds, but I ain't giving a man up for a quota."

"Listen, Hooker…"

"That's the deal," Hooker replied. "You get your wagon back, but you can find McCaffrey off your own back."

"I'd better get it back," Tollen growled, joining her men at the other side of the library. "Or you'll never hear the end of it. Nor will the No-Zone bitch."

Hooker keyed his fob. "Leah, where are you?"

"Turn left outside the library. Take a right, then another. You'll pass an old pub. I'm parked up in the car mart, behind an orange trailer."

Hooker walked to a yard, crowded with battered vehicles. Potential buyers kicked tyres and rapped on windows, bug-eyed in their smog masks. The NatSec van was parked in a row of caravans and trailers, engine ticking over. The door slid open, revealing Leah's grinning face. Inside, the vehicle was a familiar tangle of equipment and omniscreens, littered with food wrappers, sudoku books and piss-bottles. "Is he okay?" said Hooker, nodding at McCaffrey.

"Luke? He's just peachy," Leah replied, patting McCaffrey on the knee, "aintya?"

"What do you want now?" he said, hands trembling. "Why are NatSec after me?"

"They suspect you of facilitating terrorism," Hooker lied. He put his feet on the bench and pulled a water bottle from his belt. "They want to stitch you up. Now tell me, where's Lottie Rhys?"

"I told you, I don't bloody know."

"NatSec'll pull your fingernails out," said Leah, playing with the van's camera controls. "I also heard they like to take Reds on copter rides. Kick 'em out over the estuary, just for shit and giggles."

Hooker frowned. "You were telling us about Roisin. She buys tea smuggled from the Goons and works as a nurse. Anything else?"

McCaffrey took in the van's gloomy interior. An omni showed low-light footage of him entering and leaving the hall. "They were watching *me*?"

"Shit just got real," said Leah. "Ha! I've always wanted to say that."

Hooker tapped the screen, checking the date and time

display. "Luke, what did you expect? This is what NatSec do. They're fishing, hoping to identify Bloc operatives. If they're lucky, maybe even the Crimson."

"*Wocca-wocca*," said Leah, making pretend rotor-blades with an index finger. "I can see you now, falling into the river. Splash!"

"I can get you to the No-Zone," said Hooker. "Or even down to Kent, if you want to join your glorious comrades. But I need info."

McCaffrey closed his eyes, a tear rolling down his cheek. "Evie was promising. Politically, I mean. Passionate. I introduced her to Roisin. Roisin didn't seem surprised, almost like she was expecting to meet her."

"That's a start," said Hooker, "go on."

"Over a period of months, Evie and Roisin would have private chats, away from the main meeting. Sometimes in the kitchen at the back of the library, or they'd go outside for a smoke. Then, yesterday afternoon, the Rhys girl arrived. She wasn't interested in politics, I could tell. She'd come to see Roisin."

Hooker offered McCaffrey a bottle of water. He nodded his thanks and drank. "I didn't know Lottie's surname, but she was obviously from a wealthy family. She had that *air* about her. You know? Wessex."

"I bet she was nice to look at too," said Leah.

"I'm not interested in women," McCaffrey replied defensively. "Anyway, Roisin and Evie took Lottie into the kitchen. I listened at the door."

"Don't blame you," said Hooker, "you realised somethin' dodgy was going on?"

"Perhaps, but not the way you're thinking. In fact, it was nothing political whatsoever. Lottie Rhys said she was pregnant."

"Whoah, hold on," said Hooker.

Leah laughed. "This just gets better and better."

"It's not funny," McCaffrey sniffed. "She was asking Roisin if she could get hold of termination meds, because she was a nurse. Then they all left together."

"And that's it?" said Leah. "Why couldn't she get meds at a birth control clinic like everyone else?"

"How do I know?" McCaffrey snapped. "I can only tell you what I heard."

"Any idea who the father is?" said Hooker.

"Of course not. I got the gist of a thirty-second conversation, that's all."

Hooker said nothing for a moment, thinking it through. "Okay, Green-Zoners need a doctor's scrip for termination meds. I doubt a girl living in a Holland Park security bubble could get an appointment without her family knowing about it. And I don't see Lottie Rhys going to a back-street abortionist, do you?"

"You think Roisin already knew Lottie was pregnant?" Leah replied. The omnis inside the van continued playing surveillance footage, a small crowd standing outside the library. Young kids drinking beer and laughing, enjoying a rare smog-free London evening.

Hooker watched the screen. "My guess is *whatever* Lottie wanted, Roisin's job was to oblige. Turns out she was in the family way. If she'd wanted heroin or coke or stims? I bet Roisin would've offered 'em too. She's playing enabler, just long enough to get Lottie close enough to kidnap."

Leah pointed at the omni. "NatSec would've caught Roisin on camera. What time did the girls arrive?"

McCaffrey shrugged. "I'm not sure. The meeting began at four o'clock yesterday afternoon."

Leah tapped the screen to reverse the footage. A few minutes before the meeting, people began arriving in ones and twos. Mainly students, wearing summer shorts and hats, rummage bags on their backs. Leah froze the omni. Two willowy-looking girls stood outside, both wearing wide-brimmed hats, flowery dresses and sun visors. "Evie and Lottie," she said.

"Roisin was already inside the library," said McCaffrey. "Rewind a little… there she is. The woman in black."

Leah enlarged the image, showing a dark-haired woman wearing a shapeless dress and wraparound sunglasses. A black bag was slung across her shoulder, the sort favoured by couriers. "She looks completely forgettable," said Leah.

"Dark workers usually do," Hooker replied. He pulled a stick from a belt pouch and downloaded the footage. "I bet she's Crimson Brigade."

"I didn't know," said McCaffrey. "At worst I thought she was Bloc."

"Play silly games, win silly prizes," Hooker shrugged.

What happens to me now?" said McCaffrey. "Will I be arrested?"

"Depends," said Hooker. "This girl's been kidnapped, and she's a VIP's daughter. You're connected, like it or not."

McCaffrey rubbed his face, fingers trembling. "I know

people up in Birmingham. Non-political folk. Quakers. I could get a train up there and lie low. Then Scandinavia, maybe."

Hooker handed the activist a wad of RDs. "There's a grand. Sorry 'bout your nose. Anyhow, I wouldn't go back to your flat."

"Caretaker's a NatSec grass," said Leah.

McCaffrey took the money and stumbled away. He pulled a tatty smog mask from his pocket. "I never want to see you again."

"Keep your mouth shut and you won't," Hooker replied.

"He just gave you a grand. Fuck off to Sweden you ungrateful prick," Leah added. "Fucking Reds."

"Easy, Leah," said Hooker. "It's different in the Green Zone."

"I can see. They're all soft and full of shit. They need a kicking."

"You're gonna love the Reconstruction."

"I won't if it means living like this. I'll fuck off to Scotland."

"That's fighting talk," Hooker laughed. "We need to get you back to the No-Zone."

"Damn right," Leah replied, watching McCaffrey disappear into the smog. "Lottie Rhys is pregnant. Didn't see that one coming, who d'you reckon did the honours?"

Hooker uploaded the surveillance video to his fob, "Don't matter. I'm darkwiring these images to Gordy. Let's see how good Hyatt's contacts really are."

"What about the van?" asked Leah. "Torch it?"

"Return it. I did a deal with NatSec."

Leah pulled a face. "A deal?"

"I was on the Taskforce with their sergeant. She owed me a favour."

"A favour?"

"We called Tollen *The Cannibal* when she was on Taskforce Seventeen. I'll leave it at that."

"You've got dodgy friends, Hooker."

Hooker smiled. "I'm sitting with you, ain't I?"

They returned to the Merc. Tapping Tollen's code into his fob, Hooker sent the NatSec vehicle's location down the Darkwire.

"You're too honest," said Leah. "Where now?"

"Everything points towards the Goons. We'll take the Old Dover PROTEX to Woolwich, take the Lagoon City ramp."

Leah pulled an apple from an ammo pouch. She had several others taped to her fighting rig, like fruity grenades. "You gonna tell Gordy the girl's pregnant?"

Hooker made a so-so gesture. "Not yet."

They headed south, driving across the London central expressway. It took them even closer to the ever-present BluSky, painting the motorway a lurid blue. Near Southwark, they passed a NatSec convoy. Personnel carriers and trucks, machineguns mounted on hard points. "More rioting in the Goons?" said Leah.

"It'll keep NatSec busy, at least." Hooker's fob flashed. Gordy Rice's darkwire code scrolled onscreen. "Get the pictures, Gordy?"

"Hyatt fast-tracked them through the Security Service

B3i system."

"B3i?"

"Biometric and Imagery Intelligence Index. It cross-references zettabytes of datasets in seconds," Gordy replied. "Heavy shit."

"Did it shit out any heavy matches?"

"No. The technicians think the suspect's using body-worn doppling tech to change her appearance. But dopplers aren't fool-proof – the spooks got a couple of partial hits. One was from last year, on a tram in Croydonia. Another, in the Goons, in the company of a known black-marketeer. Two weeks ago, not far from the Crosland Estate."

"*Tea.*" Hooker felt a surge of adrenaline, "Roisin buys black-market tea."

Gordy whistled through his teeth. "I'm not surprised, you know there's a forty percent tax on Darjeeling? Anyhow, the smuggler's called Natly Hare. Lagoon City born and bred, previous for revenue violations, drug-trafficking, black-marketeering and multiple border infractions. She's in and out of Kent like a ferret."

"Location?" Hooker asked.

"Last known address is in Abbey Wood."

"Got it. We're on our way."

The Old Dover PROTEX towered over south London, a high-rise freeway protected by anti-rocket mesh. It overlooked the Kent DMZ, where metal signs warned of IEDs and snipers. The border was protected by fields of anti-personnel mines, a hundred metres deep, covered dog runs and motion-sensitive fencing.

Leah sped by a long-dead speed camera. "You know the Crimson Brigade won't care if the girl's pregnant. They'll kill her anyway."

Smoke rose from east. "I know," said Hooker. "We'll get to her before that happens."

Leah cocked her head. "Whoah. I thought this was a locate-only gig, Hooker, not a rescue attempt."

"Vassa Hyatt's plan is bullshit. There's no way a load of foreign mercenaries will get her out of the Goons. Especially if there's a riot and the Street Leagues mobilize."

"And we can?"

"I know the Goons better than half the fuckers who live there. I could sneak in and out if I knew where Lottie Rhys was."

"If the job changes, so does the fee."

Hooker sucked on his teeth. "You never used to be this mercenary, Leah."

"You never used to be this soft."

"If it means that much to you, take sixty percent of the fee. I'll have forty."

"Rufus, we've got these Green-Zoners by the balls. We need to squeeze. You're talking about going into the Goons and fighting. For who?"

Hooker shook his head. "Leah, you need to get that shit out of your system."

"What shit?"

"Hate? Anger? Whatever it is, it's fucking with your head," Hooker replied. "We're getting decent money for this gig."

Leah grimaced, eyes angry slits. "I can see why

Trashmob got pissed off with you. You sound like a fucking Answerer."

Trashmob shared Leah's twin obsessions – money and an enduring fear that one day the No-Zone would become civilized. "Just drive, Leah."

"Or what?"

Hooker shrugged.

Leah muttered under her breath, the Merc's speedo hitting a hundred. "I'll take sixty percent."

"Noted."

Abbey Wood was a bomb-site. The smuggler, Natly Hare, lived in a grubby backstreet of boarded-up houses. The pavement had dissolved into ankle-deep marshland, the big 4x4 churning oily mud. It was nearly dusk as Hooker walked towards the door, shotgun ready. "I'll go in. You cover me, okay?"

"No problem," Leah replied, fishing her Kalashnikov from the Merc's trunk. She took cover behind the engine block and checked her comms. "I'm right here. Full of hate and anger."

"Save it for the bad guys, partner."

"*Partner?*"

"Well, now you're takin' sixty percent I suppose you're the boss."

"Glad you finally worked it out," said Leah. When Hooker looked back, she was smiling.

Hooker nudged the door jamb with his boot. Warped and mouldy, but surprisingly solid. Pulling a thermal lance from a pouch, he slid it into the lock mechanism. It flared white, melting into the keyhole. Using the end of the lance as a lever, Hooker prised the door open. "OK," he whispered into his mic, "I'm going inside."

"Copy that."

The ground floor smelt of damp and old tobacco, the ceiling stained black. A trove of tinned food and bottled drinking water were stacked against a wall. Hooker circled the room, pump-gun trained on the stairs. "Ground floor clear," he whispered.

"Got you," Leah replied through his earpiece.

Pulling a torch from his pocket, Hooker walked towards a flight of rickety stairs. *Snick...* something tensed across his foot.

Tripwire.

The ceiling buckled, plaster falling like dirty snow. A ripping, crashing noise as something plummeted into the room – a rust-streaked machine, trailing cobwebs like crazy hair. Rubber-tracked wheels spun, a cannon whirring, sniffing for a target.

"Sentry drone!" Hooker yelled, pump-gun roaring, pellets splashing harmlessly off armour. The drone's cannon barked in reply, lighting the room white. Hooker dropped to his belly, the wall behind him torn apart, bricks tossed into the street. He racked his shotgun, aiming for the machine's optics. Pellets scarred metal, the drone making a strange clicking noise.

A green light on the cannon pod flickered. *Target acquired...*

TWELVE

Paolo's fob masked his voice, every syllable channelled through international Darkwire routers. He was theoretically traceable and identifiable – if the British GCHQ had fifty years spare. "Yes, Miss Hyatt?"

"I'd usually ask for your name and try to establish a rapport. You know the methodology, but it'd be a waste of my time and yours. I simply require proof of life. *Now*."

"You'll have it," Paolo replied. "Can you confirm Damon Rhys has arranged a press conference? One where he confesses his sins, as per our demands?"

"It's in hand," Hyatt replied.

Paolo parsed her words. No traces of nerves or evasion. "I was hoping for a *yes*. I'm afraid that isn't good enough, Miss Hyatt. Disappointing, in fact, considering our intelligence suggests you're reasonably competent."

Hyatt didn't take the bait. "I assure you, I'm working

hard as I can."

"Stalling tactics? So soon? Amateurish, Miss Hyatt. As you said, we all know the playbook for these situations."

Hyatt's voice hardened. "In which case you'd realise you're asking much, but offering little. For example, how do you intend to return Lottie?"

"The girl will be left somewhere safe inside the Green Zone," Paolo lied. "We'll provide a location, as soon as Mister Rhys makes his confession."

"I'm not privy to what his confession, as you call it, concerns. The Minister simply tells me it's in hand."

"It refers to the MADRIGAL Program, Miss Hyatt. What is it they used to say, *sunlight is the best disinfectant*?" Paolo rolled the word around in his mouth. *Madrigal.*

"Madrigal? It means nothing to me."

She really doesn't know. "You will have proof of life when you confirm the press conference. Or, should you fail to meet our simple demands, proof of death. Goodbye."

Roisin applied surgical glue to Abid's cheek. The big Yemeni was expressionless as she probed the wound with a spatula.

"Hyatt's playing for time," said Paolo.

"Why would the silly bitch do that?" Rourke replied. "It's not like they can stage a rescue, is it?"

"Rourke is right. If we cannot leave, how can they get in?" Abid agreed.

Paolo looked out of the window. It was near-dusk. "They'll try to locate the girl, but Hyatt won't go to the authorities. If they knew Rhys was about to reveal MADRIGAL, they'd stop him. NatSec might even kill him."

Rourke finished gluing Abid's wound. "What are their options?"

Paolo watched fires in the half-light, beyond the hulk of the old Thames flood barrier. "They'll have access to mercenaries, I imagine. However, I doubt they'd make it past the rioters *and* NatSec. Abid's right – these disturbances might keep us in, but it keeps them *out*. Assuming, of course, they even know where she is."

"The riot's growing," Rourke replied, joining Paolo at the window.

Paolo drew smoke deep into his lungs, felt the nicotine hit. He allowed himself a smile. "If the mob's angry now, wait until they hear Rhys's confession."

Rourke's voice was an urgent whisper. "What is it? Tell me."

"Many years ago, I worked for the Central Intelligence Agency. I've seen dark secrets, Sorcha. MADRIGAL is one of the darkest. Even I knew nothing about it."

Rourke gripped the windowsill with quick-bitten fingers. "CIA? You're American?"

Abid growled. "Why was I not told?"

"You didn't need to know," Paolo replied, studying the tip of his cigarette, "I *was* American. I have no nation or allegiance now, except the Crimson Brigade." For a second, he felt strangely homesick for Spokane.

Rourke lit a cigarette too. "We smoke too much," she said quietly. In the distance, a fireball erupted midway up a cloudscraper.

"We all need a vice," Paolo replied. Across the river,

housing blocks smouldered. Tiny shapes dropped from its balconies, trailing flame. People.

Abid stood, touching the wound on his cheek. "I must prepare myself for martyrdom," he said.

Paolo nodded. "Thank you, Abid."

Rourke nodded her agreement. "I'll let you know when the Spaniards arrive, big fella."

The fob rattled and buzzed on the table, like a dying bug. Paolo answered. It was Hyatt. "The conference is confirmed, I'll have the time in the hour. I want proof of life now."

"Of course," Paolo replied smoothly. "I'm sending the image."

"I want a live feed."

Paolo laughed gently. "Don't issue orders, Hyatt, unless you want MADRIGAL uploaded to LibNet. Then I'll kill the girl for publicity – the Darkwire snuff-streams will go into meltdown."

"I've spoken with Mister Rhys about MADRIGAL. He says without his voice behind them, your allegations are garbage. He said you'd know that."

"Which is why I demand details of his press conference. I will consider your request regarding a live feed," Paolo replied. "The girl is asleep right now."

"Wake her up."

"This conversation is over." Paolo switched off the phone.

"Is everything OK?" said Rourke.

Paolo shrugged. "Just Hyatt trying to impress Rhys by being tough."

Rourke sat on the sofa and rubbed her eyes. "Let her see the girl as she is. It might concentrate the bitch's feckin' mind."

"Perhaps later."

They turned to the live riot coverage. The NatSec lines surrounding the Commune had thinned, tacticals diverted to disturbances north of the Thames. The remainder were bolstered by nervous-looking munis, an orange-jacketed army encircling the perimeter. They huddled behind riot shields, bottles and bricks raining from the tower. A muni would occasionally break cover to fire a baton round or a choke gas grenade. There was something half-hearted about the exchange, as if both sides knew it wasn't time for the main event.

"The main NatSec force went north? It might make it easier to get out," said Rourke. "Why do you think Rhys will give the press conference *before* meeting the peace delegation?"

Paolo studied his cigarette. "A press conference takes minutes. Negotiations take days. He could host the press anywhere, which is why your agent needs to access Rhys's schedule."

"Get me out and I will. I'll be an hour, maybe a little longer. But I'll get that bloody schedule."

"Is your man answering his fob?"

"No, but he's never failed to make a meet."

They returned to the window. Below, a dark tsunami of humanity filled the streets. Paolo studied the scene with a soldier's eye. "The police are letting rioters take the west side of the estate. I see the logic – it's like a fire-break. It'll burn itself out."

Rourke pointed at the omni. "Or they've decided to throw their fascist dogs a bone. Look, the Leagues are coming out to play."

The Street Leagues are marching on Lagoon City. A statement from the Woolwich Urbanskis declares they 'intend to restore law and order to the Crosland if the police will not.' Other leagues, including the Loyal Croydonian Brethren, are mobilizing...

Paolo sipped his coffee and winced. It was cold. "Street leagues? I suppose it was only a matter of time."

Rourke began rolling a cigarette. "Kent will go crazy if they unleash those bastards. Free Medway would go up in smoke."

Paolo nodded his agreement. "Street leagues are reactionary analogues of the Bloc. Maybe the Government will eventually let them march south, to do their dirty work."

"That'd start a civil war," Rourke replied. "It'd make the Balkans look tame."

"It would be to our advantage. The People would see how hopeless the Bloc were and join us."

The newsfeed crossed to a reporter interviewing a municipal policeman, an old man wearing a blue uniform. *I'm with Chief Superintendent Bruno Banazewski, from Lagoon Command of the Municipal Police. Do you have a message for the Leagues?*

The cop wore a strip of faded medal ribbons on his tunic, mouth veiled by a grey moustache. *My message to the Leagues is simple - send your Generals to parley. And, above all, stay away from the Crosland Estate. We have the full support of our NatSec colleagues. We've had too many deaths here today to escalate the situation further…*

Paolo's fob trilled. The Spaniards. "General Ignacio wishes to see you."

"Very well," he replied, heading for the door. "Sorcha, I'll see the General now. We'll get you out very soon."

Ignacio's den was now lit by guttering candles and storm lanterns, walls covered with posters and political slogans. The General was dressed for battle, resplendent in ballistic armour and a black-painted helmet. Around his feet lay weapons, from swords to assault rifles. "Paolo, *ciao!*" he called easily.

"*Prego*," Paolo replied. "You wished to see me?"

"The fascists march on the Commune."

"Yes, I saw on the omni."

"Leagues? Just criminals in drag," Ignacio sniffed. "I should know - we sell them cotics, crack and synthetics. So, they know we have quality product *and* treasure."

"You think they're coming simply to rob you?"

"Why else march against us? They saw the police weakened when the rioting spread and took their chance. Petit bourgeois scum! Class traitors!"

"NatSec won't let them cross the cordon, and if they did your defences are too strong," Paolo replied, suspecting Karl Marx would be churning ever-deeper into his Highgate grave.

Ignacio's runner appeared, a girl in a beret carrying a hunting bow. "General, there are at least six leagues mobilizing. Including Loyal Croydonia."

"That's twelve thousand men," Ignacio replied.

"It's even more important for me to get my people out," said Paolo. "You'll honour our deal?"

"Yes of course," the Spaniard replied, stroking his beard, "Although I'll admit we require an extra… *favour*."

"Just name it."

Ignacio grinned. In the shadows, beery henchmen hefted weapons. "I want half of your cache. The explosives, I mean."

Paolo felt his trigger finger tense. He squinted, optical implant warming up. It would take only a moment to kill everyone in the room…

"Relax, my friend," Ignacio replied, flashing a smile. "I assume you're from the Crimson Brigade? I'm guessing Special Action Group."

"What do you plan on doing with the explosives?"

"I'm going to blow those street league bastards sky-high," the Spaniard laughed. "You're going to help us do it. Perhaps it's consistent with your plans, whatever they are."

"How did you know?"

The Spaniard picked up a rifle and worked the action. "Spies are worth as much as bullets, I'm sure you agree. You were seen near the basement, so I had it searched."

"They were well-hidden, and booby-trapped. Your searchers must have been good."

Ignacio bowed, a sly grin on his face. "High praise, from a soldier of the Crimson."

Paolo nodded. "Tell me, General, why didn't you simply take the explosives for yourself?"

The brawny Spaniard shrugged. "Why make an enemy

of the Crimson, when you can make a friend? And, of course, I expect you to build devices for me."

"I have some knowledge of explosives," Paolo conceded, accepting the general's handshake.

"In which case, you have a deal," Ignacio nodded, "but your people must leave now."

"They're ready."

"Get them to the lobby. My people are waiting."

Paolo raced to the apartment, knocking on Abid's door. "Get ready, Abid. Right now!"

The hulking Yemeni wore military-grade body armour over his courier's uniform. He'd converted the plate carrier into a suicide vest, pouches bulging with liquid explosive. "I'm ready," he said, hefting two Kalashnikov rifles. He slung one across each shoulder and pulled on a baseball cap.

Rourke appeared, dressed in a raincoat and woollen hat. Unremarkable as always. Across her shoulder was a rummage bag, the stock of a machine pistol glinting inside. "I suppose we'd better get on with it," she said.

"Good luck, Sorcha," Paolo replied. "For the Crimson."

"Aye, Comrade, for the Crimson," the Irishwoman replied. "Abid, tell me, what do you think The Prophet would have said about all this?"

"That victory is inevitable, *inshallah*."

"Even a heathen like me hopes he's right," Rourke replied. "Let's go."

"Yes, *kaffur*," Abid replied. 'I will lead the way."

THIRTEEN

The sentry drone's cannon spewed smoke, unspent bullets clattering to the floor. Hooker realised the ammo feed had been knocked out of alignment. He leapt at the door, the drone snapping a new ammunition hopper into position. Outside, the Merc's engine growled. Leah's voice rang in his earpiece. "Move to the left wall, Hooker. *Now!*"

Hooker flinched as the G-Wagen burst into the room, its ram scattering brick and plaster. It slammed into the drone, spinning it like a garbage can. Cannons roared in reply, bullets punching into the Merc's hood and windscreen. Hooker staggered towards the felled machine, stamping on the cannon and pinning it to the floor. The drone's optics snapped open and shut, rubberized tracks spinning crazily. Pulling another thermic lockpick, Hooker flipped the ignition. It burned and crackled, washing the slum silvery-white. Leah leapt from the driver's seat, falling on the upturned drone and clamping her hands either side of its optical array. "Do it," she barked.

Hooker punched the white-hot thermic into the drone's armorglass eye. It bubbled and smoked, globular optics fusing with the pick. Grunting, he punched the lance deep inside the drone's head, plastic and circuitry hissing and fizzing. With a high-pitched whine, it powered down, smoke seeping from its armoured torso.

"Shit," said Leah, rubbing her hip. "Who left psycho-bot up there?"

"Dunno," Hooker replied, studying the dying machine. "I can't see a two-bit smuggler being able to afford a surplus drone with a functioning autocannon."

"Maybe she ain't so two-bit after all." Leah activated the flashlight attached to her rifle, "let's take a look upstairs."

"You're going first?"

Leah nodded. "You're getting old, Hooker. Old and slow. I almost ran you over there."

Hooker eyed the battered Mercedes parked in the living room. "Thanks for the timely warning."

"Don't worry," Leah replied, grinning. "If I wanted to kill you, you'd be dead by now."

Hooker rubbed his rib, which he reckoned was cracked. "I'm sure I would. Now, let's move. You'd hear that gunfire in Dover."

They climbed the stairs, Leah darting into a doorway. Carpet smouldered where a breaching charge released the drone. "Clever booby-trap," she said.

"Feels like Crimson Brigade," Hooker replied. "Too clever by half."

On a bed lay a corpse. A woman, face-down. Leah's flashlight swept the wound in her skull. "Large calibre round. Just like Evie Kendrick's mother."

"Yeah, looks like the same shooter, don't it?" Hooker patted down the body, pulling a ration book from a coat pocket. "Here we go. Natly Hare."

"Roisin's smuggler friend," said Leah, wrinkling her nose. The room stank of death – dirty and meaty. Flies already buzzed over the glistening void in Natly Hare's skull.

Hooker switched on his torch and dropped to his belly. Reaching under the mangy divan, he rummaged through a mess of boxes and cartons. Finally, he pulled out a cheap suitcase, more mould than leather. He worked a rusty zip and flipped it open.

"What you got?" said Leah.

"Cigarettes," Hooker replied, stacking red-and-white sleeves on the bed. "Marlboro Reds – proper coffin nails."

"There's something tucked in the lining," said Leah, tapping the suitcase. "You need glasses."

"The ageism is getting old," Hooker replied. "See what I did there?"

Leah rolled her eyes.

Hooker pulled a grubby notebook from a slit in the faux-leather. "Well there's a thing – Natly was south London's most organised smuggler. She kept a sales ledger. Bush-meat, morphine, ammunition, antibiotics and this…"

12 SLEEVES MARLBORO RED (r$6000)
700g EARL GREY (r$1400)
TO CROSLAND (COMMUNE)

Leah raised an eyebrow. "Earl Grey? Dunno about the smokes, but McCaffrey said Roisin's a tea-drinker."

Hooker nodded. "The Commune International would be as good a place as any to hide a hostage. My contacts in the Goons tell me it's run by Spanish mercenaries."

"Spanish?"

"Call 'emselves the Black Rifles," Hooker replied. "They fought in Libya when I was in the army, the Germans killed most of 'em. A proper shower of shit. They pretend to be Reds, but they ain't really. Just looters and rapists."

Leah grimaced. "Yeah, I think I heard of 'em. But Roisin's Crimson Brigade, right? They're sneaky. Maybe that note was *left* for us to find."

Hooker pointed at the smouldering gap in the bedroom floor. "Or she reckoned anyone breaking in would get a drone dropped on 'em."

They returned downstairs and examined the Merc. Cannon-fire had pierced the engine block, greenish liquid pooling beneath the chassis. "As a mechanic might say, that's *proper* fucked," said Leah sadly. "Mebbe Trashmob could get the low-loader down here, we could strip it for spares."

"What about Lottie Rhys?" said Hooker, shaking his head.

"Ah, the girl. I knew there was a reason we destroyed a perfectly good Mercedes. Maybe we'll find some wheels I can hotwire."

They retrieved their gear from the Merc and left on foot. They trudged through muddy streets towards the Crosland Estate. It was only a couple of miles, but Hooker hoped there was a taxi or a tuk-tuk running. An orange-liveried pickup truck pulled out of a side-street, blue lights flashing. A NatSec carrier followed, a steel-hulled monster with oversized tyres. A muni jumped out of the pickup, sinking to his ankles in muck. "Municipal Police – drop your weapons."

Hooker slowly placed his shotgun on the least muddy piece of ground he could see. "Let me do the talking," he said.

"Yeah, 'cuz you're a natural diplomat," Leah replied, making a show of unloading her Kalashnikov.

"Keep your hands where I can see them," said the muni, joined by a colleague armed with a shotgun.

"Ain't a problem," Hooker replied.

The cops approached, closely followed by a squad of tacticals. The first muni was a tired-looking Asian kid, wearing a riot helmet at least two sizes too big for him. He pointed at Hooker. "We heard a shitload of gunfire. Papers and pockets – both of you."

"We're authorised security contractors," Hooker replied, tapping his red armband. "We've got firearms permits. We're working a MISPER case, a lead took us to a house back there."

"What, the one with the burning truck sticking out of it?" the muni replied.

"You've done the observation course, ain't you?" said Leah.

Hooker shot her a look. "Yeah. There was a sentry drone inside, which is why you heard gunfire. There's also a dead body, we're about to call it in."

"I'm sure you were," the muni replied, running a scanner over their ID. "Their permissions check out," he called to the tacticals. "Concealed carry firearms permits, too."

One of the tacticals nodded and conferred with his squad. They advanced on Natly Hare's, weapons ready. "The dead body is upstairs," said Hooker.

The muni stepped back and spoke with his partner, fobs crackling with contact reports from the estate. "Authorisation or not, we're taking you in. CID can ask you about the body," said the muni. "Murders ain't our remit."

Hooker shook his head. "Come on, this is bullshit. I'm looking for a missing girl…"

"You're under arrest," said the muni, pulling a pair of gel-kuffs from his utility belt. "Section Twelve."

"Am I under arrest too?" said Leah. "'Cuz I've got places to be."

"Yeah, why not? Consider yourself pinched," the muni replied cheerfully, "We'll sort out why at the custody centre."

"Hey, there *is* a sentry drone in here," called a tactical, "looks like they took it out with a thermic."

"That was ballsy," another tactical admitted, joining the munis. "I'll get an evidence team to bag and tag any evidence."

"You really got time for this?" said Hooker, "my brief will have me out in an hour. You've got a riot to be dealing with, ain't you?"

"Suits me just fine," the muni shrugged. "It'll get me off the Crosland for a couple of hours. It's a nightmare up there tonight."

Another tactical approached, two emerald stars marking her as an inspector. "If you're pinching these two, drop 'em off for processing. Let someone else book 'em in."

"I was going to deal with them myself, ma'am," the

muni replied.

"We're needed back on the estate," the inspector replied. "You know your way around better than we do."

Hooker kept his hands raised. "Inspector, can you ask these officers to reconsider whether we need to be arrested? We're contractors and fully authorised…"

Face covered by an armorglass visor, only the inspector's mouth was visible. It twisted into a sneer. "I don't think so, *Hooker*. I know exactly who and what *you* are." Her fob hissed. She took a step back, speaking quietly into her throat mic.

"That's your cosy night processing prisoners screwed," Leah shrugged, offering the munis a stick of gum.

"Worth a try," said the Asian cop, nodding his thanks. He pointed at Hooker. "You met her before?"

"No, I'm famous," Hooker replied. "For all the wrong reasons."

The inspector returned. "These munis aren't taking you in, Hooker – we are."

"Why?"

"I'm not a sleuth, but I'd say you're in deep shit."

Leah shrugged. "What's new?"

Hooker put his hands out for the muni's gel-kuffs, gloop hardening around his wrists, "who wants us?"

"OCS," said the inspector, smiling. "Yeah, the Gestapo have decided to grace us with their presence."

"Office of Counter-Subversion?" said Leah. "Fuck."

"D'you want us to escort you?" said the muni, eager to please. "I know a short cut."

"Will you let it go?" the inspector sighed. "Get back to

the estate and stop shirking, before I write you up for discipline. We'll take the prisoners from here."

"Where?" said Hooker.

"Millbank Tower," the inspector replied, her smile cruel. "OCS Headquarters. They'll process you there, in the land of Section Twelve. You can check in, but you never leave…"

"*Process?*" said Hooker, who'd heard stories about the goings-on at Millbank. "I've never heard it called that before."

"No less than you deserve, I imagine," said the inspector.

The tacticals trooped from the house carrying evidence sacks. A garbage can-sized drone buzzed overhead, landing on an apron of straggly grass. A tactical loaded the evidence inside the drone's belly and it buzzed away. "I've never seen that before?" said the muni. "Sending a drone to pick up exhibits?"

"That's the OCS," Hooker replied. "All the gear and no idea."

The tacticals bundled Hooker and Leah inside an armoured carrier, its cramped interior smelling of sweat and street food. Tacticals prised off their helmets while an omni played old-school Death Metal, roaring and guitar riffs interrupted by radio traffic. The eight-wheeler rumbled towards the Crosland Estate. Through an armorglass porthole, Hooker saw they'd turned off the metalled road. "We're not heading to the Green Zone," he whispered.

"No talking," said a tactical, a wiry man with face full of scars.

Hooker guessed they'd travelled another mile, when the carrier stopped.

"Get the prisoners outside," said the inspector wearily, pulling on her helmet. She was in her late twenties, Hooker guessed. Hard-eyed, a unit tattoo on her neck. Stepping outside, they stood in the shadow of the old Belmarsh high-security prison. Ivy-covered walls lit by old gas lamps, cell wings pock-marked by bullets.

"You know this place?" said Leah.

"I ain't been here since the war," Hooker replied. "I remember it burning, after the inmates rioted."

"I suppose you're something of an expert on incarceration, Hooker," the inspector smirked. "I heard you were banged-up on the Isle of Man, along with the paedos and rapists."

Taskforcers convicted during the Reconciliation Tribunals were all sent to the island's lonely prison. Hooker cocked his head. "You're starting to boil my piss, darlin'."

The inspector checked her fob. "I couldn't care less. Ah, the gentlemen from OCS appear to be running late. Constable Hasker, could you give Mister Hooker a beating to pass the time?"

"Yes ma'am." Scar-face grinned, tugging a shock baton from his belt.

Hooker brandished his gel-kuffed hands, eyes boring into the cop's. "Take these fuckers off. I'll have a tear-up with the lot of you."

Scar-face whipped his baton across Hooker's knees, the weapon crackling with electricity. Groaning, he fell to the ground.

"Just a gentle attitude readjustment, Hasker," the inspector warned. "He still needs to be fit for interrogation."

"Yes, Ma'am," Scar-face grunted, smashing the baton across Hooker's upper arm. Leah shouldered-barged the tactical, knocking him on his backside. His chin made an audible crack as it connected with the tip of her steel toe-cap.

The inspector chuckled. "Get on your feet, Hasker. Harris! Singh! Give the skank some volts. Apparently, she used to be Bloc."

Two tacticals stepped forward, shock batons trailing sparks. "Bloc?" said one. "I'm gonna enjoy this."

"Leave 'em alone," said a voice. Hooker saw a figure emerge from a black BMW Urban. A stringy white guy in a cheap suit, an ID tag hanging around his neck.

"Stand down," the inspector ordered. The tacticals obeyed like Pavlov's dogs, holstering weapons and snapping to attention.

"Can't you fucking meatheads do *anything* without beating the shit out of people?" the suit sighed. His skin was greyish and pock-marked, thinning hair plastered across his scalp.

"Watch your tongue," the inspector growled. "You're Chisholm, ain't you?"

"*Detective Sergeant* Chisholm to you. These are OCS detainees, so if anyone's gonna give 'em a battering, it'll be us."

The inspector hissed. "Until you sign for 'em, they're *my* prisoners. I'll manage 'em as I see fit."

Chisholm was joined by a chubby black guy. He wore a maroon sports jacket and cowboy boots, his fingers encrusted in bling. "This is DC Bailey," said Chisholm.

Bailey grabbed Leah's arm. "You too, Hooker, on your feet."

Chisholm smiled at the tacticals. "We'll be off then. I'm sure your unit has important stuff to do. Like licking windows and eating crayons."

"I'm reporting you for insubordination, Chisholm," the inspector hissed, "who d'you think you are?"

"Who am I? I'm the secret-fucking-police," Chisholm grinned, revealing a mouthful of wobbly teeth. "I reckon you might enjoy a transfer, maybe Free Medway? Delicious! IEDs, beheadings, kidnaps. Not to mention friendly fire, when one of them drones goes wrong."

"You're talking bollocks."

"We'll see, shall we?" Chisholm replied. "Check your email when you get back to base. Now fuck off."

The inspector grunted an order, the tacticals disappearing inside the carrier. It rumbled away, roof-gunner glowering. Chisholm and Bailey giggled and did a high-five. "That shit never gets old," said Bailey.

"What's this about?" Hooker groaned. He'd bitten his tongue, blood running down his chin. "What do you want with us?"

Chisholm spun on his heel, still smiling. "You and Miss Martinez are assisting us in a matter pertaining to National Security, under Section Twelve of the Emergencies Act."

"Sounds like an arrest to me," Leah replied.

"Sounds like you need a lawyer," Chisholm smirked.

"Oh shit," Bailey interrupted, enjoying the double-act. "On a Section Twelve they ain't allowed legal representation, Detective Sergeant Chisholm." He took a drag on a cigarette and smiled.

"I know, Detective Constable Bailey, it's a proper liberty," said Chisholm. Now, get these two in the car and let's get outta this shit-hole."

Bailey grabbed Hooker's elbow. "Easy, big man. All will be revealed at Millbank."

"The Puzzle Palace," Chisholm nodded. He ran his tongue along his gums and giggled. "You're gonna love it. Fucking delicious."

"Hurry up, Chisholm," said Bailey, getting in the car. "It's gonna kick off big-time 'round here. Man, I hate the Goons."

Leah shimmied along the BMW's backseat. "What is this bullshit?"

Chisholm opened the car window. Plugging a nostril with his finger, he blew a gobbet of snot from the other. "Fucked if I know," he said, "but I'm on overtime, so who cares?"

FOURTEEN

Paolo dressed for war – black ceramoweave armour, flame-proof coveralls, combat boots and an assault vest. He stowed magazines, grenades, spare fobs and gold in pouches and pockets. On his belt he wore his HK35 and a fighting knife. Standing by the apartment door, he motioned for the others to leave.

"What will you do with the girl?" said Abid.

"She'll be fine here. I'll return shortly."

The Yemeni frowned. "We should take her."

"No," Paolo replied, "I don't want the Spanish to know we've got a hostage."

"Paolo's right," said Rourke, checking her stuff. "Where can she escape, anyway?"

"As you say," the giant shrugged. He folded his arms, resting them on his explosive-packed chest armour.

Rourke rested a hand on the giant's shoulder. "Come on, don't you be worryin' yourself about stuff like that."

One of the Spaniards stood guard outside, rifle shouldered. He nodded when he saw Paolo and led them to General Ignacio's quarters. The General and his henchmen stood around an omni showing a three-dimensional schematic of the estate. The Commune stood at the centre, the Crosland to the west and the river to the north. Paolo cleared his throat and pointed at the map. "Our vehicle is garaged to the west, General, in the old industrial estate."

Ignacio looked Abid up and down. Then he laughed. "You're sure this one needs our help getting anywhere?"

The Yemeni shrugged. "I need to get to my vehicle without fighting."

"Don't worry, we have a tunnel between us and the Crosland," said Ignacio, lowering his voice. He pointed at two of his men, dressed in camouflaged cloaks and goggles. "This is Oscar and Miguel, they will be your guides. Be warned, you may have to wait underground for a while, until the way is clear."

"Yes," Oscar replied, tapping the schematic with a dirty finger. "Our scouts report cop activity on the other side."

"I hope we won't be delayed too long," Paolo replied.

"We'll leave soon," Oscar replied. "Comrade Paolo, we have eyes and ears everywhere. Don't worry."

Rourke nodded and checked her watch. "I'll call when I'm on the other side, Paolo."

The Spaniards escorted Abid and Rourke away, the Irishwoman giving a small wave. When they were gone, Ignacio took another swig of beer. "I was thinking of putting devices on the perimeter, by the gates to the…"

"May I?" said Paolo, spinning the schematic with a finger. "I would divide the remaining explosive into four. We build three primary devices, and a handful of smaller IEDs with the remainder. I'll need nails, petrol, tape, frangible containers and fobs. Any chemistry materials from your 'cotics labs would be helpful for making tilt switches, timers and command wires. A mortar bomb or two wouldn't go amiss, if you've any spare."

"You heard the man!" Ignacio bawled, underlings saluting as they scurried away. "We've had too much peace. It makes us lazy."

"There will be no peace here," Paolo replied, studying the map. "Push hard enough, General, and this will be the first domino to fall."

"With London next?" Ignacio replied, jutting his chin like a pocket Guevara. "And your plan?"

Paolo nodded. "Next, we hide smaller devices near abandoned vehicles and street furniture, just inside our perimeter. This will slow the enemy, channelling them into prepared kill-zones. Put snipers on likely escape routes, casualty exfil points and RVs. Then, we position larger devices along the enemy's line of advance." Paolo pointed at the earthwork palisade protecting the Commune. "The first bomb will kill the initial wave of attackers. The second IED will be *behind* them, killing reinforcements and medical teams. Without ordnance disposal assets, they'll be paralysed. We put the largest device on the palisade itself, to break their final assault."

General Ignacio accepted a fresh beer from a flunky.

"The wall? Won't it be destroyed?"

"Probably. But by then we'll be looking at many hundreds of casualties, enough to break the enemy. This isn't an army we're dealing with, it's a bunch of second-rate militiamen." *Alternatively, they might destroy this place, covering my escape...*

The General stroked his beard. "I still think the fascists could destroy the Commune by sheer force of numbers."

Paolo shrugged. "This place has had its day, comrade, and Class Struggle has an endless appetite for martyrs. I presume you have your own exit strategy?"

Ignacio smiled. "We have friends who can get us to the coast. The Black Rifles will be in Free Cordoba by the end of next week." The Spaniard turned to a second omni. A newsfeed showed crowds gathering on the western perimeter, parleying with police lining the cordon.

The Street Leagues are demanding permission to carry out what they call a 'People's Eviction...'

A skinny girl arrived, a pair of binoculars around her neck. "General, we've spotted tacticals hiding in the marshes near the northern palisade. Street leagues are marching from the east and south."

"And to the west?" Ignacio asked.

"The pigs are withdrawing. There are fires from other class struggles, as far as the Green Zone. It's spreading."

"The leaguers will replace the cops in the west," said Paolo. "We're hemmed in by the river to the north."

"I agree," the General replied. He tapped a finger on the

schematic, showing the expanse of swamp separating the Thames from the Commune. "How many cops were hiding here?"

"Perhaps three, maybe four rigid inflatables. They were wearing green, not the usual black uniforms."

"Tell the scouts they are doing excellent work," the General replied, kissing the girl on the cheek. "Gather a squad of Black Rifles. If the cops advance, fire warning shots and keep them away. If they continue, shoot to kill."

A Spaniard brought bomb-making supplies in hessian sacks. Paolo snapped on surgical gloves and divided the creamy loaves of explosive into rectangular chunks. He worked fast, assembling detonators and circuit boards, carefully placing each IED in a sack when he was finished. Paolo Falcone had been taught by CIA paramilitaries, Russian combat engineers and elderly Jihadis. He'd blown up tanks and school-buses, airliners and cruise ships, barracks and hotels. Newsfeeds hummed in the background as he worked –

Up to seven thousand leaguers have assembled a mile from the Commune International. General Zachary Fry, of The Loyal Croydonia Brethren, has announced ten thousand more will march. His spokesman tells us Fry has called a Grand Council of the Leagues, who have issued an ultimatum to the Wessex Parliament. Either allow the Leagues to march on Free Medway, or they will withdraw their support for the authorities…

"Are you finished, Paolo?" asked Ignacio, examining a bomb.

"Who's your best man with explosives?"

"I am," one of the Spaniards replied. "My name is Julio, I learnt from a Crimson Brigade bomb-maker in Tunisia."

"Good – you'll lead one of the teams, Julio. Take these smaller IEDs, seed them around the western perimeter. Put them near anything flammable or made of glass. If you have spare gasoline, leave it in plastic containers nearby."

"I understand."

"Remember, anything that maximises casualties will slow them down. Make a note of where you place each device and issue them to the sniper teams."

Julio placed his bombs in a sack, gently as eggs. He pointed at three men. They shouldered their rifles and followed him away.

"NatSec will deploy their MQ-15X UAVs," Paolo continued, smoothing nails and bolts into the last slab of explosives.

The General pulled a face. "Eviscerator drones?"

"Yes. They have two on station at any given time, equipped with nano-munition pods. Provide them with easy targets as a distraction, fodder on the scaffolds and balconies. It will make your escape easier."

"Ruthless bastard," the General laughed. He turned to an aide. "Send those fucking Frenchmen up there, the ones who keep complaining about the noise."

"My pleasure, General!" the aide replied, grinning.

Paolo nodded his approval. "They may also use Special Forces, probably their SAS and SFSG. They excel at this type of operation. One option is for half their number to land on the roof and fight downwards. The other half will assault a lower floor and fight their way up."

Ignacio scratched his balls. "Making us the meat in the sandwich. You seem very sure of their doctrine."

"I was with the defenders of the *Cite El Habib*, when the British SAS and Paratroopers assaulted the stronghold. It was a bloodbath, comrade. They are ruthless."

General Ignacio nodded, "Tunis? We fought the 2nd Panzer Division near Ras Jebel. They had a tame Archangel, I lost half my men. How did you escape?"

"I booby-trapped the approaches and posted martyrs on the roof to distract them. Sound familiar?"

"I knew you were a good prospect."

Stripping off his gloves, Paolo joined the Spaniards at a window. Sodium lights silvered the night sky, surging ranks of street leaguers overwhelming the remaining munis. Banners rippled in the wind, flares arcing into the sky. General Ignacio of the Black Rifles drew himself to his full height. "This is going to be magnificent!"

The police lines broke, leaguers dragging riot shields aside and attacking munis with spears and clubs. A few cops tried to drag their wounded away, only to be swallowed by the mob. Pieces of police uniform and equipment were tossed in the air, leaguers rampaging towards the perimeter.

Paolo gestured at the Commune's earthwork berms and palisades, protected by rows of razor wire and water-filled moats. "Our defences are strong. They won't be able to breach them without heavy equipment. Perhaps they'll lay siege? Toss dead cows into the commune with a trebuchet?"

The General pointed at a column of retreating police vehicles, blue lights winking. "The cops are running."

Paolo opened his Zippo and lit the Marlboro glued to

his bottom lip. "That, I think, is a deliberate command decision – the police are letting the mob do their work."

The General raised an eyebrow. "They sacrificed their munis?"

"Don't make the mistake of thinking they aren't as ruthless as we are," Paolo shrugged.

Flags and standards billowed above the horde. Paolo recognised them from his mission briefing – the largest was orange, emblazoned with a black Kalashnikov and the words NO SURRENDER in gothic script. The standard of the Loyal Croydonia Brethren, self-appointed defenders of the South London borderlands. Croydonia was followed by the red and mauve fist of the Deptford Avengers, then the blue hawk of the Southwark Souljas. The black skull of the Bermondsey *Totenkopf* flew amidst the smaller banners of the Woolwich Urbanskis, Streatham Kommando Posse, Tulse Hill Razormen, Sutton Trollz, *Kampfgruppe*-Millwall and the Battersea Shanksters.

"Sometimes," said Ignacio, "I wish we had our own Archangels."

Paolo smiled. "That's heresy, my friend."

The General grabbed a Kalashnikov, kissed it and laughed. "If we can't have angels, we'll fight like devils. Move my headquarters to the bunker. Give the order for the Black Rifles to stand-to!"

FIFTEEN

The BMW raced west. A news feed flickered across the car's HUD, streaming footage of the rioting in Lagoon City. "They love a ruck in the Goons, don't they?" said Bailey.

Chisholm grinned. "Savages, the lot of 'em. Send in the Eviscerators and blow 'em to fuck."

"You white boys, always wantin' to drop bombs on people," Bailey guffawed. He turned to Hooker, "what d'you say, brother?"

"I ain't your brother."

"See, Bailey?" said Chisholm, "Hooker ain't your brother. I certainly ain't your brother. And I don't think you even got a brother. That makes you one sad, lonely fucker."

They wove through the Government Zone, a blast-proof warren of checkpoints, barriers and guard towers. The Palace of Westminster squatted by the Thames, screened by transparent armorglass walls. Barrage balloons bobbed in the night sky like deep-sea creatures, searchlights dappling their matte grey flanks. Millbank Tower, the Office of Counter Subversion HQ, was the colour of old bones. Anti-rocket mesh draped across the upper stories reminded Hooker of giant cobwebs. Chicanes, like concrete dominos, protected the entrance, guarded by tacticals with slobbering guard dogs. They drove into a subterranean carpark, Chisholm opening the door for his prisoners. "I'm going to remove your cuffs," Bailey announced, pulling a spray canister from a pocket. It dissolved the gel-spheres on Leah and Hooker's hands, resin dripping to the floor like grainy porridge.

A gaunt man in coveralls stepped from the shadows. He waved a detector wand over the prisoners and nodded his satisfaction. "They're clean. No body-melded tech. No weapons. No cavity-borne explosives."

Hyatt's pouch of coins lay on the ground. "I want a receipt for that gold," said Hooker.

"You're delicious, you are," Chisholm smirked, dropping the pouch in an evidence bag. "Receipt? Whatever next? Don't worry, it's in good hands."

They trooped along a series of cold, damp corridors. Globular drone cameras followed them everywhere, tiny engines hissing. "Miss Martinez, you'll come with me," said Bailey.

"No. We stay together," said Hooker.

Chisholm shook his head. "The Man wants to speak with *you*. Martinez waits with *us*. She can grab a cup of coffee. Maybe a sandwich from the canteen? Girl looks like she needs fattening up."

Leah shrugged. "Have you fuckers got cake?"

"Yeah, we've got cake," said Bailey.

"Chocolate cake?"

"Be surprised if we didn't."

"Then I'll be alright," she said, stepping out of the lift.

Hooker fixed Chisholm with a stare. "You'd better be."

"Don't sweat it, Hooker," Leah replied. "I'll see you soon, and if I don't you'll fuck these pigs up?"

Hooker nodded slowly. "Yeah, I'll fuck 'em up. Badly."

"Heard it all before," Bailey shrugged.

They took an elevator to the top of the tower. Chisholm escorted Hooker to a door. He straightened his tie and knocked once. "You're about to meet the Big Boss, Hooker. You'd best show some respect."

"Come in," said a voice.

Hooker stepped into a room overlooking the unlit BluSky. Beyond, cloudscrapers reflected distant fires. Music drifted from an omni, ancient jazz. "This is Mister Hooker," said Chisholm.

"I'm grateful," said the man behind a desk. "You may go."

Chisholm bowed and hurried away, quietly closing the door behind him.

"Do you like jazz?" said the man. He wore a greyish suit and open-necked shirt, fiftyish and hawk-nosed. He tidied files on his desk with long, delicate fingers. "This track is from *1969*, would you believe? Miles Davis. I wouldn't say I'm a connoisseur, but..."

"Who are you?" said Hooker. He thought the man looked like a college professor, not a policeman.

"*Chief Superintendent* Bliss," he said, as if the title amused him. "Would you care for tea?"

"Water." Hooker replied, sitting down.

"May I call you Rufus?"

"No."

"As you wish," Bliss replied, producing a flask from his desk. He poured green tea into a china cup. "Let's start with an easy question. Why did you meet Vassa Hyatt this morning?"

"Who's Vassa Hyatt?"

Bliss smiled. "Let's try something else. What is the precise nature of Damon Rhys's involvement in this affair?"

"How should I know?"

Bliss touched his fob, "water for Mister Hooker, please."

They sat in silence until Chisholm arrived. The detective placed a bottle of chilled water on the desk. Hooker nodded, cracked the cap and gulped. It tasted good. Clean. Chisholm nodded and left.

Bliss produced a notebook and a fountain pen. "Vassa Hyatt is ex-MI6, although knowing them she still might be. The story is she left the service under something of a cloud, you know. Nonetheless, she's still playing the game. They look after their own, the spooks. I'll give them that."

Hooker wiped his mouth with his sleeve. "And you don't? Look after your own, I mean?"

"No. This place is like a bloody *shark* tank," Bliss smiled. "The scent of failure is like blood, draws in the predators. I find it a healthy way to do business, it keeps the gene pool refreshed."

"What about you, Bliss?"

"Oh, I'm fine. They call me *Daddy-Shark*. Behind my back, of course. *It's better to be feared than loved*, after all."

"Machiavelli?" said Hooker.

"Very good."

"There were plenty of books in the prison library," Hooker shrugged. He could be across the desk, strangling Bliss, in two seconds. Then he thought of Leah. The girl could look after herself, but she didn't know the Green Zone.

Bliss steepled his fingers, "you need to understand what's at stake. We want the same thing, don't we?"

"And what's that?"

Bliss snapped his fingers and the music stopped. "The People want security and reconstruction. And, most importantly, no Archangels. Aren't those bastards the reason we're living in this half-baked police state in the first place?"

"I don't much like 'em either, but you can't un-invent RXP," Hooker replied. "Archangels are like guns or nukes. They'll keep coming back, because they're weapons. Everyone wants weapons."

Bliss nodded. "I agree. You're a sensible man. Pragmatic. But doesn't it make your skin crawl? Knowing those… *deviants* might have the whip hand again?"

Hooker shrugged. "You think this is about transhumans?"

"Everything's about Archangels, they're an existential threat. More so than the Crimson Brigade or Black Bloc. The Reds' masturbatory fantasies of class warfare are nothing compared to what transhumans are capable of."

Hooker remembered the briefing with Hyatt. "They say

there's only a handful of archangels left. They're helping the Wessex Parliament with the Reconstruction."

Bliss made a so-so gesture with his hand. "That's the official line. But their real desire? The Archangels want to breed, Hooker. *Breed.* They've got the technology to the point where RXP will be passed on genetically."

"It's an arms race. What about the Chinese and Russians? Or the 'mericans? They all have RXP."

"Of course, the Americans do. Russia has a much earlier iteration of the procedure – the side-effects are killing their transhumans slowly but surely. The Chinese? Their facility in Tianjin was sabotaged during the war. Beijing are reviving the program, but they're a decade behind the Americans. By then it'll be too late."

Hooker glanced at his watch. "What's it got to do with me and Leah?"

Bliss tapped the omni on his desk. "Now, *this* was a good piece of detective work." An image of Natly Hare's manifest flickered onscreen, the list of smuggled tea and cigarettes. "You've linked a terrorist suspect directly to the Commune International. Furthermore, I know Rhys is being blackmailed by the Crimson Brigade."

"Why's the Commune so important? It ain't surprising, a smuggler mixing with anarchists and squatters."

"We know a Crimson Brigade intelligence officer called *Sorcha* is active in London," Bliss replied. "An Irishwoman, associated with a man described as chain-smoking *Marlboro Red* cigarettes. Our analysts have been hard at work. They found a report from the CIA in southern Italy – the Americans seized a Marlboro cigarette butt from the scene of an execution in Naples last year. They've a DNA match to a known Crimson Brigade assassin."

"Naples? Sounds like a long-shot," Hooker replied coolly. Yet his pulse raced. *Sorcha is Roisin…*

"Come on, Hooker. Marlboro? Vintage cigarettes, very rare and very expensive. It's too much of a coincidence."

Hooker folded his arms. "Perhaps."

"The DNA belongs to a terrorist using the name Paolo Falcone, Commanding Officer of the *Action Group Andreas Baader*. He's in London I'll wager, on a mission of critical importance. A kidnapping, perhaps?"

Hooker sighed. "I ain't got nothing to say."

Bliss cocked his head. "My patience is wearing thin. You told the munis you were looking for a missing girl. Charlotte isn't at the Rhys compound in Holland Park. We provide her father's protection team, after all."

"You should sack 'em."

Bliss smiled. "Oh, I shall. But on the other hand, few forces of nature are less containable than a headstrong teenage girl."

Hooker shrugged. "Well, it sounds like you've got the case solved, Chief Superintendent. You're wasting your time with us."

Bliss spooned honey into his tea. "If only, Mister Hooker. Here's the thing – we think Damon Rhys is being blackmailed to reveal classified information. That information might fatally compromise the Reconstruction. Do you want another Hate War? Maybe the Kentish insurgency will spread…"

Hooker remembered the redacted ransom demand he'd

read in Gordy's office. "What information? What's so important?"

"The details are ultra-classified. Even *I* don't know. The distro list is limited to half-a-dozen people in Whitehall and Wessex."

"What's in this for me?"

Bliss smiled like a quiz show host. A man who knows all the answers. "You wish to visit Wessex, but are unable. The Sanctioned Persons Index is a blunt instrument, I know. You have matters that need putting in order. Your daughter for example. Although I'm aware Beatriz...."

Beatriz. Her hand tracing Hooker's through an armorglass screen on the Isle of Man. So out of place, standing in the visiting room. Beatriz had her mother's cheekbones, sharp and high. Her hair was like Hooker's when he was a kid, an explosion of shiny ringlets...

Bliss's teacup clinked on its saucer. "Hooker?"

"Choose your next words carefully," Hooker replied, unclenching his fists. Breathing deeply, willing the rage away. Gordy always said Hooker had a long fuse, but you didn't want to be around when it was lit.

Bliss sat forward. Hooker thought he was enjoying himself. "Rhys is planning a press conference, probably at the kidnapper's behest. Sadly, and for the greater good, Charlotte Rhys must die, and *be seen* to have died, before her father starts yapping."

"What the fuck did you just say?"

"If the girl dies, Rhys has no reason to acquiesce to the kidnapper's demands. He won't talk. It's that simple."

"If you know where she is, why not send an Apex team?

Rescue Lottie and tell Rhys to keep his mouth shut?"

Bliss shook his head. "We don't know *exactly* where she is. Only that she's in the Goons, and quite possibly inside the Commune. And that's thirty floors of armed, feral scum."

"If you don't send help, she'll die anyway," Hooker replied. "It's a war-zone on the Crosland Estate."

"In which case, may I ask your professional opinion? Few men know the Goons as well as you."

"Ask your question, Bliss."

"Let's assume Lottie Rhys is held by Falcone's cell, somewhere inside that damn commune. No more than three or four operatives, if they're Crimson Brigade and working to their usual model. Lottie is surrounded by anarchists, street leaguers and trigger-happy tacticals. Tell me, what do you think the odds are of her being killed by the terrorists and not a third party?"

Hooker shrugged. "My crystal ball ain't working."

"Precisely my point," Bliss replied. He took another sip of his tea. "If events run their natural course, the girl might die at the hands of her captors. Conversely, she might be captured by rioters, or even escape. *We simply don't know.*"

"So?"

"We all have our orders, Mister Hooker. Mine are to shape events. Whatever happens, the world must know the Crimson Brigade executed Lottie Rhys."

"You're asking me to risk my life *and* let the girl die?" Hooker replied.

"Why not? We live in hard times. Lottie is Damon Rhys's daughter, the man who set up the tribunals that sent you to prison."

"You got kids, Bliss?"

The policeman said nothing.

"I reckoned you didn't. Lottie Rhys didn't choose her father."

Bliss poured the last dribble of tea into his cup. "Irrelevant. It's an incontrovertible fact Damon Rhys is soft on extremism. He thinks he'll make peace with the Black Bloc, but if his daughter is murdered, he won't even sit in the same room. We want Rhys on *our* side. I am going to deliver him."

"I'm still wonderin' what this has got to do with me?"

"Vassa Hyatt chose *you* to find the girl for a reason. I'm simply asking the same, except I need you to ensure she dies. Look on the bright side, assassinations are easier than rescues."

"You're a sick fucker."

Bliss shook his head. "Mister Hooker, I've given you the courtesy of candour few people receive. Will you accept my offer?"

"I want a lawyer."

"A lawyer? Given your background, I'd have thought you'd be intimately familiar with Section Twelve of the Emergencies Act."

"You think you can do whatever you want," Hooker replied.

"I know this must be galling, but I *can*."

"I'm leaving," said Hooker.

"Not before you see this," said Bliss, tapping the omni on his desk. It showed a dimly lit room, Leah trussed to a surgeon's chair. She was naked, body white as chalk. Standing over her were two masked figures, dressed in surgical scrubs and rubber aprons. Their faces were hidden behind anti-spatter visors. "You're an old hand at *coercive persuasion*, aren't you?" Bliss continued. "An unfortunate tactic, I know, but sadly necessary in extraordinary circumstances such as these."

Hooker tensed in his seat, fists balled.

"Please, Mister Hooker. There's an Apex team outside. They'd love nothing more than to toss you out of a window. It would look like an escape attempt gone tragically wrong. It happens here occasionally."

"I don't care."

"No need for bravado, Rufus."

Through the office window, Hooker saw fires to the east. Out in the flood zone, London burned. Bliss tapped his desk impatiently. "The record will show Miss Martinez was arrested for grave offences against the Reconstruction Administration…"

"What are you going to do to her?"

"I'm not a… *technician*," Bliss replied, wrinkling his nose.

"I'm going to kill you," said Hooker matter-of-factly.

"No, you aren't," Bliss replied easily. "You're going to accept my offer, and Miss Martinez will be released unharmed. Then you will be at liberty to make your… *pilgrimage* to Wessex."

"You don't know me, do you?" said Hooker.

The secret policeman smiled. "Your answer, Mister Hooker?"

"Fuck you."

Clearing his throat, Bliss spoke into his fob. "This is Bliss. Begin Miss Martinez's treatment."

SIXTEEN

Paolo watched Abid and Sorcha cross the darkened plaza, finally merging with sludge-coloured shadows. Beyond the palisade, street leaguers waved gaudy banners and flaming brands, fences bulging under the weight of their bodies.

"There must be five thousand of the bastards," said General Ignacio of the Black Rifles. He squinted through NVGs, bug-eyed beneath the brim of his helmet. "If only we had heavier weapons."

"Your escape plan is ready?"

"Of course," the General replied. "Everything is in place. Free Cordoba awaits."

"I will be back soon, General," said Paolo. Returning to the apartment, he re-checked his equipment – tripod-mounted camera, omni and the comms node for uploading images of the girl's execution. They were satisfactory. Next was the sword, razor-sharp. Candlelight reflected in liquid ripples on the plastic covering the walls and floor.

Lottie Rhys sat in her room, hands cuffed in her lap. Her hair was matted with blood, a smear of dirt down her cheek. She glowered at Paolo. "You're going to kill me now?"

"No, Lottie."

"You know I'm pregnant," she whispered. Her fingers lay on her stomach, trembling.

"You want to abort it, don't you?" Paolo pulled the encrypted fob from his pocket and took Lottie's picture. Adding a time-stamp and a one-line message, he Darkwired it to Vassa Hyatt:

Proof of Life as agreed. Now deliver.

"Why did you do that?" asked Lottie.

"To show Vassa Hyatt you're still alive and well," Paolo replied. "You see? We're negotiating your release. As long as your father sees sense, you'll live."

"I don't believe you."

Wise girl. "You will see, Lottie. Tell me, who made you pregnant?"

"I don't know for sure," she replied. "It's why I want an abortion."

"You're polyamorous?" said Paolo sharply. He held old-fashioned opinions on monogamy.

Lottie pulled a face. "No, of course not. I think I was drugged. I was at a party..."

The degenerate lifestyles of the elite were of little interest to Paolo Falcone. He'd seen, and experienced, every manner of perversion. He was grateful for the ennui that had rescued him from it. "That's unfortunate, Lottie. I'll bring you something to eat and drink soon. Until then, rest."

The omni bleeped, a newsreader reading from a pad. *We interrupt our regular feed to bring you live images from Lagoon City. The Government has declared a National Security Event, as ten-thousand armed Street Leaguers overwhelm the increasingly stretched police lines…*

Paolo stood on his tiny balcony, watching leaguers swarm around the Commune. There was no sign of the security forces, either NatSec or Munis. They'd left the job to the feral militias, roaring as one as they tore down the fences protecting the outer perimeter.

We're going live to the scene, where the Leagues are making an announcement.

The newscast showed a tall man on a podium, besieged by journalists. He was boyishly handsome, with neatly-combed hair, his three-piece suit bedecked with medals and league regalia. He was flanked by bodyguards wearing balaclavas, carbines held stiffly across their chests. Paolo recognised him as Zachary Fry, Lord Marshal of the Loyal Croydonia Brethren. "Zachary, do you condemn your leaguesmen for attacking police lines?" said a journalist.

"No," said Zachary Fry. "We trusted the Reconstruction Government to control these Reds. They wanna drag London into their insurgency, turn us into the next Medway. Now, I'm tellin' you, Croydonia ain't avin' it. We'll fight fire with FIRE."

"Do you expect to be arrested, Zachary?" shouted another reporter. "Aren't you concerned about being sent to prison again?"

"Oh, I *expect* prison," Fry smirked, "but I don't *fear* it. My message to the Government is simple – you counted on our support, and we gave it freely. Now you've attacked us for defending our land and women and kids from CHAOS. We were only there 'cuz you FAILED. We'll finish the job on the Crosland, I PROMISE you that."

"Lord Marshal Fry are you actually *threatening* the Government?" asked another Journalist.

"No, 'course not. We ain't called LOYAL Brethren for nuffin'. As you know, I served as a corporal in North Africa. I risked my LIFE for this country. I was shot twice. Loyalty is what pumps the BLOOD 'round my heart.

"BUT the Government must understand we're PARTNERS, not slaves. If they move against us, I will call for a Council of the Leagues. I'll form an army so strong, they'll LOSE London. Let's see if the military agrees to move against us, shall we? We've got many brothers and sisters serving in uniform…"

"And your message tonight is, Mister Fry?"

"*Lord Marshal* Fry," a bodyguard warned.

Zachary Fry's eyes glittered, a sheaf of black hair falling across his brow. "The Crosland will BURN. Anarchist scum will BURN. And the SAVAGES down in Kent? The Reds can come up 'ere if they think they're 'ARD enough. We'll fuckin' well BURN THEM TOO."

Outside, Paolo heard a roar.

It had begun.

Opening the door to Lottie's room, he tossed her a shrink-wrapped sandwich and a bottle of water. Locking up, he took a lift to the shelter in the Commune's sub-basement.

The walls were lined with sandbags, electric lights swaying from the ceiling. The air stank of cigarette smoke, a coffee urn stewing on a trestle table. The General nodded curtly. "Welcome, Comrade Paolo."

"The Leagues attack."

"We're ready."

"The cameras are back online General, covering the western perimeter," said a stern-faced woman in black fatigues. The omni showed the horde surging across a broken fence, smoke grenades and petrol bombs heralding their advance.

"Blow the bastards up!" Ignacio ordered.

The girl in black nodded. "Detonate the first device," she ordered into her mic.

A sphere of light bleached the omniscreen white. When the camera refocussed, it revealed a flaming crater. Gunfire from the balconies raked the surviving attackers, young leaguers wriggling like landed fish. Others retreated, dragging their injured with them. The Spaniards punched the air in delight. The omni switched to the southern perimeter. A clutch of blazing municipal police vehicles lay abandoned by the gate, leaguers dismantling barricades with picks and hammers. Young men danced crazily, firing maroons into the inky sky.

A brawny anarchist appeared at Ignacio's shoulder. Crop-headed and bearded, dressed for war. His accent was English. "The leagues always send the *Pups* in the first wave. Young kids, looking to blood themselves."

"Paolo, meet Caleb of Enfield," said Ignacio. "One of my best soldiers. He grew up in London."

"I was a pup in the Reapers," Caleb replied. "Escaped when I was sixteen. These kids want to move up the ranks so badly, they'll do anything."

Paolo offered his hand. "What next? After these children?"

Caleb studied Paolo with dark, hooded eyes. "The next tier are called *ProperPersons*. They just call 'em *Propers*. Pups are cannon-fodder, Propers are blooded shock troops. Most leagues are fifty percent pups, but the Loyal Croydonia are stronger. I reckon five-thousand Propers. After the Propers come *Yeomen*, then finally *Generals*."

Paolo studied the omni. The leaguers on the southern perimeter were being harassed by anarchist rifle fire. Many had stolen riot shields, made of armorglass capable of deflecting bullets. "How many soldiers do you have, Ignacio?"

"Just over a hundred trusted guns from my Black Rifles," the General replied proudly. "There are three hundred fighters available from other groups. But we have over a thousand non-combatants in the Commune."

Paolo shook his head. "No such thing as a non-combatant. Not now."

Ignacio snatched up his fob. "Give the order for our marksmen to kill the fascists. I will offer a bounty for the first confirmed kill of one of their so-called generals. Wait for them to form emergency RVPs for casualty clearance, then detonate the secondary devices."

"How do you feel about that, Caleb?" said Paolo. Testing. Probing. He didn't like new people, wanted to know what made them tick. "You might have kin out there?"

"Fascists," the Englishman replied. "Fuck them. I

recognise no nation, and the only flag I owe fealty to is Red."

Right answer.

"There's a call on the open fob," the girl in black reported. "The pigs want to talk, General."

"Patch them through," Ignacio replied. "Caleb, get up on the walkways. Supervise the snipers. Kill fascists!"

"Yes, General," the Englishman replied, plucking a rifle from a crate.

A weary voice crackled through speakers dotted around the bunker's walls. "This is Chief Superintendent Bruno Banazewski of the Municipal Police. We need to speak about the explosions on your perimeter."

The General hit the fob's privacy button. "Banazewski is reasonable enough, for a pig."

Paolo raised an eyebrow. "You're going to speak with him?"

"Yes. Do you disagree?"

"No, but it might help to feed him misinformation. It might buy time," Paolo replied.

Ignacio nodded and cleared his throat. "We have internal elements outside my control, Chief Superintendent. The explosions are nothing to do with me, in fact I'm trying to calm the situation."

"We've got upwards of a hundred casualties outside your perimeter," the policeman replied. "You must ceasefire and allow casualty evacuation."

"This is self-defence, Chief Superintendent. Why not get the street leagues to ceasefire instead?"

"I'm negotiating with *all* parties," the policeman replied.

"I'm sure you are," Ignacio spat, nostrils flaring. "I saw

that fascist *puta* Zachary Fry's speech. You suck league cock! When Fry's men withdraw from our perimeter, I will order a ceasefire. Until then, we have nothing to discuss, except to put our innocence on the record."

"I'm duty-bound to remind you it's not *your* perimeter," Banazewski sighed. "It's an illegal squat. You're being evicted. We have military support, which we'll use if necessary."

The General's laugh was a hearty boom. "If you have the army out there, order them to tame the fascists, not us. *They* are the aggressors."

"You were warned. Ignacio Azarola, I'm informing you there's an international arrest order against you for war crimes in Libya, Tunisia and Morocco. You'll stand trial, if you're lucky. If not, you'll die in there like mice in a trap."

"I'm not sure I'd have played that card," said Paolo, lighting a fresh Marlboro. The girl in black gifted him a smile. "Not yet, anyway."

"Chief Superintendent, I am terrified," Ignacio laughed. "Now fuck off. Tell NatSec and the Americans they can suck my huge Andalusian dick when we meet in hell!"

The anarchists in the command bunker whooped and cheered. Paolo, despite himself, smiled. "You crazy bastard."

"From you? I'll take that as a compliment," the big Spaniard replied. He cleared his fob, voice booming. "Hear this, Comrades! Black Rifles – report to the western perimeter. Wait for their ambulances, then open fire. Give the fascists no opportunities to evacuate their wounded."

More explosions rocked the bunker, sending up clouds of dust. "Are those ours?" said someone. The omni feed from a circling news copter showed fiery mushroom clouds rising above rooftops, a rag-tag convoy of ambulances trundling through the estate.

Paolo checked the gun at his belt. "I have preparations to make, but if you need me…"

The anarchist general clapped Paolo on the shoulder. "I'll call you when we do. I'm sure your mission, whatever it is, will cause this bastard country even more pain."

"I guarantee it. Our crimson banner will fly over their Parliament. I have sworn it, and it will be so."

General Ignacio readied his Kalashnikov and turned to his soldiers. "Then let's give Comrade Paolo enough time to complete his dark work. To the barricades!"

SEVENTEEN

Hooker stood in the carpark under Millbank tower. "Take that look off your face," said Bailey. "You made the right decision."

Chisholm slapped something wet on Hooker's wrist. "This looks like a shitty old graft-fob, but it ain't. You can't remove it without the right chems." Hooker felt a burning sensation, adhesive bonding to skin. Tiny fish-eye lenses dotted the device, along with a screen and a rubberized push-to-talk button.

Chisholm tapped the fob, which buzzed gently. "Good bit of kit, this. We can monitor everything you see and hear, plus geolocate you to within three metres. Here, take this."

Hooker examined a small grey tube. It looked vaguely medical, a small globule of hardened liquid suspended from the end. "What do I do with it?"

"Put the globe against your ear and squeeze. It's a nano-bot, it'll graft onto your auditory canal. You'll be able to talk to us independently of the fob."

Hooker pulled a face. "Fuck off. I'm not putting that in my ear."

"Relax. It's only an organic polymer. The grub degrades naturally after forty-eight hours."

Hooker slid the tube into his ear and felt something pop. Warm liquid, followed by a slight wriggling. Then he heard a low, clear tone.

"It's working pretty good," said Chisholm, checking his earpiece. "Seeing as we're underground an' all."

"Hooker, I've gotta warn you. If you remove either device, the techs start working on Leah," Bailey warned.

Hooker's eyes swept the two OCS men. "This is the sorta shit that comes back to haunt a man."

"Save it for the soap-dodgers," said Chisholm. "I don't like what's happening to her any more than you do."

"We are where we are," Bailey added, studying his shoe.

They drove in silence, back to the Goons. On the newsfeed, a senior leaguer declared his support for the march on the Crosland. The head of The Loyal Croydonia Brethren, promising an army to crush the rioting.

"Zachary-fucking-Fry. Lunatic," said Bailey.

"Yeah, but a useful lunatic," Chisholm replied, accelerating into the priority lane, the BMW's speedo hitting a hundred-twenty. Turning on the automated steering, he lit a cigarette.

"Ten-cent Hitler, that's what he is," Bailey grumbled.

"Croydonia's not safe, not since he took over," said

Hooker. "Zachary Fry's a race-separatist."

"Couldn't care less, I live by the Heathrow Gate," Chisholm shrugged.

Hooker smiled. "Heathrow? That'll make it easier to find you, come the time."

"Fuck off, Hooker."

They passed the Lagoon City checkpoint, parking in the shadows of a deserted office block. Bailey led Hooker to the trunk. "Help yourself."

Hooker unzipped a black ballistic bag. Inside was a holstered assault pistol, as long as his forearm. "You've got all the toys at OCS, ain't you?" he said. "New Hanyang Tactical Pro? Suppressor, recoil mitigation, nano-munitions and integrated optics. I usually work with a .38, a shotgun and a blade."

Chisholm made a face "Well, now you've been upgraded to the premium-fucking- package. This is Apex Team stuff, not medieval No-Zone bollocks."

"Yeah, even we don't get issued this kind of gear," Bailey sniffed.

Hooker shrugged on a ceramoweave plate carrier over his armorgel vest. Clipping the Hanyang's holster to his belt, he added distraction grenades, fighting knife, a coil of nylon rope, karabiner and slap charges for door-breaching. Finally, he pulled on his leather coat, hydration packs stuffed in the pockets. "You forgot the most important bit of kit," said Hooker.

"What?" said Chisholm.

"Gold."

"In the zip-up compartment," Bailey replied, pointing at

the bag.

Hooker found bundles of shiny RDs and the pouch containing Vassa Hyatt's guineas. There was also an autojet, the size of a marker pen. The needle was covered with a thick rubber cap. "Combat drugs, straight out of Porton Down's Advanced Warfare facility," said Bailey proudly. "That's a dose of super-juice."

"Respirocite?" said Hooker, examining the autojet.

"Yeah," Bailey replied, "that shit'll make you archangel-scary for twenty minutes. After that you'll be fucked for forty-eight hours. Last resort stuff."

"That sharp cost more than our lovely German car," Chisholm added. "I'd rather sign it back in when we're done."

Hooker shrugged. "I'll bear that in mind."

Bailey watched a maroon arc into the sky, trailing fiery smoke. "What's your plan?"

Hooker held up the fob fused to his wrist. "Listen and find out."

They drove deeper into the estate, the occasional NatSec patrol holding street corners. Beyond the cordon, munis stood in riot-shielded huddles. "We're almost there," said Chisholm. "I'm getting a feed in my earpiece. The leagues have marched on the Commune."

They passed a burnt-out pub, blackened timbers pointing skywards. "Drop me here," said Hooker.

Chisholm stopped the car. "One last thing," he said. "Don't contact Gordy Rice. We'll know if you call him, and if you do our deal's off."

"Think about Leah," said Bailey.

Hooker readied the assault pistol, slide snapping into

place. "Think about what I'll do if she's hurt."

Chisholm pulled a face. "We're listening, Hooker. To every-fucking-word."

Boots crunching on gravel, Hooker navigated trash-strewn pavements and boulevards, hand on his gun. Finally, he found the familiar maisonette, walls sprayed with obscene graffiti. Checking the street for watchers, Hooker pressed a buzzer set next to an armoured door. A voice bled through the intercom. "Fuck off."

"It's Rufus Hooker."

"Then double-fuck off."

"Let me in, Logan. I've got coin."

"Coin?"

"A shit-load of gold."

The door opened an inch, releasing the stench of fried food and body odour. "Come in," said a fat man. "Quick, 'fore some fucker sees you."

"Doubt anyone remembers me," Hooker replied.

"You ain't easily forgotten, you murdering shit," said the fat man, blubbery lips fringed with a greasy beard. A mauve light-stud twinkled in each nostril.

"Neither are you, Logan," Hooker replied. He peeled a wad of dollars from his pocket and tossed them on a sofa. "There's some dough, so y'know where I'm coming from."

Logan's tongue flickered while he counted the banknotes. "What is it you need, Sergeant Hooker?"

"You know I'm not a Taskforcer anymore." Hooker walked to the window and nudged open the armour-mesh blinds. The street was empty. "As if you didn't know."

Logan smirked. "I loved seein' you get banged-up at

that Tribunal. I'd be lying if I said I didn't."

"I'd be lying if I said I wasn't thinking of punching your teeth out."

Logan flopped on a sofa, grinning. Littered with pizza crusts and crunched-up tissues, the omni projecting an urgent gang-bang in three fleshy dimensions. The fat man lit a skanj joint, blowing a plume of dirty-sweet smoke. "What do you want?"

"The *Commune International*. I need to get inside."

"The anarchist dump?" Logan shook his head, jowls wobbling. "It's full of tooled-up Reds. I had you down for a lot of things, Hooker, but never stupid."

"A thousand guineas. Get me inside the Commune and it's yours. I know you can do it, Logan."

"Gold? Show me,"

Hooker threw Vassa Hyatt's bag on the table-top. "Look inside."

Logan unzipped the pouch, picked up a guinea and bit it. "Okay, but I need to make a call," he said, pointing a sausage-finger at his fob.

"Do it."

Logan spoke in *Tois,* a fast-moving mixture of Creole, Slav and Romany slang. Different from No-Zone Babble, but Hooker understood it well enough. Logan told someone to come over. *Fast.* "Who's your contact?" he asked.

Logan smiled, grease glistening on his beard. "A local girl. One of her boyfriends is a rope-head from the Commune. Reckon he might help, if the price is right."

Hooker looked for somewhere clean to sit, but thought better of it, "how long?"

Logan flicked the Omni to a news feed. Leaguers swarmed across the Goons, followed by camera drones from a dozen news stations. "Not long. Do you think they'll let those bastards in?"

"They already have."

Logan harrumphed. "The Crosland won't take a liberty like that lying down."

Hooker shrugged. "Croydonia's marching. There's thousands of 'em. This ain't like the old days, when the Goons had its own league."

"Thanks to you dirty bastards," Logan spat. "Now, wait here."

Watching the door, gun ready, Hooker waited. Logan finally reappeared with a skinny, white-haired girl. She wore a dress made of spiky grey rubber. "This is Desire," said Logan. "She can help you."

Desire studied Hooker with a hollow-eyed stare, silver-painted lips drawn into a scowl. Light-studs fringed her jawline, glowing pink. She smiled. "This is him? Handsome. I do like me a bit of black."

Logan popped open a can of beer. "Meet Rufus Hooker. Used to be a Taskforcer."

The girl screwed up her face. "Taskforcer? Why would I help one of those cunts?"

Hooker smiled, weapons visible as his coat gaped open. "How old were you in those days? Or where you still swimmin' 'round daddy's ball-sack?"

"My mum told me 'bout it." The girl attempted a coy smile, tracing a pattern on the carpet with her toe. "She said Taskforcers'd kill people just for lookin' at 'em the wrong way."

Hooker took a step closer, making Desire flinch. He smiled, and it was cruel. "I'd love to talk about the rights and wrongs of the Hate War, but I'm in a hurry. I need to get inside the Commune International."

"There's gold," said Logan. The girl went to touch a guinea, but Logan shooed her away.

"Yeah," said Desire, licking her lips. "I can do that."

"How?"

"My last boyfriend? He was a rope-head, German fella. He takes stuff in and out of the Commune. Ciggies and 'cotics." Desire lowered her voice. "They've got a tunnel. A *secret* tunnel. Police don't know nuffin' 'bout it."

"Your German friend can get me inside?"

Desire nodded. "We were fobbin' earlier. He wants to get out, before the leaguers burn the place down."

"OK, let's do it."

Desire's eyes narrowed. "How much? He'll want paying proper. Not mugged off."

"There's a thousand guineas. You and Logan sort it out between yourselves."

"Sixty-forty to me," said Logan.

"Fuck off," Desire snapped. "What risks you takin' lardy-boy?"

Hooker held up a hand. "I said work it out between yourselves. Now fob your man."

Desire crossed her bony arms. "My fobs at my sister's. You ain't going there, I'd get skinned if they knew I was helpin' a Taskforcer."

Hooker checked his watch. He saw the gold-fever in

Destiny's eyes – she'd be back. "Be quick."

Desire nodded. "Y'know the alleyway, off the Linton Mead?"

"Sure."

"There's some garages, 'cross from the lagoon. They got blue doors. Meet me there in twenty minutes."

The girl reached for the gold. Hooker grabbed her hand and squeezed it, just enough to hurt. "You get paid *once* I'm inside. Wanna find out if your old lady was right about Taskforcers?"

The girl looked at Logan, light studs blinking in his nostrils. Logan nodded. Smirking, the girl slipped out of the door. "She's a good girl," the fat man said, licking his lips.

Hooker watched the girl go. "Don't fuck me over, Logan."

Logan drained another beer. "Why would I? I'm getting paid to send you somewhere you're likely to get killed. It's like Christmas 'far as I'm concerned."

Hooker left Logan's place, sticking to the shadows as he made for the river. The Thames glittered, reflecting moonlight and fire. The strange monastery sat mid-river, lit by yellowish torchlight. Hooker magnified his goggles, watching robed monks studying the estate through binoculars. He thought the Answerers were crazy bastards, then chuckled. *I'm the one trying to break inside a war-zone.*

"What's so funny?" said a voice in his ear. *Chisholm.*

"Fuck off, I'm trying to work."

"We checked your friend on the legacy systems. Theodore Logan – registered informant with the Taskforces. There's a report saying you killed his cousin."

"Logan told me where he was. They had a beef."

"And you trust *him*?"

Hooker carried on walking. "If you don't shut up and let me get on with it…"

"You'll do what?"

"I'll fail. That creature Bliss will send you to Chatham. Then, if you're really unlucky, I'll find you there myself."

Chisholm softened his voice. "I just want you to know the system's working. We can hear you."

"Great. Now leave me alone, or find the girl yourself."

When he reached the garages, Hooker climbed onto a nearby roof. Three figures approached, light studs twinkling in one of their faces – Desire. The others were *rope-heads*, Goon slang for a dread-locked anarchist. They stopped and lit cigarettes, fidgeting from foot-to-foot. The men wore long rubberised coats and galoshes, reminding Hooker of pictures he'd seen of old-fashioned trawlermen. Climbing back down to street level, he walked towards them. "This is the fella," said Desire, lighting a joint.

One of the rope-heads offered a brawny hand. "Hey. You want to get inside the Commune?"

"Yeah."

The rope-head's accent was German. Harsh to Hooker's ear. "Typical mad English – everyone else wants to get out."

"He's got gold," said Desire. "Lots of gold."

Hooker looked the German in the eye. "I've also got a fifty-shot Hanyang Tactical Pro."

"You will have no trouble from us, my friend," the German replied, smiling. "No use having gold if you can't spend it. Desire, you'll find us somewhere safe to hide? We have a deal?"

"You can stay with me tonight," Desire replied, running a fingernail under the German's stubbly chin. "Don't worry, I'll keep you both warm. Tomorrow my sister will drive you to the border, or you can take the coach to Dover."

"I'd get your hair cut first," said Hooker. "Let's go."

"I think he's right," the second rope-head smiled, opening the door to a garage. "We need to cut our hair *and* hurry."

The garage floor was covered with layer upon layer of filthy carpeting and rotting linoleum. The two rope-heads began peeling them away, finally revealing a panel. It was cleverly camouflaged, fitted flush with the rough concrete floor. "Down there," said the first rope-head, prising it open with a knife. "Follow me and stay close, *ja?*"

Hooker nodded. "Where's the exit? Inside the Commune or outside?"

"Just inside the western perimeter," the rope-head replied. "There will be guards."

"That's my problem."

The rope-head dropped into the tunnel with a splash. Hooker followed, NVGs painting the world green. "This place has gone to shit," the rope-head whispered. "Maybe a year ago, it was good. Peaceful. Then Ignacio of The Black Rifles came."

"They aren't *real* anarchists," the other squatter added. "They're no better than fascists."

"How many Black Rifles?" asked Hooker.

"A hundred, maybe more?"

The hatch scraped shut above them, Desire making *flap-flop* noises as she re-covered it with carpet. The first rope-head slid a heavy padlock through a clasp. The lock was electronic, designed to frustrate conventional picking. "We've got to make it look like nobody came through," the rope-head explained. "This tunnel is secret – strictly controlled by the Black Rifles."

"So how come you're allowed here?"

"We maintain it. The Spaniards are too lazy to do it for themselves."

"They sleep all day," the other German shrugged.

The tunnel was a full two metres wide, cantilevered with scaffolding poles. The walls were carved through layers of rubble and aggregate, held in place by a mixture of plastifoam, wooden stanchions and chicken wire. Luminous roof tiles provided dim green light. "You built this?" Hooker asked.

"Thirty of us. German engineering," said the rope-head proudly. "We invented an organic solution to dissolve the debris. It made it easier to dig out. It's the main smuggling route in and out of the Crosland."

His friend nodded. "It's deep enough not to show up on thermal imaging. The pigs have no idea we can get in and out."

Hooker felt the slab of grey putty hugging his wrist. *And you've just told the National Security Constabulary.* "How often does it flood?"

"Once or twice a year, usually in the spring. In places, we are only a few metres from the riverbed." They waded along the tunnel, murky river water waist-deep. The rank odour of sewage filled Hooker's nose.

The first rope-head held up a hand. "Someone's coming."

"Who?" Hooker whispered.

"*Scheisse*! Black Rifles…"

EIGHTEEN

Paolo sat in the dark, awaiting Rourke's call. His fingers brushed the brainstem injectors in his pocket, each containing MADRIGAL'S secrets. A compelling story, but Paolo knew nobody believed in *truth* anymore – desiccated by a mixture of cognitive dissonance and Critical Theory. The Crimson Brigade agent remembered a lecture in Bari, a political officer explaining how the babel of technology had deconstructed veracity, like a mortician with a corpse. The Crimson Brigade had used lies to its advantage for many years, but it was a weapon that cut both ways.

No, unless MADRIGAL was corroborated from Damon Rhys's mouth, the mission would fail. In a world inured to lies, only unambiguous fact would suffice. A confessional, in front of cameras and baying journalists. Damon Rhys' tears would prove more than a thousand dossiers, his daughter's grisly fate more compelling than the story of how the world caught fire. Paolo Falcone smiled – had he not taken a mixture of drama and cloying sentimentality and weaponised it? And the siege outside? Perhaps it was the cherry on the cake.

The timer on Paolo's fob gnawed at the minutes. Yawning, he studied the girl on the omni. Lottie Rhys lay watching the lightbulb in the ceiling, hands resting on her belly. Was she thinking of the foetus gestating inside her? He fobbed Vassa Hyatt. "You have proof of life. When is the conference?"

"Approximately an hour."

"Too long."

Hyatt sighed. "You *do* want the media there, don't you? They're all in Lagoon City now. Some of them have even told me I'm trying to spin the news cycle away from the riots."

"Is that also your job?"

"I'm not a media manager, I'm a security agent."

Paolo's voice was scratchy through the doppler. "I want Rhys to announce he's going to discuss his participation in the CIA Special Access Program known as MADRIGAL. You have thirty minutes."

Hyatt sounded relaxed. "Impossible. I can't magically transport the national media across London, can I? I need more time."

"We know the girl's pregnant, Miss Hyatt," said Paolo.

Hyatt paused. Her voice wavered for a moment. "I have no response to that."

"I'm sure you don't," Paolo replied, turning the screw. "The circumstances behind her pregnancy sound quite…

disturbing. Maybe I'll film her talking about it before I execute her."

Hyatt's voice was strained. "Do you think interrogating then beheading a pregnant teenager is the way to win support for your cause?"

"Absolutely," Paolo replied, ice in his words. "Your government bombs children every day, not forty miles from London. So, I think your people will understand why the elite's brats face the sword. They might even embrace the social justice of it. Oh, and we both know they'll love the *drama* of it."

"That's your answer? Undergraduate revolutionary bullshit? Very well, I'll pass your demands onto Mister Rhys," Hyatt spat, ending the call.

Paolo lit a cigarette. Hyatt had been composed and professional, until he mentioned Lottie's pregnancy. Was it a lever they'd not properly pulled? *Dammit, why hadn't Sorcha debriefed the girl properly?* He unlocked the door to Lottie's room. "When we spoke earlier, about your pregnancy, you mentioned you were drugged."

The girl bared her teeth. Her hair, matted with blood, half-covered her eyes. She reminded Paolo of a cornered fox. "Fuck off, terrorist."

Paolo crouched beside the girl. "I'm just a soldier, Miss Rhys. I hold the rank of Colonel in the Crimson Brigade. Furthermore, in my world, drugging a woman in the circumstances you describe would never happen. The people who did it would be executed."

Lottie scowled. "So-says the man with the sword and a chopping block?"

Paolo pulled a protein bar from his pocket. "Take this. I told you, the sword is for show, merely a piece of theatre to scare your father. Now, tell me exactly what happened. It could be important."

Lottie mashed the bar into her mouth. When she'd eaten it, she shrugged. "Why?"

"If there's something your family wants to hide, I can use it to get you released more quickly."

Lottie shook her head.

Paolo smiled. "Alternatively, I could torture the information out of you."

Lottie glanced around the room. Outside, the occasional chatter of gunfire. She dabbed crumbs from her chin and put them in her mouth. "You might anyway."

"What other choice do you have, Lottie? This place isn't safe. I'm the only one who can get you out of here."

"Are we in Medway?"

"Perhaps," Paolo lied.

Lottie looked at the space between her feet. Charred floorboards and greasy linoleum. She rubbed her wrists, raw from handcuffs and rope. "Okay, I'll bite. A few months ago, Dad took me to a party in Wessex. For the Speaker's birthday."

"*Speaker?*"

"Yes, Speaker of the Winchester Parliament. It's a very important job, like a sort of referee. Dad went to Cambridge with her, she's my Godmother actually. It was quite a stuffy party, too many speeches about politics."

"Politics? I thought you were interested. Didn't you work for the New-Democrats in the States?"

Lottie's laugh was bitter. "I spent three months going to drinks with senators, most of who just wanted to sleep with me."

Nothing changes. "I'm sorry to interrupt. Please, tell me about the party."

"Etta, one of the other girls, had some skanj. So we hid in the garden and smoked it. I don't often smoke skanj, but I was bored…"

"Was Vassa there?"

"Vassa? She's everywhere. She came into the garden to see me, so I was worried she'd tell my father I'd been smoking. Turns out she was okay about it. She even brought a bottle of champagne."

"What happened after that?"

Lottie pushed her hair away from her eyes, bruised and bloodshot. "There was a good-looking guy at the party, Tristian. He was more mature than the others. He'd been to college in America, so we spent ages talking about that. We had a smoke and finished the champagne. Then he kissed me."

"You're an attractive young woman," Paolo shrugged. "Why wouldn't he?"

Lottie blushed. "There are rules for people like me."

Paolo found himself laughing. "You're at a party, smoking skanj and drinking champagne? You chose to kiss a handsome young man. Lottie, those *are* the rules."

"I know you'll find this odd, but Tristian was below my… standing. And I was a virgin. That's very important in Wessex society."

"*Standing?*"

"I have three suitors, all from high families. They've been chosen by a professional matchmaker and approved by my father. All of them are genetically, socially and psychologically compatible. Eventually, after I've graduated from Oxford, I'll marry the one I like best."

Paolo shook his head. "It's like something out of the 18th Century."

"Wessex is another world compared to London," Lottie replied. "Dad says we're rebuilding the country, so it can be just like Wessex. We need elites. He says there isn't time for… *meritocracy*. That comes later, when…"

Paolo sneered. "He sounds like an archangel. What happened with Tristian?"

Lottie studied her fingernails. "I was dizzy, then I suppose I passed out. When I woke up, I was lying down in a room with purple lights. Like ultraviolet. Anyway, Tristian was holding my hand, saying *everything's okay*. I was so cold, my teeth were chattering. Then I passed out again. Maybe it was a dream?"

"What happened after you woke up?"

"I was in the garden, with some of the other girls. They said I'd been gone for an hour. Tristian had gone home. The thing is, I didn't feel like… you know?"

"Like you'd had intercourse?"

Lottie blushed. She nodded and stood up. "May I stretch my legs?"

"Of course."

"And a cigarette? Please?"

Paolo shook his head. "Smoking? You're pregnant."

"Really? Says the kidnapper with an execution

chamber?"

Paolo shrugged. "I'm not going to harm you. Carry on with your story."

Lottie's forehead creased in concentration. "I might've been a virgin, but I understand reproductive biology. There was none of the discomfort I'd expect from my first… *time*. I began to wonder if I'd imagined it, until I missed my period. Then I took a pregnancy test."

Paolo tapped another cigarette free. *Yes, this might work. I could threaten to reveal the girl was impregnated at a cattle market for genetically-pure aristocrats. Rhys would hate that - the prurient interest would make the whole thing even more sensational.* "Lottie, there's something I don't understand. If your father had already identified potential husbands, why d'you think this happened?"

"I wondered about that myself. I really don't know… I don't talk to him about that sort of thing."

"Who *do* you talk to?"

"Evie. Evie's mother. Evie thought I should have an abortion. There was no way I could go to my doctor for termination meds, he'd tell my father I wasn't a virgin. So I asked if she knew anyone…"

"Evie knew Roisin was a nurse, of course. And here we are," Paolo smiled, getting to his feet.

"Where's Evie?"

"With her mother," Paolo replied. "She knew nothing of this."

Lottie walked to the shuttered window. "Who's shooting outside?"

"Get back from there, it's dangerous."

The girl laughed as Paolo grabbed her shoulder. "You need to stay here until things calm down. Now, I'm afraid I'm going to have to tie your hands again."

"What is it you want from my father?"

"Just the truth, Lottie. The truth sets us free."

"The truth about what?"

Paolo pulled plasticuffs from his fighting rig. "Soon you'll watch his confession for yourself. Then everything will make sense."

Leaving the girl, he returned to the command bunker. General Ignacio was stripped to the waist, a bottle of cognac in his fist. He bawled commands into his fob, eyes flitting from camera to camera. His torso glistened with sweat, hands on hips as he directed the battle. "How many IEDs remain?"

"Only the device on the western perimeter," said a fighter monitoring a bank of omnis.

"Excellent. Send reinforcements, tell them to fight hard for the palisade – make the fascists want it! When they take it, order a withdrawal. When the fascists advance, blow it up."

"Yes General. We have thirty guns on that position right now."

"Send more. The situation on the southern perimeter?"

A girl in black fatigues replied, tapping on her pad. "There's a sizeable force of leaguers a hundred metres from the gate. Our scouts report generals from three of the biggest leagues."

Paolo cleared his throat, and the room fell quiet. "General Ignacio, may I offer my analysis?"

The General nodded. "Go on, Paolo."

"I believe the higher-echelon leaguers will attack from

the south, *after* their rabble breaches the western perimeter. Part-distraction, part-pincer movement, if you will. The generals want the glory of taking the Commune for themselves."

The General folded his arms. "I agree, unless the cops or army intervene at the last minute. Do you have any information?"

Paolo shook his head. "None. I suspect the authorities have lost control now their dogs are unleashed. Their only tactical option is to keep drones on station, degrading our defences from the air. Letting the street leagues win is to their advantage now."

The General grimaced as he paced the bunker. "You think the Government are backing the Leaguers?"

"Without a doubt. Our comrades in Kent will think twice about spreading the insurgency north if leaguers hold the Goons."

The girl in black's voice was urgent. "The western palisade is under assault now."

"Tell the reinforcements to hurry. Keep a live feed on the south," the General ordered. He tugged a flak jacket over his chest and grabbed a rifle. "Now we all fight."

Paolo moved closer to the Spaniard. "I need a favour."

"Just ask," said Ignacio.

"I need someone for… dark work. Someone with a strong stomach."

"How dark?"

Paolo shrugged. "I have a prisoner. A class traitor. They require executing, in the event I'm unable to do it myself."

"You can have Caleb, the Englishman. He's got blood

under his fingernails, I trust him completely."

Paolo shook the Spaniard's hand. "This is a glorious moment, my friend. They'll talk of this battle down the ages."

The mercenary laughed. "I hope to be there to hear it – I'm not dying today!"

NINETEEN

Hooker heard voices. The splash of boots in water. Clamping his smog mask over his face, he slid beneath the surface. The water was cold and sludgy, with a chemical stink.

"*Hola Comrades!*" called one the rope-heads, four figures wading towards them – three men and a woman. Hooker watched them through night-vision – the first man was a giant, stooped in the low-ceilinged tunnel. Two other men in capes carried shotguns. The last was a woman wearing a shapeless hat, a rummage bag over her shoulder.

"Comrades?" the rope-head repeated. "It's only Gunther and Max. We're doing maintenance on the cantilevers. No problem, okay?"

Shotguns coughed in reply. The first rope-head bounced off the wall, a fist-sized hole in his belly. The second's head dissolved in a cloud of wet gristle. "Let's move," grunted one of the gunmen.

"Was that necessary?" asked the woman.

"Were these your men?" said the giant. Hooker thought his accent Arabic. He wore some type of work uniform beneath bulky body armour. Armed with two AK rifles, a ballistic bag slung across his back.

A gunman racked a new shell into his pump-gun. "The Generals orders were simple – *nobody* enters the tunnels after the alert is sounded. On pain of death."

"*A la mierda,*" said another voice.

Hooker thumbed the Hanyang's fire selector, grips buzzing in his palm.

Weapon ready.

An amber icon appeared in his goggles. He didn't need to raise the weapon, or aim. Just look. *Stare – blink – stare…*

Hooker's goggles broke water, eye movement painting target vectors, thermal imaging picking out heat signatures. He squeezed the trigger, the Hanyang making a ripping noise as explosive-tipped darts tore into the first gunman…

…with a blink, he lit up the second, nano-flechette ripping through his torso. His head and shoulders toppled into his lower body cavity, like something from a grotesque cartoon. In the half-light, Hooker saw the giant aim both rifles, the woman tugging something from her bag.

Shit.

Hooker looked, blinked and fired, flechette gouging a lump from the giant's armoured shoulder. *I aimed at his head.* A globe of searing light filled Hooker's goggles – *the bastard's armour has countermeasures.*

The giant charged, roaring in pain, weapons blazing. No more than twenty metres away and closing, flares popping from his body armour like a gunship on a hot LZ. The sonic whine of bullets hurt Hooker's ears, a round slamming into his plate-carrier. He was thrown backwards, gel-armour gripping his body.

"Abid!" the woman hollered, pulling a stubby submachinegun.

Then, a prayer, a soulful roar coming deep from the giant's chest. The giant pulled something on his armour, some kind of rip-cord…

It's a bloody suicide vest.

Hooker's weapon spat flame, a stream of bullets tearing off the giant's arm at the elbow. The Hanyang's slide snapped back – *weapon empty.* Return fire sliced by Hooker's head as the woman returned fire. She scurried away, back towards the Commune. Gunk bled from the giant's suicide vest, liquid explosive swirling and fizzing in the water. Grunting with pain, he grabbed his half-submerged bag. Bundles of loam-grey stuff bobbed on the surface.

Plastic explosives.

Hooker half-swam, half-staggered for the bullet-chewed tunnel wall. Pocked with nano-munition strikes, black water trickling from the edges. He kicked, hard as he could, against the wall and the crater widened as the trickle became a stream. Hooker mashed himself into the gap, gloved hands tearing at brick and wire. Something gave, like a rotten bone. A corroded joist, more rust than steel.

The *shahid's* prayer grew louder, the giant pressing himself against the wall, clutching the stump where his arm had been. He was smiling.

Hooker tore at the hole with his knife, muscles

straining, sinews burning. Water gushed into the void, the Thames desperate to claim the tunnel as its own. The giant exploded with a howling roar. Pieces of flesh, bone and equipment spattered the walls, peppering Hooker's armour. He fell, ears ringing, into a watery vortex, face stung by debris.

Then nothing, apart from shapes of dark, fractal light.

Then Hooker gasped, eyes flicking open, ears aching and throbbing. He checked the watch strapped to his wrist – he'd lost ten minutes of his life. It felt like an hour. Coughing water, he gobbed the taste of sewage from his mouth. Overhead, night-time clouds were tinged with flame, the stink of burning trash on the wind. He reached for his holster – the Hanyang was gone. His oxygen mask lay by his side, a sharp pain in his forearm where a shard of metal stuck from the fob on his wrist. He probed his ear with a finger, felt sticky with blood and tiny pieces of grit. The NatSec audio grub was broken. *They can't hear me. They'll torture Leah.*

"Are you okay?" said a voice. A London voice, raspy and rough. "Take these antivirals. You swallowed a load of shitty Thames water."

Hooker looked into a horror-movie visage. Gnarled and twisted, the monster's eyes were iridescent spheres, each tipped with a glittering lens. Something glistened wetly in the sockets, stopping them sliding out of the melted parody of a face. Sitting up, Hooker realised he was on the ziggurat, in the middle of the river. The monastery of The Answerers. The creature's lipless mouth moved, exposing uneven yellow teeth. "Rufus Hooker?" The voice was laboured and wheezy, sibilant against a broken tongue. "It's been a while, but I'd recognise that face anywhere."

Hooker thought the voice familiar. Tufts of coppery hair between the pads of burn tissue on the creature's face stirred his memory. "Yes, I'm Hooker."

The monster grunted wetly, lips making half-a-smile. "They used to call me Cooper. Section leader on Taskforce-12. You were TF-17, right?"

Hooker studied the fob on his wrist and sighed. "Yeah."

"We covered you in Sheppey. Gordy Rice was your boss."

Hooker remembered the red-headed Taskforcer, commanding a troop of Land Rovers fitted with heavy machineguns. Sheppey had been brutal, a network of prisons overrun by convicts. A month of bitter fighting, hand-to-hand. "Gordy's still my boss," Hooker replied.

"Some things change, others stay the same," said the monk.

"Like me being up to my neck in shit, Cooper."

"I'm called Brother Samuel now," the monk replied. He wore a rust-coloured robe, rubber sandals on his feet. A small group of similarly dressed men stood nearby, holding flaming torches, "I'm reborn."

"Oliver Cooper wasn't it?" said Hooker. "I thought you were dead."

The creature gently pulled the fob away from Hooker's wrist, dabbing bloody skin with an antiseptic wipe. "Oliver Cooper is dead. I *am* Brother Samuel."

Hooker coughed, the taste of sewage on his tongue. "I remember now. Taskforce-12 was wiped out on Sheppey."

Brother Samuel touched his face. "Swaleside prison. They lured us into an ambush and detonated a half-ton of napalm. Sixty-six dead, twenty-three MIA."

"I'm glad you made it," Hooker replied.

"It's strange, watching your own funeral on the omni. The shit that gets spoken about you…" Brother Samuel finished fixing a dressing to Hooker's wound and shook his head.

"How did I get here?"

"Brother Ranjit. He was out on the water, seeing if he could evacuate civilians from the estate. Then he saw wreckage on the water. The wreckage was *you*."

A hooded monk stepped forward, fine-featured and slim. "I'm Brother Ranjit. You were unconscious – I couldn't pull you in the boat, so I towed you back. Your smog mask's air supply saved your life."

"Thanks," Hooker replied. "I owe you."

"No," Samuel replied, tucking his hands in his sleeves. "Helping without asking for anything in return is all part of The Answer."

"The Answer?"

"Well, it's all about the question too," Brother Ranjit chuckled, passing Hooker a towel and a flask of coffee.

"Thanks," Hooker replied, crowded by curious monks. "Have any of you got a fob I can borrow?"

Brother Samuel pulled back his robe. Underneath he wore a belt studded with pouches. He produced a fob and switched it on. Hooker winced, peeling the dead NatSec fob from his wrist, taking a bloody patch of skin with it. He pulled the liquid memory chip from the device and slotted it inside the new fob. A series of codes scrolled across the screen. Hooker tapped on one and waited.

"What are you playing at?" said Chisholm.

"I'm on the container island, out in the river. The monks rescued me, I was in a tunnel under the Commune, but there was a bloke down there with a suicide vest…"

"We saw," said Chisholm. "A proper fuck-up. If I were you I'd get my arse moving, before we tell the beauticians to start on your girlfriend."

"Yes," said another voice, business-like and cold. Bliss. "Contacting us was the right thing to do. What's your alternative plan for infiltrating the Commune?"

"I'm working on it."

"Work harder. Faster. *Smarter*. We have an extraction plan *if* you succeed." Bliss ended the call.

"What's that about?" asked Brother Samuel.

Hooker pointed across the river. "I've got to get inside the Commune."

"And they say *we're* crazy." Samuel's eyes swivelled in their sockets, tiny motors whirring. The other monks laughed. "Why?"

Hooker stood up. "There's a kidnapped girl over there. If I don't find her, NatSec are going to torture my friend."

"I see," Brother Ranjit, frowned. The monks gazed across the river, at the smoke-wreathed Commune. Copters chuntered overhead, floodlights carving scoops of light from the darkness.

"I'm struggling to see how you're gonna pull that one off," said Brother Samuel. "Not with the leagues laying siege."

Hooker got to his feet, wiping his goggles with the towel. "Will you help?"

The monk pulled up his cowl, covering his war-scorched

face. "Just before Ranjit dragged you out of the water, we were watching the newsfeeds. There've been explosions, hundreds of casualties…"

Hooker, grim-faced, grasped Samuel's shoulder. "I don't have a choice."

"Perhaps we can help, but I'll have to speak with the others. There will be a price, though. The Answer demands it." Samuel's eyes glittered.

"You keep talking about The Answer. What is it?"

"What we believe in. Belief systems require beliefs, Rufus."

"Although we are, I'd argue, a meta-belief," Brother Ranjit added mysteriously.

"Whatever," Hooker replied, stamping water from his boots. "I'll pay your price. Just get me across the river."

Brother Samuel nodded slowly. "Let's see if you'll pay, Rufus Hooker. Not everyone can…"

TWENTY

Paolo keyed his fob. "Sorcha?"

The Irishwoman was breathless. "We were ambushed, in the so-called *secret* tunnel. Abid's dead."

"You were double-crossed by the Spaniards?"

"I don't think so. Feckin' trigger-happy bastards started a gunfight with some other squatters. Said something about the General's orders. Abid was badly wounded, he activated his bloody vest. The tunnel is flooded now, I'll never get out."

"Where are you?"

"Just inside the perimeter, near the palisade. It's quiet now."

"The lull before the storm. Come back, Sorcha, we 'll rethink the plan."

The Irishwoman sighed. "Paolo, I think it's over. My agent isn't answering his fob. And even if he does, there's no Abid…"

"It's not over yet," Paolo insisted. "We've other cards to play."

"I don't see..."

"Just come back, Sorcha," Paolo snapped, ending the call. He tapped his fob, opening an emergency Darknet feed to the Command Council. He was loathe to contact the Centre, especially in a denied operations area. No doubt he'd have to justify his decision to a desk-jockey Commissar, if he ever returned to Kyiv. But something about Lottie's story intrigued him. In another life, Paolo had worked intelligence cases. He felt a familiar itch.

FLASH MESSAGE

CODENAME RIVERSHRIKE. REQUIRE URGENT MISSION-CRITICAL INTELLIGENCE REGARDING MALE SUBJECT OF INTEREST (POSS. RESIDENT IN WESSEX) CALLED 'TRISTIAN' (SURNAME UNKNOWN), MALE, AGE 18-25, UK NATIONAL, EDUCATED USA. PRESENT AT SOCIAL GATHERING FOR SPEAKER OF WESSEX PARLIAMENT WITHIN PAST TWO MONTHS.

MESSAGE ENDS

He was still running Evernet searches when Rourke returned, red-faced and panting. Her clothes were soaked, trailing filthy water. She dumped her rummage bag, weapons clattering on the linoleum floor.

"Tea?" said Paolo easily.

"And there was me, not knowing you were secretly

Irish," said Rourke. She scanned the data scrolling across the omni. "You've sent a flash message to the Centre? Jesus, Paolo, why? Who's *Tristian*?"

"Tristian? The man responsible for Lottie's mysterious pregnancy, one way or the other," Paolo replied, prising open the tea caddy. He put the kettle on a camping stove and lit it. "I need you to contact *every* source in your network. Put them to work, I don't care how old or new. Activate them now."

"Why?"

Paolo told Rourke about the speaker's party in Wessex, and Lottie's disturbing encounter with a young man called Tristian. "I think there's more to her story. Something we've missed."

"Just because Hyatt was cagey when you mentioned the pregnancy? I need more than a *hunch* to risk my entire network."

"Hyatt was never evasive before. It shook her, Sorcha. More importantly, Lottie says Hyatt plied her with champagne the night she met Tristian. Lottie already has suitors identified for her, yet Hyatt was happy to let her flirt with another man."

"Yes, I've heard the elites prefer arranged marriages," Rourke replied. "I'll grant you, that does sound off. D'you think the girl's telling the truth?"

The kettle boiled. "I don't think she has the wit to lie. Not now."

Rourke patted her pockets, producing a neoprene pouch. Inside was a fresh fob. "I'll do it. My entire network, although they'll all be burnt. Now, is there any chance you could get me a bloody towel?"

Paolo found clean towels and a blanket. He fixed a cup of Earl Grey and placed it in front of the Irishwoman, along with a plate of biscuits. "D'you need anything else?"

"Chocolate, if you've got any," she replied, loading an encrypted chip into her fob. "I need you to run searches when I get anything. Is that Darknet node working?"

Paolo pulled a slab of Swiss chocolate from a draw and passed it to Rourke. "Yes. It's encrypted for contact with the Centre."

Rourke broke off a black square of chocolate and popped it in her mouth. Then she began tapping messages into the fob, running them through an encryption matrix before firing them into the ether. Urgent call-in codes, ordering agents to contact their handler. The first reply came in seconds. "That one's my tame journalist," she said. "He might be feckin' useful for a change, he's usually drunk."

"For a change?" said Paolo.

"This kid Tristian, arsing around at Wessex garden parties and seducing young girls? Gossip column bollix, so it is. He's good for that sort of thing, usually knows who's screwin' who."

Three more agents responded. "That's my municipal peeler, a Green Zone council clerk and my best agent. I call her Margot. She usually delivers."

"What does Margot do?"

Rourke put another piece of chocolate in her mouth, fingers trembling. "It's not often you recruit a data entry supervisor at NatSec's Security Vetting bureau. High-level clearance, she sees a lot of useful stuff. I use her very-feckin'-sparingly."

"If she's compromised…"

"Don't go there," Rourke replied. "I've tasked the entire network to identify anyone called Tristian with links to America or Wessex. It's an unusual name, so at least that's something."

They waited in silence, Rourke washing down the rest of the chocolate with lukewarm tea. Paolo sat by the window, studying the siege below. The leaguers were still pinned down by marksmen, each wave drawing closer to the perimeter. He'd call Hyatt soon, allow her to talk him out of the execution.

There was a knock at the door. A big man, dressed for battle. Caleb, the Englishman. Paolo led him inside. "This is Rourke. She's a trusted comrade."

"Who's this?" Rourke replied.

"One of the General's bannermen. He's here to make sure the girl is dealt with properly if we're… indisposed."

Rourke didn't look up from her fob. "Tell him he can he wait outside. I'm working."

"*He* has a name," the Englishman growled. He jutted his chin, a grimace on his war-painted face. "I am Caleb of Enfield, Bannerman of the Black Rifles. I've volunteered for dark work. I do it out of respect for the Crimson Brigade, so the least you could do is show some manners, *woman*."

Rourke's lips made a snarl. "Paolo, get this…"

"Forgive my friend," said Paolo, steering Caleb towards the door. "She's just been in a gunfight. We lost a comrade."

"So? We've all lost comrades," Caleb spat. "I'll be outside if you need me."

"You're meant to be an expert in handling human

assets," said Paolo. He banged his palm on the table, tea splashing from Rourke's cup. "Act like it."

"I feckin' hate the English, I've had enough of them," she spat. She held her hands, palms down on the table. It didn't stop them shaking. "Five *years* in this shithole, when I could be in Free Cordoba or Red Kyiv."

"Are you prepared for death, Sorcha?" Paolo replied. "I am. I have been for fifteen years. If *you* are not, work harder. This operation isn't finished, dammit."

Rourke's fob buzzed, juddering on the table like an upended bug. "Hi, it's Roisin," Rourke replied, slipping easily into her alias. "Margot? Thanks for getting back so quickly. You're working at this time of night? They've sent you to the communications centre? Yes, that's grand my love, let me grab a pen."

Paolo passed a notebook and pen to Rourke. She scrawled notes, eyes tight with concentration. "Margot, you're a life-saver. If you could find out anything else, I'd be grateful. Yes, it's time to get you out. Don't worry, there's a plan." She ended the call and exhaled.

"What did she say?"

"Margot ran searches against NatSec's personnel database. She says it'll look suspicious when they run an audit, she'll have to be brought out."

"Fob her the extraction RV and password," Paolo replied. The measures in place were threadbare – no more than a passage to Kyiv. The agents knew the risks.

"Margot found two men called Tristian on the database, but one is in his fifties and lives in the Midlands. The other is twenty-six and attended Exeter University, which is in deepest darkest Wessex. His full name is Tristian Edward Gramercy."

"Gramercy has NatSec security clearance?"

Rourke smiled. "Indeed, the bastard does. Margot says he underwent enhanced vetting because he works for a government contractor. That's fairly normal, but when she accessed a linked record she hit a special marker."

"A marker?"

"A trigger informing OCS the record's been accessed. Margot's certain it means Gramercy's linked to an intelligence service. Possibly foreign."

Paolo paced the room. "What does Tristian do that requires vetting status?"

Rourke wiped her brow. "He works for the *Anglo-American Reconstruction Taskforce*. He spends half the year in Wessex, the other half in…"

"…Langley, Virginia," said Paolo. "AART is a CIA front organisation, has been for years. Dammit, Lottie Rhys was seduced by a US agent of influence."

"Why?" said Rourke.

Paolo's fob trilled, a message scrolling across the screen. "It's the Command Committee. They're corroborating Margot's intelligence. They don't have his surname, but they do have a subject called Tristian linked to the CIA. And there's something else."

Rourke mopped her brow, "for feck's sake, what?"

"He's a suspected *Archangel*."

Rourke leant forward in her seat, eyes wide. "I'm not big on coincidences, Paolo. This whole thing is linked."

"Of course," Paolo replied, pacing the room. He rummaged in his pockets for cigarettes. "MADRIGAL. Why didn't I see it?"

Sorcha's eyes widened. "Does that mean the girl's baby will be an Archangel too? Is that even possible?"

Paolo lit a cigarette. "All transhumans are meant to be neutered under international treaty, if the Rudenko-Xiaoping Procedure doesn't render them sterile first. There's also the science – the hereditary feasibility of germline DNA transmission and so on."

"I don't believe that for a moment," Rourke replied. "And neither should you."

"You're right, of course." Paolo pulled one of the brainstem injectors from his belt pouch and passed it to the Irishwoman. "It's time for you to see this, my friend."

Rourke took the injector and popped the cap. The needle glittered, five inches of surgical steel. "Look at that bastard. I hate needles. Would you do the honours, Paolo?"

"Pull back your hair," said Paolo pressing the needle-tip into the nape of Rourke's neck. "Let the truth set you free."

TWENTY ONE

Monks crowded the vault, hooded and whispering. Lanterns hung from the ceiling, bathing the chamber with a lemony glow. Wild flowers garlanded the walls, incense burners smouldering. "Welcome to our monastery," said Brother Samuel proudly.

"What's happening now?" said Hooker.

"The Conclave. It's how we decide things."

The monks stood as Samuel stepped onto a podium. He raised his hand, eyes flashing silver in the candlelight. "I respectfully seek permission to address you all, Brothers and Sisters."

"Aye," they replied.

Brother Ranjit bowed. "Please, Samuel, go ahead. And to your friend, we extend a warm welcome."

A hundred hooded figures clapped and 'ayed' their approval.

"Er, cheers," said Hooker, joining Samuel on the platform.

Samuel cleared his throat. "This is Rufus Hooker. I knew him in my old life, when we fought in the Hate War. Hooker was brave, but we did terrible things. We are killers. Hooker went to prison and paid for his crimes. I fled, and did not. This is a constant source of shame. I would atone properly for my sins."

"You were gravely injured, Samuel. Besides, we've all done things we regret!" cried someone from the back of the room. "The Hate War stained us all."

"There's no monopoly on guilt in this place," agreed another. "Who is without sin?"

"Perhaps his arrival is a *sign*?" suggested a third.

Samuel nodded his thanks. "Indeed, it might. Which brings me to my request. Brothers and Sisters, Hooker needs our help. There is a girl, a *hostage*, in the Commune International. I seek permission to take fighters ashore to help him find a way inside. We have no intention to make war, unless we are attacked first."

"I say our help is boundless, *if* Mister Hooker has an Answer," said Brother Ranjit.

"It can't be no coincidence, Ranjit rescuin' the man from the river," said a monk at the front of the room. She was an elderly West Indian woman, silvery-white dreadlocks tumbling from beneath her hood. "Maybe he's meant to be here? Maybe we're supposed to help?"

Hooker nodded sagely. *Thanks love.*

Samuel folded his hands in his sleeves. "Perhaps, Sister. Could it be that there are invisible webs of synchronicity, interconnected by mysterious science? Spiritual physics, even? A new manifestation of spirituality, of the sort every religion has pondered since time immemorial. Ranjit believes the Archangels might even be a manifestation of this... *evolution.* But we need to ask Hooker. Does he understand the consequences of The Answer?"

Hooker glanced at his watch. "It would help if you asked the bloody question,"

Brother Samuel cleared his throat. "We come from all faiths and none. We respect the foundations of faith. We love all of the Gods and their Prophets."

"Peace be upon Them," intoned the monks.

"One of the values we appropriated, proudly, is that of Forgiveness," Samuel intoned. "For without it, there is no future."

The hooded crowd rose to their feet. *Without Forgiveness, there is no future*, they repeated. Several clapped, tears streaming down their faces.

"We've even been accused of being a bogus faith, Mister Hooker," Brother Ranjit added, clambering onto the podium. "But are we, instead, *post*-religious in the accepted sense of the word? I don't think peace and harmony are the sole preserve of the divine."

Hooker wondered what the loon was talking about, but nodded politely anyway.

Samuel held Ranjit's hand, a beatific smile on his ruined face. "The Answer, Hooker, *is* Forgiveness. Forgiveness *is* The Question. For us to help you, you must *forgive*. Forgiveness is sacrifice. It should cause pain, and puncture pride. When that pain heals, it will make you stronger – like scar tissue, binding a wound."

"I say this *is* The Answer," said a smiling Brother Ranjit, eyes gleaming. "Everyone in this room has forgiven *someone* who wronged them. They've all felt the sting of weakness and pride. Everyone has moved on. We have found… The Answer!"

The speeches strangely reminded Hooker of his prison shrink, but if he'd learnt anything inside it was when to keep his mouth shut. The monks clapped. Several collapsed into their chairs, happy tears in their eyes. Bottles appeared, cider and brandy and wine. If the Answer *was* a religion, Hooker reasoned, it certainly wasn't the worst he'd encountered. Brother Samuel lowered his hood. "Rufus, your friend is being held by NatSec under threat of torture?"

"Yes."

"You must promise to forgive those who took her. You must do them no harm, and ask them to do the same of others."

"Yes," said Ranjit. "One person at a time. Absolution is a virus. A good virus. A *healing* virus."

Samuel stepped closer to Hooker. "You'll be held to this, Rufus. By powers both temporal and otherwise. Don't make a promise you cannot keep."

Hooker met Samuel's gaze. "I don't have a choice."

"Yes you do, Rufus, but our choices are connected. Forgiveness is about the destination, not the journey," Samuel replied. "Make a promise to my brothers and sisters."

Hooker looked across the room. "The policeman who took my friend is called Bliss. I'll forgive him. Okay, I might be a bit stern…" *And I can't see Leah being too merciful…*

"That's fine," said Ranjit. "We said forgive, not necessarily love. That's all we ask."

Hooker pulled the mezuzah from a cord around his neck and kissed it. "This thing is very precious to me. I swear on it."

The monks erupted in applause. Several climbed onto the platform, to shake Hooker's hand and slap his back. "Forgiving doesn't mean you have to forget," said a woman with a heavily-scarred face.

Samuel turned to a gnarly little monk. "Brother Francis, ready the boat. Warn the shore party," he said.

"Weapons, Samuel?" Francis replied.

"Yes, issue weapons."

"I thought you lot were all peace and love," said Hooker.

The monk called Brother Francis grinned. "Don't mean we're mugs."

"There's a proud warrior-monk tradition," Samuel added.

Brother Francis went to hop down from the podium. "Hooker?"

"Yes?"

"You're gonna keep your promise, right?"

Hooker nodded slowly. "I am."

"Then let's get on with it."

They hurried to a platform, where davits held a rigid inflatable aloft. Another monk appeared, passing weapons among the group. Hooker was given an ochre robe and a vintage rifle. Samuel lowered the RIB. "Let's go," he said, outboard motor growling.

The Thames was choppy, the wind bringing hot ashes and the smell of cordite. There were five of them, armour concealed under woollen habits. Brother Ranjit knelt at the prow, a staff in his hand. "What was that?" he said, wincing at a jack-hammer noise.

"Smart munitions," Hooker replied, flipping down his goggles. "Eviscerator drone, prob'ly."

A golden cloud mushroomed skywards. "That was a big bastard," said a monk called Brother Cormac, a stringy Irishman.

Brother Samuel checked his medical pack. "Rufus, the Commune's run by anarchists called the Black Rifles. They're led by a Spaniard, Ignacio, who's a hard bastard. But we've no dispute with him or the squatters. We don't want to be fighting. D'you understand?"

"Just get me inside the perimeter. I'm not asking anyone to fight."

"We will if we're attacked, although most wouldn't raise a hand against an Answerer," Samuel replied. "Even the Goon kids ignore us. I'm not sure I can say the same about street leagues."

Brother Ranjit's hands rested on the rifle across his lap. "If the leaguers want to fight, they won't find us wanting."

"Feckin' roight," said Brother Cormac in a broad Dublin accent, scratching a tattoo-covered neck. Under his robes he wore knives of every description, strapped to leather cross-belts. An old M4 carbine lay across his lap, a leery smile on his face.

"Brother Cormac was in the Foreign Legion," said

Samuel. He motioned at the other monk in the boat, "and Brother Francis served in North Africa."

"1st Rifles Commando Group," said Francis proudly. "Answerers don't fight often, but we never come off second best."

"What about you, Ranjit?" said Hooker. "Where did you learn to fight?"

"Southall," he replied. "During the war I fought with the Singh Militia. We drove the Sons of the Caliphate all the way up the Thames Valley. I was at the Siege of Reading."

"At the end?" asked Hooker. Everyone knew of the Siege, a bloody slaughter many considered the Hate War's bloody zenith.

"I was there when they martyred themselves," he nodded, eyes downcast. "The Jihadists were misled. I forgave them all."

Samuel piloted the boat into a gap in the river wall, nudging its prow onto a concrete ramp. The riverside was protected by a fence, its gate draped with razor wire. Signs in a dozen languages warning people to keep out. "That doesn't apply to us," said Ranjit matter-of-factly, "we have a key."

"How so?" asked Hooker.

"We trade here, with the locals," he explained, a note of pride in his voice. "Chickens and bees and home-brewed beer. We also make tools and clothing."

"And I grow the best old-school skanj in the 'goons," Cormac chuckled, "better than Merseyside artisan shite. Don't know what the fuss is about."

Brother Ranjit pulled a metal key from his robes. He hopped nimbly from the boat and unlocked the gate.

"Follow me," said Samuel, plugging a steel carving of an outstretched hand onto the tip of his staff. He swivelled it, blue flame rippling from the fingertips. "It shows we're Answerers," he smiled. "Although you could bash someone's head in if you had to."

"You can use it to light ciggies, too," Francis added.

The shore party walked along the ramp, which led to an escarpment north of the Commune's perimeter. It was protected by a wall of rusting vehicles topped with of razor wire, a high earthwork berm visible beyond. Samuel held his quarterstaff high, bathing him in pale blue light. "Answerers!" he called into the gloom, "we mean no harm."

"I can't see anyone," said Hooker.

"Samuel's eyes," said Francis. "They've got better night optics than your goggles."

The monks approached the wall of junk, gaps filled with a mixture of concrete and rock-foam. "Over here," said a raspy voice.

A group of women and children huddled nearby. The voice belonged to an injured tactical, her leg crudely bandaged. "Never thought I'd be glad to see Answerers," she rasped. "We need to get out of here sharpish."

"We will help you," said Ranjit. The civilians nodded their thanks, clothes torn and faces dirt-streaked. Children cried, gently shushed by their mothers. Samuel pulled his hood over his face to avoid scaring them.

The tactical eyed the monks warily. Sixtyish and hard-faced, a scar running from her forehead to lip. Probably an ex-Taskforcer, thought Hooker. "These are my prisoners," she growled. "You see, if they're under arrest I've got authority to move 'em away."

"Yeah, but they'll still get charged on the other side," said Hooker. "I saw your Chief on the omni, he said everyone would be done under Section Twelve."

"Fuck him, clueless bastard. When was the last time he set foot on a two-way range? I'm letting 'em go soon as we're clear of this shithole. I've had enough of this bollocks." The tactical ripped the NatSec badge from her armour and hurled it into the night. "Fuck, that hurts," she groaned.

"Hold on my love," smiled Brother Cormac, swinging a medical bag from his shoulder, "you're in pain."

The tactical nodded her thanks as the monk passed her an autojet. "Morphine," he said, "good stuff."

"Do I have to forgive someone now?" the tactical replied, teeth gritted.

"Wouldn't hurt, would it?" said Cormac. "Give it a try, eh?"

Hooker knelt next to the tactical. "How d'you end up here?"

The tactical studied Hooker for a moment. "Do I know you?"

"Might do. I was Taskforce," Hooker replied.

"Which one?"

"TF-17."

The tactical winced. "Gordy Rice's pirates? Wish they were here now – my squad broke when the leaguers attacked. I got rushed by a gang of pups from the Urbanskis. Anyhow, two civvies dragged me away. Then someone let off a bomb. Before it stopped working, my fob was broadcasting casualty figures into the hundreds."

"What happened to the pups?" asked Hooker.

The tactical mimed trigger-pull. "Got 'em with my back-up piece. Six less scum to worry about. Slipped on their blood and broke my leg."

"She killed them all," said one of the women. "Even the injured."

"Injured man can pull a trigger," the tactical shrugged. "I can feel the morphine working now…"

"She saved our lives," said a dark-haired woman. Her accent was French. "We knew a way through the barricade. We thought we might find a boat here."

"A way through? Can you show us?" said Brother Ranjit. "You can hide in our monastery, we'll take you to Essford in the morning. To the Red Cross station."

"You'd do that for 'em?" said the tactical.

"Why wouldn't we?" said Samuel, face still shadowed by his cowl. "Just think about forgiveness. That's all we ask."

"Okay, I'll do it," said the Frenchwoman. "Follow me."

The other women spoke urgently in French, Hooker guessing they were trying to persuade her to stay. Then they hugged, the children starting to cry. "Get on with it," said the tactical sharply, "the sooner you go, the sooner you'll get back. And take care, for fuck's sake."

Then the night roared, fiery globes hammering the tower and palisade. "What the hell was that?" said Brother Francis. "Eviscerator," said the tactical matter-of-factly. "Wouldn't want to be on the other end of that bastard thing, it's got a mind of its own."

"I can see marksmen, hidden on balconies," said Samuel, silvery eyes gleaming. "The drone's strafing their positions."

The tactical tapped a screen on her wrist. "They fly an X-shaped vector. I reckon you've got five minutes before it comes back on station."

"You heard her – let's go," said Hooker, pointing at the wall of rusted vehicles.

Samuel hefted his staff. "Ranjit, you and Cormac stay and look after the civilians. Francis, you come with me and Hooker, OK?"

Ranjit went to say something, then nodded. "Of course, Samuel."

Cormac reached inside his pack, "take my medical kit."

The French woman introduced herself as Florence. She picked her way along the wall of bonnets, doors and chassis. Finally, she stopped. "Here," she said, fingers sliding into a crease in the rusting metal. There was a loud click, and a door panel slid open.

"Okay," said Hooker, readying his rifle. "Let's go."

TWENTY TWO

"We need another hour," said Hyatt. "Mister Rhys is going through the press release with his legal team – he's preparing to put the record straight."

"An easier tactic would be to simply tell the truth," Paolo replied.

"It isn't just Mister Rhys impacted by this. Besides, it needs to be accurate if it's going to be credible. Please, can you cut me some slack?"

Paolo smiled. The woman didn't realise her stone-walling was convenient. "Against my better judgement, I'm granting you an hour Miss Hyatt. Use the time wisely." Ending the call, he checked Rourke. She sat in a chair, head lolling to one side. Her eyes flickered crazily as she absorbed data from the brainstem injector.

Paolo didn't hear the explosion, plunging the apartment

into darkness, walls wobbling like jelly. Clambering to his feet, he watched something bank lazily over the river. A drone. Moonlight played across it's beetle-black fuselage, cannon-pods spitting fire. Flipping a table against the window, he wedged it in place with the couch. Finally, he dragged sandbags from the kitchen, making a crude barricade.

"Huh? What the hell?" said Rourke, snapping upright. Her chin was sticky with drool, eyes bloodshot.

"Drone attack," Paolo replied. "Get down."

"MADRIGAL," the Irishwoman gasped, fingers fluttering in her lap. "All that stuff's really true?"

"It is, and now we've got a girl who might be carrying an Archangel in her belly…"

Torchlight cut through the darkness. Caleb. "You okay?" the Englishman called. "Anybody hurt?"

"We're alive," said Paolo. "It was their drone, it strafed our floor."

"It's gone?" said Rourke, staggering to the window. Outside, a fresh wave of leaguers began storming the walls.

Caleb shook his head. "It'll be re-arming, I reckon. Bastard thing was targeting marksmen on the lower floors. You can't shoot 'em down without rockets."

Paolo returned to the omni, its power node flickering. "Twenty percent left on the battery. Caleb, we need to get out of here."

The Englishman nodded. "The General has a plan, but he won't be taking passengers."

"Nor would I expect him to. I have my own arrangements."

"You've got a magic wand you've not been telling me

about?" said Rourke. "Damn I'm thirsty."

Caleb pulled a water bottle from his belt and passed it to the Irishwoman. "Cold sugar-water," he said. "It'll give you energy."

Rourke nodded her thanks and took a gulp. "I could murder a cuppa."

Paolo touched the omni, scrolling through hacked data. "NatSec have a forward aviation base, a place called Biggin Hill. It's only twenty miles south, there's a squadron of Wildcat copters based there."

"You're gonna to steal a copter from NatSec?" Caleb laughed. "Can you even fly one?"

Paolo raised an eyebrow. "I'd hardly steal one if I couldn't. Caleb, wait here with Rourke and the girl until I get back."

"About the girl…" said Caleb.

"There's a change of plan," Paolo replied. "We're taking her with us. I'm going to see Ignacio about clearing the roof – I'm going to need somewhere to land."

"Yes, Colonel Paolo," Caleb replied. He took up position outside the door to Lottie's room, Kalashnikov ready.

"Steal a copter? You're crazy," said Sorcha.

"Just wait for me to return," Paolo replied, leaving the room. "Ready weapons. Protect the girl."

Rourke nodded, pulling the machine pistol from her bag. "Where you going now?"

"To see the General."

The Commune's corridors and stairways echoed with moans and the occasional gunshot. In the command bunker, General Ignacio studied a bank of omnis, issuing orders to his staff. "The enemy Generals drag their feet in the south," said a riflewoman.

"They're letting their men take the brunt of the assault?"

"Yes sir," the riflewoman replied. "They're conferring about casualties, I think."

"Good," the General replied. "Ah, Paolo. Did you hear the drone?"

"It blew my apartment's windows out. I suspect the rental value just headed south."

The Spaniard let out a belly laugh, "Are you making your escape?"

"More or less."

"How?"

"The only way there is – through the Leaguers."

"Impossible."

Paolo shrugged. "I have a plan, but I need a favour."

"You need only ask."

Paolo's voice was matter-of-fact. "I'm going to land a copter on the roof. There's junk up there. Can you arrange for its removal?"

"You make it sound as simple as stealing apples. Okay, I'll send a work party. They'll have to use the scaffold, though. We're repairing the lifts – the power is screwed." The tower was criss-crossed with scaffolding, used for everything from maintenance to graffiti-painting.

Paolo bowed. "Again, my thanks. My report to the Command Committee will mention the valour and loyalty of the Black Rifles."

Ignacio's smile was wily. "The money and gold were reward enough."

"*Until the Crimson Banner flies,*" Paolo replied. The salutation was usually shouted, accompanied by a raised fist. From Paolo Falcone's mouth it was prayer-like. A quiet promise.

"'TIL THE CRIMSON BANNER FLIES!" hollered Ignacio of the Black Rifles. Licking stray brandy from his beard, he grabbed and kissed the nearest female fighter with passionate gusto. The rest of the soldiers laughed and cheered. Paolo smiled as he left the bunker, remembering the days when a man would be arrested for less.

Sentries, armed and armoured, swung open the lobby's blast doors for Paolo Falcone. Outside, anarchists erected fresh barricades, others taking ammunition and water to the palisades. Smoking craters peppered the ground, the able-bodied dragging casualties to an aid station. Crouching in the tower's shadow, he unzipped an assault pack. Inside were weapons, gold coins, a Blue Force tracking fob and a set of black fatigues. The jacket bore the insignia of NatSec's elite Apex commando unit. He slid two axes into a back harness – black carbon iterations of the Native American tomahawk. He'd been taught to use them a lifetime ago, at the CIA paramilitary school near Fort Hood. Noting that Paolo was ambidextrous, an elderly veteran of the Afghan wars had taught him how to fight with two blades.

Finally, he opened a cigar tube. Inside was a gold-and-scarlet autojet, covered in Mandarin script. A dose of the experimental Chinese respirocite called *Kwan Kung*. Twenty-five thousand US Dollars, the black-market dealer promising a *state-of-the-art combat augmentation experience.* Paolo jabbed the needle into his thigh. He felt euphoria, almost sexual in intensity. It was even better than the genetically-modified opium he'd smoked in the ruins of Kabul.

Now, something more than human, the Crimson Brigade agent disappeared into the night. Quickly gaining speed, forty kilometres an hour, he sprinted towards the perimeter. Vaulting the palisade, he landed in no-man's land. A gaggle of rifle-armed squatters, huddled in a trench, watched open-mouthed as he flashed by. The Generals gathered in the back streets beyond, readying axes and swords and spears. Paolo's augmented hearing detected hushed conversations, men talking tactics and intent. Yes, they were waiting for the Western perimeter to fall. Paolo stepped from the shadows, an axe in each fist.

"A tactical?" a leaguer growled. "What the fuck?"

Paolo smiled.

His first victim was a blue-clad Urbanski, burly and moustachioed. He rushed Paolo, only to have his jugular pierced by a whispering tomahawk. More generals charged, gaudily dressed in surcoats and gold. Paolo's blades sliced through armour, a killing arc biting deep into muscle and flesh. He feinted, dodging a spear-thrust, then pirouetted with axes akimbo. Two more generals screamed, clutching at jelly-wet entrails. Seeing a raised riot shield, Paolo leapt, using it as a platform. Tomahawks flashed, and more men died.

Finally, a pile of corpses lay at his feet, the moon-washed concrete slick with blood. The leaguers rallied, men in orange surcoats and black helms. Warriors of Loyal Croydonia. "Who the fuck are you?" one bellowed.

Paolo laughed, axes ready. "Does it matter? Is this all you've got?"

The Generals bellowed and screamed, hefting weapons and promising death. Paolo attacked, axes making a steely blur. With a ripping noise, a severed head spun away into the night. Barely feeling a baseball bat slam into his side, Paolo chopped off an arm. More men, woad-painted, rushed to attack. They died too, only to be replaced by more. Paolo fought silently, faced blood-masked, dopamine flooding his brain. The ecstasy rush intensified. A blood-frenzy, twin axes stealing souls. It was obscene. Waves of power, no – *pleasure*, coursed through his veins. The respirocite made him a Dark God, and these cattle his sacrifices. Dull-eyed sheep, trooping to his blood-soaked altar. He'd enjoyed many identities and been many people, but right now he preferred this version the most – Paolo as Destroyer. Avatar of Butchery. *This must be what it's like to be an Archangel. No wonder they would rather die than surrender their power…*

Then, gunshots. Intuiting a bullet's arc, Paolo leapt for a wall, making a parkour across the rooftops. The remaining leaguers formed a shield wall, shuffling towards him with spears ready. Paolo's reply to their chanting was an incendiary grenade from his HK35. The explosion was muffled by the weight of bodies, a flash of light followed by the screams of the wounded and soon-to-die. Watching the leaguers burn, gaudy surcoats blazing, Paolo scanned the rooftops. He saw what he was looking for – a globe-shaped camera, feeding images to Ignacio's control bunker. He raised a fist in salute. Then, checking his Blue Force tracker, he checked the coordinates for the Biggin Hill airbase. The route took him through the Crosland estate's gauntlet.

Taking a gulp of smoky night air, he ran.

TWENTY THREE

The French woman, Florence, pointed at the barricade. "I've shown you the way through. Can I go?"

Hooker watched the skies for the relentless drone. "Sure, but before you go, d'you know of a bloke in the Commune called Paolo. Or a woman called Roisin?"

"Paolo? The Italian? He lives at the top of the tower, with a big Arab guy and a woman with dark hair. But I've never heard of... *Ro sheen*?" she replied, struggling with the pronunciation.

"Paolo and his friends – are they squatters? Anarchists?"

"People think they're hackers, or maybe 'cotics smugglers," Florence replied. "They are okay, though. Friendly. Paolo always looks very smart, he has good manners."

"Thanks," Hooker replied, giving Florence his

remaining guineas. "When you get to the Red Cross station, tell them Rufus Hooker sent you."

"I will," she replied, taking the gold, "bless you, *Monsieur*."

Francis disappeared inside the wall. He returned a few minutes later, smiling. "This leads to the perimeter. Brother Samuel, I reckon we'll be OK if you show that magic-bloody-wand of yours."

"No problem," the big monk replied. "Let's hope they honour our neutrality."

Hooker and the monks squeezed inside the tunnel. The air was stale, scented with rust and oil. Their feet clanged on metal, weapons making scraping noises. "All we need is a fucking trombone," Hooker grumbled.

"Ranjit's got a tambourine," said Brother Francis, snickering. "Right, let's get our monk-shit together."

"Love and peace, baby," Brother Samuel chuckled. He twisted the metal hand at the tip of his quarterstaff, blue flame curling from its fingertips.

They emerged into a no-man's land of bodies and burning vehicles. The last line of defence, the palisade, lay before them. Smaller barricades had been pulverised by explosions, bullet-riddled ambulances littering the battlefield. Medics crouched behind them, taking cover from the gunfire spitting from windows and balconies. "Follow me," said Brother Samuel.

They walked towards palisade, red and black flags snapping in the hot night wind. Combatants scurried through wreckage created by missile strikes, throwing themselves to the ground when snipers opened fire. "How many leaguers d'you reckon?" Brother Francis asked, taking in the carnage.

"Thousands – the Commune's surrounded," Hooker replied, watching fighters lurking in the ruins. Some wore the blue surcoats of the Woolwich Urbanskis, others the orange of Loyal Croydonia. The Urbanskis sported extravagantly waxed beards, the Brethren clean-shaven and crop-headed. Those with crossbows or firebombs occasionally broke cover to open fire, before scurrying back to safety.

Brother Samuel raised his staff, blue flames swirling about its tip. "We are Answerers! We mean no harm."

More warriors appeared – fresh street leaguers, carrying stolen police riot shields. The Sutton Trollz, wearing monster masks. They watched the monks warily, weapons ready. Hooker's hand gripped the rifle hidden beneath his cloak. "That must be three league's worth of Propers and Yeomen. I've never seen so many."

"It's the cream of the Urbanskis, Trollz and Loyal Croydonia," Brother Francis replied. The Propers wore red cloaks, the Yeomen black. Then, finally, a small delegation of Generals, older men in lacquered armour. One raised a flag, a jagged rune representing the Grand Alliance of the Leagues. The leaguers bellowed as one, straining at the leash, eager to attack.

Brother Samuel whistled through his teeth. "This is going to be a legendary tear-up."

"Ain't ever seen anything like it," Brother Francis agreed. "And I used to go to Millwall when I was a kid..."

"But they ain't shooting at us," said Hooker in amazement, the palisade drawing near.

"Not yet," said Brother Francis. He stopped to offer a

field dressing to a wounded pup, who grunted his thanks.

The palisade was seven metres high. "Answerers!" called Brother Samuel. "We're here to help the wounded."

"Come up," shouted a man wearing a crash helmet. He pointed at the leaguers. "just don't expect us to forgive any of those bastards."

"There'll be forgiveness in good time, my friend. We have morphine."

"Answerers! They have medicine," someone hollered. A ladder snaked down the wall, aluminium slats threaded into parachute cord.

Brother Francis went first, digging a muddy boot into the wall.

Then gunfire.

Eyes bulging, a bullet struck Francis' back. Another punctured his skull, a third tearing into the back of his thigh. He fell, tangled in the ladder. With a roar, a skirmish line of Urbanskis and Trollz charged, weapons gleaming from the light of a hundred fires. Some carried long ladders, others rope and grappling irons. A stolen fire engine followed, warriors crouching on its hydraulic platform. "Move," Hooker shouted, pushing Brother Francis' body free. The Urbanskis roared a war cry, a roiling wave of fury. Grabbing Francis' weapon, Hooker began hauling himself up the ladder. Brother Samuel followed, unflinching despite the bullets peppering the palisade around him.

At the top of the wall was a trench. They rolled inside, two of the anarchists grabbing Samuel as bullets whistled overhead. "Come on, *plata ojos.*"

"The medical station's halfway between here and the

tower," said a gunman in a greatcoat. "Take your medicine there, quickly."

"Be careful of the cable, or you'll trip," warned another, pointing at a muddy length of hose running across the trench floor.

Hooker looked at the cable. Half-sunk into the palisade, snaking away into a metal box. A fob was duct-taped taped to the lid. "Is that what I think it is?"

"IED. A big one," one of the defenders grinned. "We're gonna make them fight hard for this position, make the fascists commit reinforcements. Then we'll blow the bastards up."

"Won't that let 'em in?" said Hooker.

The anarchist smiled. "It's a very big bomb."

"Let's get going," said Brother Samuel.

The defenders opened fire with crossbows and rifles as the leaguers advanced. A volley of arrows, crossbow bolts and rifle shots spattered the length of the palisade in reply, killing several Black Riflemen. With a roar, ladders rattled and grappling hooks bit into dirt. "Go," said the anarchist, working the bolt on his rifle. "Quickly!"

Hooker and Brother Samuel descended a ramp into a courtyard. The squatters had rigged storm lamps to a medical trailer, a red cross painted on the roof. Three figures sat huddled on top, heads bowed. A row of walking wounded waited patiently outside, smoking and looking nervously skywards. Hooker touched Samuel's shoulder. "Can you see who's on top of the trailer?"

"Wounded tacticals," the monk replied, squinting. "The drone won't shoot a target with friendly Blue Force trackers, will it?"

Hooker and Samuel nodded at the doctor supervising the medical orderlies. She was red-haired, dressed in a bloody apron and rubber boots. "I'm Doctor Porter, *Medicine Sans Frontiers*. Always good to see Answerers. Are there only the two of you?" Her accent was of Wessex, well-spoken but strange.

"Yes, we're it," said Samuel, unshouldering his pack. "We lost a man on the wall. I've got morphine, antibiotics, blood plasma and field dressings."

"I'm sorry for your loss," the doctor replied, lighting a cigarette. "We're doing okay here at the moment – mainly shrapnel, burns and crush wounds. Not too many gunshot injuries yet."

"It'll get worse," said Hooker. "There are thousands of the bastards out there."

"So I understand," said Porter, blowing smoke from her nose. "Come on, let's be having you. I can always use more orderlies."

"Sure," Hooker replied, making for the Commune. "Gimme a couple of minutes."

"Okay," the doctor replied, checking the medical supplies in Samuel's bag.

Hooker waited until the doctor disappeared inside the trailer. "Samuel, are you OK to stay here?"

"I'd prefer to," he said. "I'm not here to fight. I'll help the wounded."

"When I'm done, I'll get you out. There's an extraction plan."

Brother Samuel looked around, a smile twisting his

ravaged features. "I don't need rescuing."

Hooker raised an eyebrow. "Give it half an hour. You got a spare fob?"

"Sure," the monk replied, passing a handset from the collection on his belt. "This one's an old 5G model. It works, but on a ham cell network. Pretty secure."

Hooker thanked the monk and ducked into a doorway. He tapped Trashmob's code into the ancient cell-phone. "It's Rufus."

"Fuck off, Rufus, I'm trying to sleep," Trashmob yawned.

"I'm in trouble."

"You're always in trouble."

"Yeah, but not as much as Leah. She's been pinched by OCS – I need a favour."

Trashmob woke up. "Go ahead," he said sharply.

"My man uptown, Mister Dark Work?" said Hooker, referring to Gordy.

"No names on this line, right?" Trashmob replied. "I know who you mean."

"Good. Can you get word to him? His comms are being monitored. I need a full Darkwire, nothing that can be traced or hacked."

"I've got someone in the Green Zone who'll can do it," Trashmob replied. "How's Leah?"

"Last time I saw her she was in a torture chamber, Trash. The fuckers have gone too far this time."

Hooker heard something smashing over the line. Trashmob got his name partly because he liked trashing things. "I'll fucking kill them," he growled. "Gimme a name…"

"Not now, mate. Just get this message to my man." Hooker read geolocation data off the fob's tiny screen. "Tell him the parcel is believed to be on the top floor of the main block at the following…"

"Fuck me, Rufus, the Crosland? You're in the middle of a fucking riot."

"You know GPS code off the top of your head?"

"Everyone needs a hobby. You want anything else passing on?"

"Tell him NatSec have Leah. I've got new orders – get rid of the parcel. I repeat – get *rid* of the parcel, OK? *Not* deliver it."

"I've got it. Your man will have the message in ten minutes."

"Thanks, Trash."

"You need me over there?" asked Trashmob. "I'll call in my QRF. We've got six gun-trucks and a dozen technicals."

"You could bring the whole of Echo-Seven down here and not make any difference."

"Okay, but if you need us, just give the word."

Hooker approached the Commune's front door. The lobby had been converted into a strongpoint, reinforced with breeze blocks and sandbags. "I need to go inside," he said to a burly sentry.

"Sorry, brother," the sentry replied, Kalashnikov shouldered. "No entry – not even for an Answerer."

"I'm helping at the aid station. The doctor asked me to fetch clean water."

"Which doctor?" the sentry replied.

"Wessex-woman with red hair. I think her name is Porter."

The sentry stepped aside. "OK, go quickly…"

A mighty explosion shook the ground, throwing Hooker and the sentry to the floor. His ears ached, something wet dribbling down his cheek. A gout of flame flared on the palisade, pebbles and mud falling like dirty rain. The sentry crawled towards a wall of sandbags. "They've let off the IED. The leaguers must have broken through."

Above them, the sound of cheering. Hooker peered up at the scaffolding that snaked about the Commune's walls, masked figures anchoring synth nodes in place. Red and black banners unfurled, hoarse-voices singing. "That's *Santa Agueda!*" said the sentry, pulling himself to his feet.

The first leaguers began picking their way through the smouldering palisade, stepping over the bodies of fallen comrades. The Trollz bore the brunt, dozens of bodies blown to ragged chunks. They were followed by Yeomen of the Urbanskis and Loyal Brethren, flying now-ragged banners. "Whatever your plan was, it didn't work," said Hooker.

"We weren't expecting so many," the sentry replied. "I have faith in our General."

"I'm glad someone does."

"You've got a gun?" said the sentry, watching Hooker pull a rifle from his robes.

"Even monks have bad days," Hooker replied, snapping the FN's folding stock in place. He peered over the sandbag wall and took aim.

The sentry shouldered his Kalashnikov. "Get ready, brother. Here they come."

Leaguers began boiling through the breach, led by men with riot shields. Hooker and the sentry fired into the human wall, every casualty replaced by two more warriors. Anarchist snipers swept the plaza from the balconies, gunfire stitching across the killing ground between palisade and Commune. Hooker changed magazines, the sentry providing covering fire. Another rank of leaguers fell, bloodied and groaning. The survivors scattered and took cover, others locking shields to reform their wall. "Drone!" someone hollered.

The stubby-winged Eviscerator was, for a moment, silhouetted against the moon. Cannon-fire strafed anarchist positions, explosions rippling across walls and balconies. A volley of rockets, twisting in the sky like fiery snakes, obliterated the remaining perimeter strongpoints. Wounded defenders stumbled from the rubble, only to be overwhelmed. Axes and spears flashed and bit into flesh, the anarchist's rifles and SMGs seized and passed around the woad-painted ranks. Hooker watched the drone peel away. "NatSec are giving the leaguers air support?"

"They're all fascists," the sentry replied, sliding a fresh magazine into his AK. "Keep shooting!"

The leaguers, emboldened by the airstrike, hurled rocks and petrol bombs at the strongpoint protecting the lobby. A flurry of spears killed a defender, pinning him to a wall. Leaguers swarmed the medical station, tearing it apart with picks and sledgehammers. Injured anarchists were executed by jeering warriors, the captured tacticals on the roof decapitated, severed heads kicked like footballs. In the lamplit courtyard, the doctor fell, dragged into a scrum of warriors. Some yelped and began unbuckling their belts until Hooker opened fire.

Three, four… *five* men fell, but the doctor disappeared inside the writhing mob. Blue-armoured Urbanskis appeared with shields, making another wall.

Hooker saw something glowing, near the edge of the enemy line. A blue flame. Brother Samuel appeared, swinging his fiery staff, a fox chased by hounds. He swung the stave about his head, leaguers swerving to escape its flaming arc. One fell, hair alight, screaming and slapping at his smouldering head. Hooker squeezed the trigger with a calloused fingertip, exhaling as he fired. Again and again. Every bullet found its mark, Samuel's attackers tumbling like skittles.

"That monk? He's the craziest bastard," said the sentry, "*magnifico.*"

Brother Samuel shook his hood free, the leaguers' charge faltering as his monstrous features were revealed. The monk turned his head towards Hooker and smiled a lipless smile. "Get inside the Commune, Rufus," he shouted. "Now!"

Hooker went to climb over the sandbag wall, but the sentry stopped him. "Don't be a fool, brother."

Samuel tossed the staff at the leaguers, flames guttering at their feet. He fell to his knees and threw back his head. His eyes were silver as the moon. "I forgive you all," he called, into the cruel black night.

The leaguers bellowed in triumph as they fell upon him.

TWENTY FOUR

The rain cooled Paolo's drug-heated flesh, the wind carrying faraway whispers. Drone engines. Paolo's heightened senses divined other aircraft – the subsonic hum of a surveillance plane, different from the churning propellers of the NatSec blimp. The drone worried him most. The Eviscerator. No combat drug or gel-armour would protect him from its nano-munitions or demented AI.

The PROTEX towered before him. Beyond lay a jumble of low-rise housing units, marking the outer edge of the estate. Most were boarded-up by the authorities, to protect the raised motorway from vandals and snipers. His tracker gently buzzed, alerting him to a new comms signature. It was feint, bleeding from a warehouse to the west of the PROTEX. The code *AN40* flashed across the tracker – two personal fobs, on a low-frequency encrypted channel. Visible, but undecipherable. Probably a small unit, perhaps a police reconnaissance unit. To the south, other call-signs emitted a babel of electronic traffic. It signalled larger forces, moving on multiple routes. Paolo figured AN40, the smaller signature, made for the path of least resistance. He headed west, towards *Alpha November Four-Zero*. Then he'd jink south, towards Biggin Hill. If he could, he'd steal or commandeer a vehicle.

Reaching the cinderblock warehouse, he climbed onto the roof. Below was a grey BMW, two men lounging against the hood – one skinny and white, the other bulky and black. The skinny guy was smoking, the other drinking from a flask of coffee. Paolo parsed the evidence – cigarettes, coffee, cheap suits and a ride neither looked like they could afford.

Cops.

The Crimson Brigade agent crept, gecko-like, across a pitch-covered roof. Craning his head, he picked up snatches of conversation. "Where's Hooker's fob pinging?" said White Guy.

"Looks like he's inside the Commune footprint," Black Guy shrugged. "Relax, Chisholm. I'm even beginning to think the fucker'll pull this off."

"Nah, don't like it. Too convenient, losing our fob like that. And his story about the monks?"

Black Guy shrugged beefy shoulders and swilled coffee. "You saw the feed with your own eyes. That explosion in the tunnel looked real enough to me. Or do you think he hired a giant Arab to blow himself up?"

Paolo winced. *The mission was compromised by NatSec?*

White Guy fished a fob from his jacket, briefly revealing a shoulder holster. "It's Bliss," he said, wandering in a nervous circle. Paolo couldn't hear what was being said, but White Guy wasn't happy.

"What's occurring?" said Black Guy.

"The technicians. They damaged the Martinez girl."

"They started the treatment already? Why?"

"Bliss, innit? He don't need no reason, does he? Maybe he wanted Hooker to know he weren't bluffing. Or he thought the girl might know something."

Black Guy whistled through his teeth. "Did she cough?"

White Guy shook his head. "Nothin' we didn't already know. Their 'mancer is a cripple, lives in Wandsworth. Ex-army infowarfare operator. We're sending a team to bring him in, maybe he's got something."

"Makes sense," Black Guy replied, "but harming Martinez? Bad idea."

White Guy ran a hand through thin, greasy hair (Paolo could smell the styling wax). "It's Bliss, ain't it? He'll do what he likes."

Black Guy shook his head. "If I was him, I'd make sure Hooker dies up there."

"If the man wants your advice, Bailey, I'm sure you'll be the first to know."

Paolo's skin itched. *They've got an agent inside the Commune, looking to rescue Lottie Rhys. He's being coerced. Someone called Hooker.*

White Guy checked his watch. "Anyhow, we've been here too long. Let's move somewhere else."

Paolo jumped from the roof, weapon ready. He shot White Guy, a bullet grazing his shoulder. Another whistled through Black Guy's upper arm, a clean in-and-out. "Drop your weapons," Paolo ordered.

Two handguns clattered on concrete. Hands behind heads, the cops sank to their knees. "I'm Chisholm, NatSec OCS," White Guy hissed through gritted teeth. He took in Paolo's uniform. "You're Apex?"

"It's fancy dress," Paolo replied, shooting him in the thigh. The secret policeman rolled into a ball. "That's the femoral artery. Now you require urgent medical attention."

"What d'you want?" the cop groaned, hands trembling, blood pooling beneath him.

"Identify your asset inside the Commune. What is his objective?"

"Rufus Hooker," said Black Guy, hands clasped behind his head. "He's a bounty hunter, knows the Goons inside-out. We've sent him to find a kidnapped girl, a Green-Zone kid."

"But you intend to betray him?"

"That's down to our boss, okay? He's a proper bastard," Black Guy replied. "For Christ's sake, don't shoot me."

"Describe Rufus Hooker."

"He's a black fella, built like a brick shithouse – two metres tall, one-hundred-fifty kilos, crazy eyes. Scary-looking fucker."

"How did you know where to look for the girl?" Paolo felt the Blue Force tracker buzz on his wrist. Fresh call-signs slid across the screen, converging on his position.

White Guy saw the tracker. "Reinforcements. That's fucking delicious..."

"I'll concede your point," Paolo replied. The night was laden with clues – the scent of vehicle fumes, weapon oil and testosterone. Well-armed men, psyched-up for violence. The chug of diesel engines carried on the wind, the static squelch of comms. He shot White Guy between the eyes, the nano-munition blowing off the top of his head. His body toppled forward, the sludge inside his skull spilling onto wet tarmac.

Black Guy threw up. "What do you want to know?" he coughed, a stain darkening the crotch of his trousers.

"The girl. What led you here?"

"Hooker figured it out. He traced a smuggler called Natly Hare to the Goons. He managed to link her to the Crimson Brigade."

"Thank you." Paolo replied, shooting Bailey in the heart.

Two armoured carriers rounded the corner. Paolo scrambled into the cops' BMW and hit the ignition, fast-reversing, arms braced on the wheel. His ear implant picked up snatches of radio traffic – *Suspect vehicle – NatSec-flagged BMW Urban. It's showing a covert Blue Force callsign, Alpha November Four Zero. At least two officers down. Request ADVENT call-signs ASAP…*

Roger that, Delta Zero Actual, ADVENT is guns-free and will be on station in sixty seconds…

ADVENT. The callsign for the Eviscerator.

Paolo motored towards the PROTEX, bullets splashing harmlessly off the BMWs armorglass windows. He fobbed Rourke. "NatSec have an operative inside the Commune, a man called Rufus Hooker. He's looking for Lottie. The Answerers are helping him."

"Today just gets better," Rourke sighed.

"Hooker's described as well-built, black…"

"Paolo, I've got a problem here… I think Caleb *knows*."

"About what?"

"The girl," said Rourke. "About her pregnancy. Who she is."

"How?" said Paolo.

Sorcha's voice was a husky whisper. "I think he heard us talking. Before the drone strike."

"I'll deal with it when I return. But you must warn the General about the intruder." In the rear-view mirror, headlights grew larger. Paolo drove hard. His tracker buzzed, the screen showing a red triangle vectoring towards him.

The Eviscerator.

Paolo mashed his boot into the accelerator. *200kmh.* The PROTEX split – right for Croydonia, left for the border. He chose the border, roaring down an exit ramp and onto a pot-holed road. Shanties flashed by, suspension rumbling. Gaslit and quiet, nobody on the streets. Paolo glanced at his tracker as the Eviscerator's icon, at an altitude of two kilometres, began to merge with his.

He stood on the brakes. The speedo flickered, the BMW shuddering as it decelerated. *60kmph.* The red triangle overshot, banking hard to correct its speed.

40... 25...

Paolo rolled from the car, remembering his jump training at airborne school. Making a ball, rolling on hard ground, the BMW trailing flame. Nano-munitions swarmed the 4x4 like fiery hornets, peppering the car as it screeched into a dumpster. It rolled once, burning, landing in an abandoned shop front. The entire building warped, as if punched by a giant fist, volleys of rockets slamming into the walls.

Paolo was on his feet, already sprinting through back streets and alleys, scattering feral cats and mangy foxes. He stuck to the gas-lamps, knowing they'd blur his heat signature. The tracker on his wrist showed him in a place called Petts Wood, *twelve kilometres from Biggin Hill.* He navigated fallow fields and scrubby woodland, respirocites burning through his veins.

Finally, beyond the walls of a long-abandoned factory, a razor-wire fence. Lights blinked beyond, neatly spaced and burning white. Signs warned of electricity and dogs, of being shot on sight. There was a concrete gatehouse, protected by sandbags and blast barriers. The sign outside read –

NATSEC (No.1 Region) AIR SUPPORT UNIT

Pulling on a navy-blue beret, Paolo stamped the mud from his boots. His ID showed him as Inspector Nordstrom of NatSec Apex Team 7. Apart from the coveralls, his kit was non-issue, but Paolo knew Apex commandos wore what they damn well liked. A Land Rover rumbled towards him, headlights glowing. Paolo waved it down. "Evening, sir," said the driver, a young NatSec technical officer in fatigues. He wore an air support flash on his sleeve, a helicopter inside a sky-blue triangle. "You okay?"

"Been fighting, over in the Goons," Paolo replied. His English accent was flawless, with the glottal stops typical of the south. He wiped his brow with a sleeve. "My vehicle broke down in Petts Wood. Fuckin' 'lectric piece of shit."

"Petts Wood? How d'you get over here?"

"I ran, son."

"You're Apex? I knew you lot were meant to be fit…"

"Yeah, I'm Apex 7. Special Projects. I'm on combat

stims, but I'll be coming down soon. I need to speak to your duty officer – I'm on a classified piece of work."

The officer nodded, glancing at the tomahawks on Paolo's back. "Yessir. I'll have to check you in with the gatehouse, though."

Paolo got in the Land Rover. "Sure, no problem."

They passed dog handlers and security guards, stopping at a bunker with armorglass windows. A bored-looking sergeant sipped from a plastic cup, playing card games on his pad.

Paolo acknowledged his salute. "I'm Nordstrom, Apex 7. I need to speak to the duty officer."

"N.O.R.D.S.T.R.O.M. Is that correct?" The sergeant said, tapping at an omni. "I'm afraid your name ain't on the system, sir."

Paolo slid his ID into a card-reader. The Crimson Brigade quartermaster in Rimini assured him it was genuine. "I just transferred back from NATO in Milan. I was gone for two years, they warned me this might happen."

"They did a system upgrade last month… typical IT bollocks," the sergeant shrugged. "Funny, your ID is current though."

"Sergeant, I don't wanna be difficult, but this is urgent."

The sergeant looked at Paolo for a moment and nodded. "Look, why don't I give you a visitor's pass, sir? Then I can raise a service ticket for your global profile."

Paolo's hand crept from his pistol, "I appreciate it."

The NatSec officer drove them across an airfield, past a World War Two fighter resting on a plinth. Maintenance crews stood in the gloom, drinking from steaming beakers.

Two helicopters stood on an apron, pilots talking to clipboard-carrying crew chiefs. They parked outside a portable cabin. "There you go, Sir. Duty officer tonight is Inspector Campbell." He keyed his fob, "Alpha-Sierra Zero? You've got a visitor outside the ops hut."

A woman in a flight suit appeared at the door, sleeves rolled to her elbows. She was black and fine-featured, with the high cheekbones Paolo associated with East Africa. "I'm Campbell," she said, eyes settling on his beret. "Apex? Do I swoon now or later?"

Paolo smiled. "Now's good, but I can live with later. I'm Tom Nordstrom, Apex Team 7."

"Special Projects, eh?" Campbell looked him up-and-down. "How can I help?"

"I need a recce flight, over the Crosland Estate."

Campbell folded her arms. "It doesn't work like that – we've got protocols for booking sorties. Who's your authorising officer?"

Paolo's knife flashed, tip pressed against Campbell's jugular. "Inspector, you're going to fly me to the Crosland, or I'll open your neck and do it myself."

"What the fuck are you on?"

"Combat respirocites, actually," Paolo replied, the pilot's breath hot on his cheek. "Now, let's go."

TWENTY FIVE

The lobby was littered with sandbags and barrels of armorgel, defenders firing through wall-slits. Ragged kids brought fresh water and ammunition, relaying messages and lighting cigarettes. "The perimeter's fallen," reported a sentry into his fob. "Yeah, we're holding the lobby. Dunno for how long."

Hooker lowered his rifle. "How do I get upstairs?"

The sentry shook his head. "You don't. We hold here."

Hooker touched the edge of his Answerer's cowl. "With respect, I'm not under your orders. I'm here to look after the wounded."

"I guess not. Your brother out there was brave, he bought us time."

"He was a good man," Hooker replied, passing his rifle to the sentry. He'd only one magazine left for it, and the FN was too bulky for close work. "Now, take this and good luck."

The French girl, Florence, said Paolo lived on the top

floor. The thirty-fifth. Studying a fire map, he identified the stairwells and elevators, which he knew would probably be broken. He chose the longest route, figuring it would be the least busy. No time for fighting. Checking Brother Francis' sub-machinegun, a subcompact MP5, Hooker mounted the stairs two at a time.

Fifth floor, heart pounding, squatters ignored the monk in Answerer's robes. On the eighth, Hooker stopped. Dumping the heavy robes, he emptied his water bottle in two long gulps. Through a broken window, he watched leaguers bringing up trailers loaded with breeze blocks. Cover. The shooting from the Commune was ragged now, defenders conserving ammunition. Each side pelted the other with arrows and bolts, bricks and bottles.

The tenth-floor stairwell was blocked with rubble. Hooker switched route. Squatters sat huddled in candlelit doorways, smoking skanj and brewing coffee. Some nodded greetings. "I'm trying to get upstairs," Hooker asked a young woman. "The way I've come is blocked."

She pointed down the gloomy passageway. "There's a fire escape at the far end," she replied. "But it's dangerous up there. Y'know, drones. Stay away from windows."

"I'll be okay."

She wrapped her coat around her, although it wasn't cold. "None of us will be okay. We're going to die."

Hooker shrugged, "you won't die if you get out. Get on a fob, tell the cops you want to surrender."

"Too late, ain't it? The General's men will shoot us as deserters." The woman pulled a bottle of vodka from her coat and drank. She stopped when a speaker mounted on the wall began crackling.

Attention, Comrades! A fascist intruder has infiltrated our Commune. He is described as a big man, black, possibly linked to the Answerer monks. On strictest orders of General Ignacio, this class-traitor is to be executed ON SIGHT. There is a reward for any Comrade who kills him.

Squatters eyed Hooker, hefting clubs and knives. They said nothing, circling like jackals. "You don't wanna do that," he warned, shouldering his MP5.

A hooded squatter stepped forward, a knife in his fist. "You a cop?" he said.

"No."

"He is," said another. A bearded lump with an axe, reminding Hooker of a Viking. "You can tell."

"Definitely a pig." A third man, slapping club into his palm. "He can't shoot us all, can he?"

Hooker's MP5 barked three times. He'd already decided to shoot the Viking first. Three men fell, a neat hole in each of their foreheads. "I *can* shoot you all," he growled. "I don't want to, but I will."

"Murderer," a woman spat from a doorway.

"Definitely," Hooker shrugged. "There's twenty-seven bullets left in this magazine. There's what? Twelve of you?" *Just like the old days.*

The squatters melted away. Hooker, weapon shouldered, padded along the corridor. At the end was an elevator, doors caked in rust and old paint. Scrawled instructions in English, German and Spanish explained the lift stopped at some floors but not others. Hooker pressed the button for the twentieth and, lights flickering, the lift limped skywards. The doors opened into a battle-scarred lobby, corpses strewn like mannequins. Hooker checked the bodies for ammunition, but found nothing. Only a cheap fob. He pocketed it anyway – you could never have too many fobs. Below, leaguers lashed cables to the Commune's doors. Holding shields above their heads, they limbered the cables to a tipper truck. Missiles rained down, concrete and petrol bombs and even buckets of shit. Wounded leaguers were dragged to waiting ambulances.

Hooker's secure fob chirruped. *Gordy.* "Rufus, where the hell are you, son?"

"Is this line safe?"

"Darkwired burner, fresh out of the box. I got Trashmob's message."

"NatSec pinched me and Leah – they knew we were working for Hyatt," Hooker replied. "Leah's at Milbank Tower now. An OCS man called Bliss is threatening to have her tortured." He explained what Bliss had ordered, and why.

"Bliss? Horrible bastard," said Gordy darkly. "Our paths have crossed once or twice before."

Hyatt's voice cut in. "Did you just say OCS wants Lottie dead?"

"Did you hear the part about Leah being tortured?" Hooker growled.

"We'll make sure Leah's safe," Hyatt replied. "We've got a plan to get you out of there, once you've found Lottie."

"Best you get on with it," said Hooker. "There's an army of leaguers outside, but I got a feeling they'll be inside soon."

"We're tracking your fob – find Lottie and get on the

roof. Then message me. Understand? Remember, the *roof*. Don't try to get outside of the Commune."

"I couldn't if I wanted to. Promise me you'll get Leah out of Milbank."

"You've my word."

"I'll hold you to it," Hooker replied.

"Just go," Hyatt ordered, ending the call.

The uppermost floors seemed deserted. Hooker climbed two more flights of stairs, finding only a fire escape. The walls were sheared away by rocket fire, beyond a twisted steel ladder nothing but the night sky… and a hundred-metre drop to the plaza below.

Shit.

The only route left was a companionway, planks laid over scaffolding, crudely bolted to the exterior wall. Taking the nylon rope from his belt kit, he attached either end to a carabiner and clipped onto the scaffold. Probing the platform with his boot, hot wind tearing at his clothes, he climbed gingerly outside. Vertigo made him hug the wall, like a baby at its mother's tit. Below, other squatters traversed a web of scaffolding, connected by ladders and gantries, a higgledy-piggledy mess. Some of the figures carried guns, others spears and axes. Several wore harnesses attached to bungee ropes, fighters bouncing from platform to platform.

Hooker tugged the fob he'd found on the dead body and switched it on. It's signal would pulse into the night, alerting NatSec's electronic warfare teams – a high-technology version of a sentry lighting a cigarette in the dark. He placed the handset on the platform, the scaffolding swaying as a more squatters swarmed up ladders. Gunshots rang out, the whine of bullets hitting steel. He pulled the mezuzah from his armour and kissed it, rain stinging his face. Thinking of Beatriz, and faraway Wessex, Rufus Hooker began hauling himself up the tower.

TWENTY SIX

Paolo followed the pilot, Campbell, to a waiting copter. A decrepit, military-surplus Wildcat, battle-damage patched with armorgel strips. "This is my bird," she said quietly. "I'll need to talk to my ground crew."

Paolo nodded. "Say a cross word…"

"I'm a *pilot*, not a cop. The rank's honorary. I'm on contract, for Christ's sake…"

"That's a novel twist on the Nuremberg defence." Paolo's blade touched the small of the pilot's back, "wear fascist uniform, take fascist risks."

The ground crew nodded a greeting, Campbell returning the crew chief's salute. "I hope she's ready – I'm taking her up now. This Apex officer needs a taxi ride."

"Apex? Yes, Boss," the crew chief replied, seeing Paolo's beret. He turned to his team, wiping his hands on a rag.

"Right, shift your arses."

"She's fuelled up," said a young technician. He handed Campbell her flight helmet and a spare for Paolo. "Anything else, Ma'am?"

"Nothing, thanks, Mercer. We're in a hurry."

"No flight engineer or gunner?"

"It's a half-hour job," Campbell replied. "Besides, the inspector here is flight-qualified."

Paolo nodded. "We'll be fine."

"There's no flight plan on the grid, ma'am," said one of the ground crew, a crop-headed woman in fatigues. She tapped at a pad. "Unless this thing's fucked for a change."

"There is *no* flight plan for this operation," said Paolo, watching the ground crew focus on the Apex flash on his sleeve. "This is dark work. Understand?" *Dark Work*. NatSec used copters for enhanced interrogation. Take six prisoners up. Return with one. *Talk or drop.*

"I understand," the Crew Chief nodded.

Inspector Campbell nodded. "Good, so let's have a sense of urgency, *please*. We need to get this man where he needs to be."

They were soon airborne, the Wildcat flying north towards Lagoon City. The control tower hailed them over the radio, but Paolo shook his head. "Just fly."

Campbell flew no more than a hundred metres from the ground. Her finger hovered on the navigation console, a schematic of southeast England appearing onscreen. "Okay, where to?"

Paolo pointed at the horizon. "The Goons. Do it visually, else your control will pick up any coordinates you enter. Just follow the flames."

They were soon over the estate. By the river's edge loomed the Commune International, bullet-pocked and trailing smoke, tracer splashing off the upper levels. Campbell pointed at the Wildcat's control panel. "Tactical air ops are asking for my permission code. There's a no-fly embargo over the tower."

"Ignore it and land on the roof," Paolo ordered, scanning the landing site with his eye implant. There was enough room to land, as the General promised.

"On the bloody roof? You could walk on the flak over there." Campbell hit a button, anti-missile countermeasures flaring from the Wildcat's weapon pods. She banked over the river, voices crackling urgently over the tactical net.

Paolo pressed his knife to the pilot's throat. "I could set automatic flight control, kick you out and land myself. You choose."

Campbell nudged the cyclic forward, the Wildcat nosing towards the Commune's roof. "Cut me again and I'll crash this bastard," she spat.

Paolo kept the knife against the pilot's jugular. "No you won't."

"Put the blade down. If I'm landing, I do it my way – I'll gain altitude then drop straight down."

"Then do it," Paolo ordered. Something caught his eye. *Movement on the Commune's exterior, higher than the other defenders...* He activated the copter's FLIR display, thermal imagers sweeping the tower.

"What's that?" said Campbell.

"A crazy bastard, near the top of the scaffold," said

Paolo, locking the camera on a figure scaling the tower. *Heading for my floor.* It was a dark-skinned man, heavily-muscled. Hand in his pocket, as if searching for something. *Hooker. The NatSec agent. It had to be…*

"I see him," said Campbell. "Look – he's being followed." Below, more dark shapes swarmed in pursuit.

"Hold steady." Unclipping his seatbelt, Paolo clambered into the copter's passenger bay. Pulling his HK35, he wrenched the side door open.

Campbell shook her head. "No way, I'm taking her down."

Bracing himself in the doorway, Paolo went to paint a sight vector on Hooker's torso. *Too fast.* Paolo held his breath. Target nearly centred. Any moment now…

Movement right.

Campbell pivoted in the pilot's seat, a snub-nosed pistol in her hand. She fired, a bullet slamming into Paolo's ceramoweave vest. He spun and squeezed the trigger, a nano-munition piercing Campbell's flight helmet. The dead pilot slumped in her seat, blood leaking from her visor. Warning alarms screeched from the copter's gore-spattered instrument panel, ground fire plinking against the fuselage. The copter lurched, avionics whining, the undercarriage clipping the edge of the tower with a sharp crack. Paolo jumped, legs like pistons against the Wildcat's fuselage door. His fingertips brushed concrete as the copter spun away into the night. It fell like a dead bird, crashing into the plaza, flaming smoke roiling skywards.

The Crimson Brigade agent hung from a ledge, rain spattering his face. Peering into the abyss, he saw a wooden plank suspended on a scaffold. He dropped, catlike, balancing on it like a surfer. Below him he saw the man he *knew* was Hooker. Hauling himself up beams and poles, Hooker made for a doorway carved into the exterior wall. Paolo remembered it was made for the maintenance crews, experienced climbers who tended the Commune's solar panels and evernet dishes. If Hooker got inside, he'd be only minutes from the apartment.

From Lottie Rhys.

Paolo's eye implant picked out the rivets that secured the scaffolding to the tower. He fired two armour-piercing rounds, projectiles with tungsten penetrators. With a flash of white light, they bit into steel. Creaking and yawing, a beam swung crazily from wall. The big man clawed and flailed, trying to swing back towards the doorway. Paolo aimed again, augmented hearing filtering two sets of noise – the subsonic whisper of stealth-enabled aeronautics…

The other sound was bitter and deep. *Laughter.* Hooker was laughing.

A light winked below them both, on a wooden platform amidst the scaffold-maze. Paolo focussed and saw a fob, tiny screen glowing.

Then, like a wasp sensing jam, came a stubby-winged aircraft, swooping out of the darkness. Paolo winced. *The Fob. The drone's sniffed the fob's signal…*

The Eviscerator appeared, hovering near-silently, attracted by the electronic bait. It was a machine of preposterous angles, rows of phallic-looking weapons bulging urgently beneath its wings. System specifications flooded Paolo's optical implant – *Warning! Autonomous Airborne Interdiction Platform detected. You are being targeted by 30mm*

Jackhammer IV cannons and Almaz-Antey Werewolf antipersonnel rockets…

The drone's targeting systems relied on heat-seeking optics. And thanks to the respirocite, Paolo was a burning man. The Eviscerator fired at multiple targets up and down the tower, spattering the walls with fire. Shrapnel tore a chunk of flesh from Paolo's calf, the respirocite numbing the pain. Panting, he let himself drop to another plank, the drone jinking like a kitten playing with a ball of wool. It shuddered mid-air, weapon ports spitting flame. A rocket exploded somewhere above. A body toppled from above – a Black Rifleman, headband fluttering like bandages as he fell.

Paolo's hands scrabbled for the wall, fingers piercing concrete. He checked his weapon's ammo load – only a handful of high-explosive and fragmentation rounds remained. Painting target vectors on the drone's comms array, he squeezed the HK35s trigger. Detecting incoming fire, the drone cut its engines and dropped, counter-measures popping and fizzing. A lucky high-explosive round struck its starboard wing, making a flurry of sparks. The Eviscerator's engines roared back to life, soaring away into the night.

Paolo half-fell down a ladder. His calf hurt now, a sharp, biting pain. The respirocite was waning, nanobots evaporating, weakness flooding his body. Soon he'd be unable to fight, and there was still no sign of Hooker. Dropping to the entrance hewn into the wall, he ducked inside the tower, HK ready. He saw wet boot prints. *Hooker made it…*

The Commune's thirtieth floor was used for skanj production, a lush micro-forest of genetically-modified skunk. The odour made Paolo gag. He shivered suddenly, a spearpoint of pain driving into his chest. Damn, the come-down off the respirocite was brutal. Then, a noise. Boots on concrete. Gulping air, Paolo pulled a morphine autojet from his pocket and stabbed it into his thigh. This thing wasn't over. There were still cards to play.

Perhaps it was time for the Joker.

TWENTY SEVEN

Hooker fell through the doorway, chest heaving, fingers raw. Muscles burning from the desperate scramble across the scaffolding. *Who the fuck crashed a copter into the side of the building?*

He looked around, realising he'd stepped into a jungle. Skanj everywhere, feathery plants smouldering. Shattered hydroponic systems dotted the ceilings, walls scarred by rocket-strikes. The farm's heat signature would have been an irresistible target for the drone. A fire escape read *FLOORS 31-35.*

He was close.

Then, a noise. Heavy breathing. Wheezing, like an asthmatic. A gaunt-looking man appeared, skin tight against his skull, hands raised. He wore NatSec fatigues, inspector's rank flashes on the epaulettes. "You're Hooker?" he said.

"Who wants to know?" MP5 ready, Hooker made a sight picture of the stranger's head. The stranger was no more than three metres away.

"The man who killed the two OCS cops who sent you here."

"You're NatSec?"

The man hawked something on the floor. Glistening red. "I am Colonel Paolo Falcone, of the Crimson Brigade's Special Action Group. I'm not your enemy."

"That wasn't you trying to shoot me off the side of the building then?"

"And you didn't leave a fob for the drone to lock onto?" The man in black's smile was mirthless. "My blood ran hot – I'm recovering from a respirocite high. There's little time to explain, but there's something I must show you."

Hooker's finger slid inside the MP5's trigger. "Bullshit. Where's Charlotte Rhys?"

Paolo's eyes shone, "*Bullshit?* Why is my weapon holstered? Why'd I tell you I'm drug-fatigued? You have me at a disadvantage, Hooker. What do you have to lose?"

"The girl. Where is she?"

"Want to help Lottie? Then there's even more reason to talk. I'm going to reach into my pocket. I assure you it's not for a weapon."

Hooker was ready to fire. "Slowly," he said. "Move very slowly."

Paolo produced a silver tube. "This is a neural uploader. Have you heard of the technology?"

"Yeah," Hooker replied, "It injects information straight into your brain, right?"

"More or less."

Hooker raised an eyebrow. "If you think I'm going to let you stick a needle in my skull, you can fuck off."

Paolo nodded. "I'd be sceptical too. After all, you're being blackmailed by the NatSec Office of Counter Subversion. I also know your friend's being tortured."

"Leah?"

"I don't know her name. I do know they've started working on her."

"Then it's even more important for me to find Lottie Rhys."

"I've no plans to kill Lottie, Mister Hooker," Paolo shrugged. He offered Hooker the autoinjector. "She's far too valuable."

"Valuable?"

"When the facts change, so does my mind."

Hooker studied the injector, clinical and clean. "Why not just tell me what's inside this thing?"

"Seeing is believing," Paolo replied. "Consider the evidence before you decide your next move. I assure you, this information is *leverage*."

Hooker lowered his weapon. "Okay, persuade me – why should I trust *you*?"

"Why shouldn't you? You've the look of service about you, Hooker. You were a soldier, maybe? A loyal man. Yet here you are, blackmailed into a suicide mission…"

"What's in it for you?"

"The truth," Paolo replied. "Truth sets us free. Upload the truth. *Taste it*. Then we parley."

Something itched in Hooker's brain. Vassa Hyatt. Bliss.

Charlotte Rhys. *Beatriz…* the mezuzah burnt his skin. "Parley?"

Paolo lay his weapons on the floor. A sophisticated-looking HK, a knife and two tomahawks. Finally, he plasticuffed himself. "You'll be able to stop the information dump anytime you choose. You'll be fully conscious and able to function normally. Shoot me, even. Now, I think I'll have a cigarette. The pack's in my left ammunition pouch, if you wouldn't mind?"

"A Marlboro Red?" said Hooker.

The Crimson Brigade agent smiled. "I knew they'd be the death of me. Now, place the autojet in the nape of your neck and push the button. It's relatively painless."

Hooker lit Paolo a cigarette. Then, MP5 ready, he touched the injector to the base of his skull. Paolo nodded, smoke trailing from his nostrils. "Do it, Hooker."

Hooker pressed the button.

Brain-freeze. Like a kid gobbling ice cream too quickly. I remember ice cream. Flavours, milky-sweet. Beatriz loved ice cream. Cookie dough…

Now vertigo. Images. Data. Voices… Paolo Falcone looks relaxed, even with a gun at his head. He's smoking a Marlboro, which has been his favourite brand for ten years. How do I know that?

Hooker winces, tries to focus. Something's mapping the contours of his brain. Like a tiny crop-duster, seeding fresh engrams into his subconscious. *[Neurological Fact: An engram is a biophysical process that generates memories]*

[Please try to relax. Neural uplift can be disorientating while Npas4 manipulation completes. Data package delivery in

five seconds…]
[Three seconds…]

[…Prepare for payload delivery]

Hooker sees a room. He's in it, but he isn't. It's shadowy and quiet, like the waiting area at a doctor's surgery. He sees cracks in the roughly plastered walls, condensation glittering on a spider web in the window. Yet he's still in the stairwell of the skanj-stinking Commune, his gun at Paolo's head. Paolo's saying something, but Hooker can't hear. But he can smell the Marlboro, cigarette smoke sharp in his nose.

A broken man sits slumped in a chair. His face is a tapestry of black and mauve from a sustained beating. A figure appears, dressed in fatigues. *[This is a soldier of the Special Action Group* Andreas Baader, *operating in Southern Italy against the NATO / Fascist alliance.]* The soldier touches a cattle prod to the prisoner's chest, and he convulses like a ghoulish puppet.

"It's time," says a voice from the corner of the room. *[The voice belongs to Colonel Paolo Falcone, conducting the debrief of a High Value Prisoner]* Paolo Falcone's voice is gentle. "Are you ready?"

"Water? Please…"

[The prisoner's name is Martyn S. Weir. At the time of this memory capture, he's a forty-two-year-old paramilitary operations specialist, contracted to the Special Activities Division of the US Central Intelligence Agency. His primary role is Human Intelligence identification and development. The interrogation

takes place late last year in Bari, Southern Italy. Weir has already surrendered the identities of the top intelligence sources run by the CIA inside the Crimson Brigade]

The man in fatigues hands Martyn Weir a bottle of water. The prisoner sips gratefully, purplish lips struggling to make a seal around the bottleneck. "Say thank you, Martyn," says Paolo.

"Thank you."

"Please explain how you became aware of Operation MADRIGAL."

Weir ignores the water dribbling down his chin. "Basically, it was a screw-up. Prior to deploying to Italy, I volunteered for a type IV neural upload - they wanted to test a new language module, and my Italian ain't too good.

"Anyhow, they gave me a standard brainstem shot. The technician who performed it was a kid called Trio Fernandez. Turns out Trio had stolen a shitload of random CIA data from a hacked Special Access server. He'd managed to convert it all into a neural upload format to smuggle out of the facility – 'cuz they can't search your *brain*, can they?"

"Not yet," Paolo replies, studying his fingernails. "Give them time. Please, continue."

"I receive the info dump. I immediately figure I've been given seriously compartmentalised Intel, the sort of thing I don't need to see. Afterwards I ask Trio what the fuck's goin' on. It only takes a couple of minutes to get the story outta him."

"Please, tell us about Mister Fernandez," says Paolo. "The circumstances are important."

"Trio's girlfriend was mixed up with a hacking

collective. Y'know, libertarian anarchists or some kinda bullshit like that. She pussy-whacked him into going rogue, but Trio was hardly spy of the century material. He had the injector in his pocket with the stolen data, but there was a security check that day. He panicked and got 'em all mixed up. So instead of intermediate Italian, Trio squirted MADRIGAL into my brain." Weir almost smiles. "Just my fucking luck."

"Why didn't you report the error?"

"Soon as I knew what it was? I figured I got two choices – keep quiet or get lobotomised by the agency."

"So, what did you do, Martyn?"

"I'm trained to improvise. I told Trio I was sympathetic to the cause, and arranged to meet him away from the office to talk about our next move. I met him in a carpark and ran a K-Bar into the back of his skull. I dumped his body in the Potomac."

"Was that necessary?"

Weir nods. It hurts, and he winces. "Hell yeah. The CIA's counterespionage monkeys are seriously medieval when it comes to that kinda shit. Data from a *Beyond Top Secret* Special Access Program?"

"Tell us what you learned."

Weir closes his eyes, as if reading from a script. [*This material is in his brain, so he can quote it verbatim*] "Operation MADRIGAL was the covert US response to emerging gene-augmentation and Transhumanist technologies, especially the Rudenko-Xiaoping Procedure (RXP). MADRIGAL'S objectives were –

"ONE: Develop parallel technologies to Rudenko-

Xiaoping to guarantee the United States enjoyed continued technological hegemony in the field of augmented humanity;

"TWO: Disrupt other international actors attempting to obtain or develop augmented humanity technologies;

"THREE: Implement a long-term strategy to restore the pre-2025 international order, namely by covertly seeding global institutions and governments with augmented transhuman agents of influence. Their mission was to rejuvenate liberal democracy around the globe."

"Old wine, new bottles," Paolo sighs. "Tell us about the outcome of the third objective, please. That's of specific interest to me."

Weir nods, brow beaded with sweat. "MADRIGAL went bad. Really bad. The initial cohort of operatives decided liberal democracy was bunk, 'cuz they could do a better job. They were super-people, right? They infiltrated governments and intelligence agencies, ended up leading armies. They took over terrorist movements and organised crime groups. Their budget was unlimited, and once they were up and running they rigged the financial markets too.

"They called themselves the *Archangels.* Their inner council was the December 13th Group, which coordinated transhumans from other nations who wanted the same thing."

"The same thing?" says Paolo.

"A World Government. Run by Archangels. The Russians and Chinese had their own transhumanity programs, and their super-people were equally frustrated by the status quo. They had more in common with each other than the nations they served."

"Was this the CIA's intention all along?" Paolo asks.

"No way," says Weir shaking his head. "The material I saw doesn't support that – the whole thing was a fuck-up. Nobody understood their agenda until the wars started. The file says when they finally captured one of the December 13th plotters, she claimed the group's motives were beyond the understanding of *Cattle*. That's you and me, by the way."

Paolo nods. "Those of us who never underwent RXP treatment?"

"Exactly, but finally a dozen of 'em turned against the rest. That led to a split, a war among the transhumans. The turncoats won, and were pardoned for taking out their comrades. The survivors were neutered, and RXP was banned."

"Who outside the US Government knew the truth?"

Weir takes another sip of water. "The file specifically mentioned someone in the UK. They were eventually indoctrinated into MADRIGAL, after civil war broke out there. The Brits called it the *Hate War*, right?"

"Yes, aptly so. Name this person," Paolo orders.

"He was called Damon Rhys, the UK Security Minister. Rhys was personally briefed by President Mendoza, and sworn to secrecy."

"Mendoza died last year, of course. And the Americans pledged trillions of dollars to atone for this debacle?"

"Yes they did. They called it the *Atlas Program*," Martyn nods. "As long as the Brits kept quiet, they'd get trillions of aid dollars pumped into their economy. The French and Germans never got the same offer. Look what happened to them."

"Is there anything else you remember, Martyn?"

"No. That's it. Man, havin' this stuff in my head? It's like carrying a fucking brain tumour around."

"Let me divest you of that burden." Paolo Falcone steps into view. Something flashes in his hand. A sword, curved and over a metre long.

[Upload ends]

Hooker felt a sudden rush of nausea. He thought he was going to be sick, then – nothing.

"There you have it," Paolo shrugged, leg bleeding. He stubbed out his cigarette on the dirty concrete floor.

"The *Americans* created the Archangels?" said Hooker.

"Sort of. In an unusual piece of role-reversal, the CIA stole the technology from the Chinese. The Americans improved RXP immeasurably, to the point where a clique of transhuman fascists was inevitable. But who could have predicted that terminal-stage Capitalism was the ascension of the rich into a separate *species*? Damon Rhys concealed the truth. He chose to take blood money instead. Dirty money."

"And that's what you want Rhys to tell the world?"

Paolo nodded. "I give people the truth. From truth comes freedom."

Hooker shook his head. "Freedom? You really believe that? Ain't you a Communist?"

"We live in a time of hard ideologies," Paolo shrugged. "I consider mine least-worst. This government will fall, as will the nest of Archangels incubating in Winchester."

Hooker looked around. Outside, the sound of fighting grew louder. "How does this change anything?"

Paolo's face was clammy and grey. "I assume you came here with an exit strategy. Help us escape and Lottie Rhys lives. Your friend will live. We shall take bloody revenge on the bastards who did her harm – bring the roof down on their heads."

"I want to see Lottie first."

Paolo held out his hands. "Cut the plasticuffs, Mister Hooker, and I'll take you to her myself."

TWENTY EIGHT

More stairs. Never had Hooker missed escalators so badly. Paolo had to stop to catch his breath, breathing ragged. A chunk of his calf was missing, the wound bloody and raw. "Respirocites," he shrugged. "Never take two fixes in one day."

"They really work?" Hooker still had the combat stims Chisholm had given him, tucked in his belt pouch.

"Yes, but the comedown is an… ordeal."

They arrived at a door fitted, with an iris scanner. A bearded man, dressed in combat gear, stood guard outside. He hefted a Kalashnikov, warily eyeing Hooker.

"It's okay Caleb," said Paolo.

"Welcome back," the man replied, looking Hooker up and down. His accent was English. "Was that *your* copter that hit the building?"

"Sadly it was. This is Hooker, he's going to get us out of

here."

Caleb licked his teeth. "He's sounds like the man who…"

"The intruder? He does indeed." Paolo held up a hand, "Mister Hooker was coerced into coming here. But now he isn't - we've made a deal."

Caleb bristled. "Does General Ignacio know about your *deal*?"

Paolo smiled. It reminded Hooker of a movie he'd once seen about a killer shark. "Careful, comrade. Don't overstep your mark."

Caleb aimed his rifle at Paolo. "The General didn't know about the girl. When were you gonna to tell him?"

"It was safer he didn't know. Have you spoken to him?"

Caleb's eye twitched. "Not yet. The comms are screwed, leaguers have taken the lobby."

"I'd be grateful if you didn't mention it," Paolo replied. "I'll tell him myself."

Caleb took a step back, making a sight picture. "You've taken us for a ride, Paolo. I wouldn't be surprised if the girl's the reason…"

Hooker's weapon barked. Caleb's staggered, eyes wide. The Black Rifleman crashed to the ground, hands fluttering at the bullet wound in his chest.

"You beat me to it," Paolo sniffed. "I'm getting old."

"You and me both." Hooker replied, smoke curling from his gun. "Who the fuck is the General?"

"Ignacio of the Black Rifles. If he knew the truth about the girl…"

"He'll want a ransom, not a confession?"

"Yes, something like that. I think Caleb lied about telling him - Ignacio's gunmen are probably on their way now." Sighing, Paolo coughed phlegm on the concrete floor.

"How? The drone'll pick 'em off that scaffolding."

Paolo shook his head. "There's another elevator – the Germans built it for moving skanj down from the thirtieth floor. From there, it only stops on the fifteenth and in the basement. They never marked it on the fire map, which is how I assume you plotted a course up here."

Hooker plucked the grenades from Caleb's belt. "I'm still wonderin' why you think I'd help you escape?"

Paolo squinted into the iris scanner, the lock snapping open. "What choice do you have? It's the only way you'll save Lottie. I assure you, there's no way you'll send her back to Damon Rhys."

"I made a deal."

Paolo stopped by the door, voice low. "Speak with the girl first – it's all I ask."

The apartment smelt of smoke, floors littered with rubble. The living area was crudely barricaded with sandbags and furniture. "Paolo?" said a voice, "in here, with the girl."

The room was candlelit. A soiled mattress on the floor, a bucket to piss in. The girl was slumped against the wall, dressed in a dirty orange jumpsuit. "Lottie?" said Hooker.

A dark-haired woman stood next to the girl, eyes narrowed. Hooker knew it was the woman who'd called herself Roisin. She cradled a gun in her hand, finger resting along the trigger guard. "Who was shooting outside?"

"Caleb told the General about the girl," Paolo replied.

"He's dead now. Hooker, this is my colleague, Rourke."

"I told you he'd overheard us," she said.

Paolo shrugged. "So why didn't you kill him?"

"Don't be funny," she said, nodding at Hooker. "Who the hell's *he*?"

"I'm here for the girl."

The woman pulled a face, "Paolo what the hell's going on?"

"Not now," Paolo replied. "Hooker, whatever your extraction plan is, activate it now."

Rourke studied Hooker with interest. "He can get us out of here?"

"I didn't say that," Hooker replied. He rested his hand on Lottie's shoulder. "Are you okay? I'm gonna take you home."

Lottie shrank from his touch. "Are you one of *them*?" she said. "A terrorist?"

"No."

Paolo stood over the girl. "Hooker, she's carrying an *Archangel* in her womb. They drugged her and impregnated her. She's the fascist's very own Virgin Mary, don't you see?"

Lottie glowered. "What did you just say?"

Rourke stood up, pistol ready. Her smile was cruel. "The boy you talked about, the one you kissed at the party in Winchester? He's a CIA agent called Tristian Gramercy."

"We think he's an archangel," said Paolo. "My guess? You've been chosen for the next phase of the Project. Your father used you, Lottie. You're a brood mare."

Lottie stared at the wall. Hooker gripped her hand. "We've got to get you out of here."

"You've got aviation on standby, I assume?" said Paolo.

Hooker shouldered his MP5 and flicked off the safety. "What were you gonna to do with her?"

"Take her somewhere safe. Kyiv, or Free Cordoba. She'll be looked after, and her child will…"

"You want it, don't you?" said Lottie, teeth bared. "The baby. You want it. It's just a weapon, isn't it?"

Hooker caught Rourke's eye, but the Irishwoman looked away. "Yes, Lottie. I make you right on that one."

"No, not a weapon," said Paolo. "It's almost a miracle, don't you see? They said it couldn't be done, that archangels could never breed. Our scientists will want to know how it was achieved, germline transfer is …"

Hooker shook his head. "I've heard enough. Lottie, get up. Grab the back of my belt and stick close to me. We're leaving."

Lottie nodded, threading her fingers through Hooker's web belt.

"No!" said Rourke.

Hooker towered over the Irishwoman. "Lottie, this is the one who murdered your friend Evie. Killed her mother too – I saw the body myself. You're just a science experiment to these people."

"Nor will she be safe with her father," Paolo replied. "With us Lottie has a chance of a different life. A *virtuous* life."

Hooker pressed the send button on his fob. The signal for Gordy pinged into the ether. In the corridor, an alarm trilled. "The Spanish," said Rourke, checking the action on her pistol. "Hooker, if you think our plans for the girl were bad…"

Paolo unholstered his HK. "I suggest we settle this *after* we've dealt with our friends from The Black Rifles."

Hooker was already out of the room, Lottie close behind. With a ripping sound, the apartment's front door burst off its hinges, something bouncing on the floor.

Grenade.

Wrapping Lottie in a bear-hug, Hooker crashed into the nearest room. The explosion sounded like a monstrous cough, concussion shaking the walls. "Not in here," Lottie cried. "No…"

Hooker took in the gloomy, black-walled room. Flags and a chopping block, a sword lined up in front of a camera. "Lottie, get down," he whispered. "Low as possible. Do it *now.*"

"Is the girl okay?" called Paolo.

"Yeah," Hooker grunted. He peered around the corner, gunmen crowding the doorway. Weapons barked, riddling the walls with bullets. A ricochet slammed into Hooker's upper arm, numbing it beneath his armorgel. Ripping a grenade from his belt with his good hand, he lobbed it at the doorway. A gunman shouted in Spanish, hurling himself on top of the explosive. His body bucked crazily, purplish offal spattering the walls. With a roar, the remaining Black Riflemen charged.

Paolo and Hooker poured fire into the tiny corridor, weapons rattling like buzz-saws and chopping the first wave of attackers to pieces. The cocking lever on Hooker's SMG snapped forward. *Weapon empty.* Nano-munitions from Paolo's HK35 sparkled in the half-light, ripping into a gunman's chest. He grunted and fell, only to be replaced by two more. The Crimson Brigade agent flinched, bullets hammering his armoured vest. Hooker reloaded and opened fire, two more Spaniards joining the barricade of corpses blocking the doorway. Rourke crawled out of cover, firing wildly.

"Get down!" Hooker ordered, readying another grenade. He pitched hard, bouncing it off the wall and through the front door. There was another muffled explosion, followed by screaming.

Paolo was still firing, teeth gritted, face masked with blood. Hooker went to join him, a bullet punching into his chest. He fell back inside the black room, gasping for air. Heart hammering, ribs burning, armorgel burning into his skin. He didn't know if the vest could take another hit. "Lottie?" he gasped.

The girl tugged the sword from the executioner's block. She didn't look strong enough to heft it. "We're going to die," she said.

"No," Hooker gasped, coughing blood. He fumbled in his belt pouch, fingers clutching the respirocite autojet. "I need your help – I've been shot. Take this and fight. If you don't, we're both dead."

"Is that a military stim? I've seen them in movies," Lottie replied. "Where do I inject?"

"Your thigh will do. Quickly, do it now."

She flipped the cap, fingers shaking. "What will it do to the... *baby?*"

"I dunno."

Lottie shook her head, steel needle glittering. "I can't."

Hooker fixed her eyes with his. "Then the baby'll die anyhow."

Lottie slammed the autojet into her thigh, through the leg of her grubby jumpsuit. She winced, tears beading the corner of her eyes. Hooker fumbled in his pocket for a foil package. A trauma-pack. He rolled it across his chest, feeling a Ketamine buzz "Lottie?"

"Oh *fuck*," the girl sighed, eyes rolling. She tumbled backwards, a tangle of orange-clad limbs. Her mouth frothed, sword clattering to the ground.

"Go!" bawled a voice from the corridor. "Get in there, you useless bastards!"

Paolo's voice was calm. "I need help, Hooker."

"I'm shot."

"We're all shot."

Hooker stumbled towards the corridor, Kalashnikov ready. The Crimson Brigade agent was waiting. He made a series of hand signals. *Hostiles to the left of the doorway. At least three.*

"Paolo," said a voice in English. "Surrender, you bastard. The leaguers are coming!"

"That's General Ignacio," Paolo whispered. "Kill him if you can."

A fighter appeared in the doorway, pausing to step over the bodies littering the corridor. He wore heavy body armour and a full-faced helmet, a belt-fed machine gun cradled in his arms. Paolo fired, peppering the gunner's thighs and groin with armour-piercing rounds, blowing him off his feet. Another took his place, also armoured. His shotgun roared, Paolo spinning like he'd been punched by a giant fist. Hooker felt the sting of shotgun pellets across his arm and face, the Kalashnikov dropping to the floor. In the black room, Lottie shook like a drunk, grinning and gibbering.

Pulling his knife, Hooker lunged at the armoured shot-gunner, blade sinking into his throat. Eyes bulging like eggs, the dying man smashed his weapon against Hooker's head. They both fell to the blood-slicked floor, the armoured hulk pinning Hooker to the ground. More men appeared, bulky in black-painted armour. One spoke in accented English. "The black guy is over here, General. He's in a bad way, but I think it's the NatSec *bastardo*."

The man they called *General* strode forward, a pistol in each fist. He wore his coppery hair long, a lop-sided smile splitting his handsome face. "Was this fascist Paolo's man all along, I wonder? What is it to be Comrades? Interrogation or execution?"

"Do motives matter now, General?" said one of his soldiers, a gingery weasel with a northern accent.

"Execution," growled a man with a patch over one eye.

The other gunmen nodded. Hooker saw something ripple in his peripheral vision, a flash of orange. And a sound – halfway between a cackle and a hiss. The red-headed man's head toppled from his shoulders. Then a grunt, a black sword biting into the General's shoulder. His arm fell to the ground with a wet thud, pistol clattering into the corridor. The head rolled across the floor, a look of surprise on its face. The three remaining gunmen spun, struggling to aim rifles in the cramped corridor. Lottie slid between them, lithe as a snake, sword chopping and slashing. A gunshot rang out, a fighter mistakenly blasting another in the chest. "I am Ignacio of the

Black Rifles!" growled the one-armed man, eyes wide. "I'm…"

"Dead?" Lottie Rhys replied, drawing the sword across his gullet. She stood over a pile of corpses, face agleam with blood, eyes blazing with dark fire. She cocked her head like a bird of prey, hefting the blade in doll-like hands. Her skin oscillated, mottled red and mauve, tendons and muscles bulging like the innards of some strange creature.

"Not me, Lottie," Hooker gasped, pointing to the door, "there might be others outside. Kill them all."

"Yes," Lottie nodded. "I can do that."

Hooker dragged himself into the torchlit corridor. He saw only a fraction of the slaughter, Lottie screeching and howling. She fell amongst the last of the Black Riflemen, hacking them down with her sword. The girl's blood-stippled head swivelled, owl-like, eyes scanning for threats. "It's like I'm watching myself do this," she gasped. "It's unreal, the power…"

"You're doing great," Hooker replied. "Look for a fire escape."

Rourke appeared in the corridor. She cradled Paolo's HK35, aiming at Hooker. "What have you done to her?" she screeched, "what about the *baby*?"

Lottie smiled. "What do you care, *Roisin*?

"Lottie, put the sword down," Rourke replied. She reversed her grip on the pistol, finger clear of the trigger. "See? I won't hurt you. I promise."

"You? Hurt me?" Lottie laughed. She hurled the sword, the tip skewering Rourke through the guts. The Irishwoman fell to her knees, eyes wide. Lottie tugged the sword free and handed it to Hooker, before scooping him up in her arms.

Paolo appeared, hair sticky with blood, a tomahawk in each hand. His coveralls were shredded by shotgun pellets, scorched ceramoweave gaping underneath. "Rourke?" he said, grimacing with pain.

"I killed her," said Lottie. "You're next."

"Perhaps not," Paolo replied, stepping over Rourke's body. "I know where the fire escape is."

"Then show us," said Hooker.

The Crimson Brigade agent led them to a red-painted door. Inside was a small room, a metal ladder leading to a ceiling hatch. War cries echoed in the corridor behind them. "Leaguers," said Hooker.

"It was only a matter of time," Paolo replied.

Lottie climbed the ladder, Hooker close behind. Boots thumped on concrete, a face-painted leaguer lurching around a corner. He grinned drunkenly, hefting a spiked mace. Paolo stepped in his path, tomahawks ready. Other woad-painted warriors arrived, eyeing Paolo's police fatigues with surprise. Loyal Croydonians and Urbanskis, dressed in leather and steel, weapons bloodied.

Ignoring Paolo, one of the leaguers pointed at Lottie. "Tasty little bitch 'ere, boys," he leered, "form an orderly cue for fresh pussy."

Paolo Falcone smiled a bloody smile. "I'm not sure you should've said that."

TWENTY NINE

Paolo's tomahawks flashed, severing the leaguer's hand. Pivoting at the waist, he round-house kicked the fighter into his comrades. "Who's next?"

The leaguers faltered for a moment, leery of the strange axeman. Lottie punched the hatch open and pushed Hooker outside. She hissed, dropping the sword. Hooker pulled something from his pouch. "Grenade!" he hollered.

Paolo scrambled up the ladder, leaguers scattering. The Crimson Brigade agent rolled onto the roof as the grenade went off, smoke billowing from the hatch. "That was too close," he spat.

"You're alive, ain't you?" said Hooker.

Paolo looked skywards. "Where's our ride?"

"Dunno," Hooker replied. "All I know is they're tracking my fob."

From below came the *clang-clang-clang* of boots on the

metal ladder. Lottie dropped to all fours, arching her back and howling. Bounding to the hatch, she plucked out a leaguer like a bear pawing for salmon. "Fresh *pussy?*" she laughed, hurling him from the roof, screams lost on the wind. The next leaguer out of the hatch had a pistol. He opened fire, a bullet whining past the girl's head. Hooker drop-kicked the shooter's face like a football, smashing his skull like a piece of bag fruit. The pistol bounced across the roof, the leaguer dropping into the seething mosh-pit below. Lottie panted like a dog. "This is incredible, I feel like I'm on fire, but the fire's sweet. Like honey..."

Paolo limped over to the girl, pulling something from his fighting rig. "Take this hydration pouch. The fire'll burn out soon enough, girl. Take deep breaths."

"Why do you care?" she spat, snatching the foil sachet. She tore it open, gulping the chilled liquid. "You were going to behead me, weren't you?"

"I care because you're the *only* fully combat-capable person up here."

Lottie sneered, standing by the open hatch. She hissed and laughed. "Are you scared?" she goaded the leaguers below.

"Step back, Lottie," Hooker ordered, picking up the leaguer's pistol. He gasped, a sudden dagger-pain in his chest. His armorgel might have saved him, but the bullet had busted more than a few ribs.

"I want to fight," said the girl.

"No, you don't," Hooker replied, looking out across London, blue-black in its vastness, quicksilver moonlight riming the lagoons. Beyond lay the Closed Zone where, even now, there was movement beneath dozens of geodesic globes.

Earth-moving equipment and diggers, Hooker guessed. American. Blood-geld for The Emergencies.

Paolo nodded at the globes. "Don't be taken in. It's a lie. An illusion. The Archangels will return, and you'll live as slaves. Or there'll be another war. If we take the girl, maybe we can…"

"Give it a rest, for fuck's sake," Hooker replied.

"Force of habit, I guess."

Hooker pointed at Lottie, "all we can do now is hold and wait."

Lottie ran a claw through her hair, streaking it red. "Wait for what?"

"Help, Lottie. An old friend promised help would come."

"What sort of help?"

"I don't know."

They retreated across the roof, taking cover behind the junction box of a long-dead ventilation system. Hooker tapped metal, hoping it was dense enough to stop a bullet. The top of a riot shield appeared from the roof hatch, an Urbanski crouched behind it. Hooker checked the pistol's transparent magazine – eight rounds. Lottie found a wooden fence post and hefted it. Making a fighting stance, on the balls of his feet, Paolo readied his tomahawks.

The leaguers were all gold-torqued generals. The front rank wore ballistic armour, decorated orange and black – the cream of the Loyal Croydonia Brethren. They beat a crude tattoo on their shields, war-hammers pounding armorglass. More leaguers fell in, forming up behind the wall of shields.

Some held metal spears, long enough to jab past the first rank. On each flank were more generals, cradling shotguns.

Hooker fired twice, the first round glancing off a shield. The second tore open a spearman's throat, the dead man disappearing inside the phalanx. Shotguns roared pink-white flame, pellets spattering the junction box. More leaguers arrived, lesser-ranking Yeomen spilling from the hatch. Generals barked threats and curses, urging their men forward.

"I appreciate you coming to find me," said Lottie.

Hooker tried to grab her arm. "Lottie, no…"

Lottie charged, making an orange blur, howling as she leapt into battle. "Magnificent," said Paolo drily, pulling himself to his feet. "Whatever happens, make sure the girl doesn't fall into the Archangels' hands."

"I told you, I made a deal."

Paolo gripped Hooker's arm. "This isn't about deals or politics anymore, Hooker. It's about something else."

"Like what?"

"Who we are," Paolo replied. Smiling grimly, he followed Lottie Rhys into the shield wall.

Hooker could only watch, pistol ready, body ketamine-numb. Lottie hurled herself into the leaguers, kicking a General between the legs and punching another in the throat. Men jabbed with spears, a shot-gunner scrambling to reload. Paolo jinked into the scrum, slashing with his cruel black tomahawks. A black-armoured warrior bellowed, locking his arms around Lottie's waist, turning to the spearmen behind him. Lottie twisted, eel-like and threw her head back, smashing his nose. Breaking free, she seized a shotgun and blasted the front rank with birdshot. A spear pierced her thigh as Paolo lunged, hacking at the leaguer wielding it. A fighter grabbed Paolo's leg in a clumsy tackle, another smashing a shield into his face. Stunned, Paolo fell to his knees. A leaguer wrenched a tomahawk from his hand, screaming in triumph. The mob bayed, weapons glittering in the torchlight.

"To me, Lottie!" Hooker hollered. He aimed and fired, killing one of the shot-gunners. He fired again, downing the warrior struggling with Paolo. The girl rolled free, using a spearman's corpse as a shield. She threw him into her pursuers and bounded away. A general drew a revolver from his belt and stuffed the barrel in Paolo's face.

Hooker saw Paolo close his eyes.

There was a muffled shot, and the Crimson Brigadier died. The leaguers stomped his body and roared. They hacked Paolo's head from his shoulders and kicked it off the roof. Then they turned towards Lottie and Hooker.

Hooker fired again, the general who'd shot Paolo spinning as a bullet pierced his skull. The leaguers raised their weapons to the sky, axes and spears and maces. They charged, a battle cry on their lips. *No Surrender!*

"I'm sorry," said Hooker, ripping the mezuzah from his neck. He felt the metal, skin-warm in his fist, and thought of Beatriz...

His fob, clipped to his collar, crackled.

"*NatSec ADVENT Alpha Zero? You getting' this?*" said a voice, an easy Texan drawl. "*NatSec ADVENT Alpha Zero, this is VENDETTA Four-Seven Actual, stand-down your aerial assets.*"

"Huh?" said Lottie. "Vendetta *what?*"

"My fob. Someone's patched me into the local tac-net."

Hooker broke cover and fired, sending another general tumbling. The leaguers circled their wounded comrade, shields raised. From the fob bled a reply to the American's challenge.

This is NatSec ADVENT Alpha Zero, please identify yourself, VENDETTA Four-Seven Actual. This is an unknown callsign on this tac-net... Hooker knew ADVENT Alpha Zero was an airspace control call-sign, responsible for aviation over the combat zone.

Hear this – I am Lieutenant-Colonel Vail, of the 1st Raider Battalion, United States Marine Corps. We ARE deployed under the Bilateral Assistance Treaty, and we ARE extracting an American national from your AOE.

This is ADVENT Alpha Zero, we have NO permissions for any VENDETTA call-sign, please standby...

The American sounded like he was enjoying himself. *You ain't listenin' to me, are you son? This is a Warhawk strike boat, we're comin' in hot and if we even sniff your drones on our six we'll open fire. We are fully authorised by YOUR government to do so. DO YOU UNDERSTAND, NatSec Alpha Zero?*

The controller's voice wavered. *Your presence is unauthorised, VENDETTA Four-Seven Actual. This airspace falls under UK law enforcement jurisdiction. Please change course.*

Bullshit – consult your chain of command. We're locked

and loaded. VENDETTA Four-Seven Actual OUT.

It was as if the night itself roared and wailed, something blocking out the moonlight. The leaguers stared in disbelief at the ugly war-machine hovering overhead. "Aztecs," said Lottie.

"Huh?"

"This is what it must have been like, the first time they saw a Conquistador galleon."

The sky was filled by the Warhawk's mottled grey fuselage, VTOL thrusters belching blue flame. Hooker made out the stars and stripes on the tail array, stubby cannon tracking targets across the roof. A voice boomed from loudspeakers. *Rufus Hooker? This is the United States Marine Corps. Is our national with you?*

"You American?" asked Hooker.

"No."

"Then pretend," Hooker replied, staggering from cover, arms raised. He pointed at Lottie and nodded. With a metallic whisper, smart munitions raked the roof. The leaguer shield wall ceased to exist, replaced by a scorched expanse of butchery.

Lottie Rhys fell to her knees, mouth bubbling with bloody spittle. Armoured figures descended on fast-ropes, weapons ready. Snapping Lottie into a harness, they swooped back to the strike boat's belly like trapeze artists. Another squad descended and found the roof hatch, where a marine readied a long-snouted flamethrower. With a hiss, liquid fire streamed into the void below. The marine was like a pest controller, calm and indifferent.

Gauntleted hands seized Hooker's arms. "You're gonna be fine," said a marine, voice robotic through helmet comms. "We got a corpsman on board. He'll patch you up good, okay?"

"Lottie's American?" Hooker replied. He scanned the marine's mud-coloured armour, spotting the stars-and-stripes on his breastplate.

"'Guess she is now."

"Vasquez, this guy needs a doctor," said a second marine, pulling a trauma pack from her fighting rig. She pressed in gently to Hooker's chest. "There you go."

Hooker mumbled his thanks, painkiller pumping into his body. Then he was aloft, strapped to a marine and hauled inside the strike boat. Two medics worked on Lottie, a third setting up an intravenous drip. "What the fuck is this kid *on?*" said one of the corpsmen.

"Combat respirocite," Hooker replied. "She took it maybe ten or fifteen minutes ago."

"What type of juice?"

"All I know is our Apex teams use it."

The medic nodded. "Brits? Kolyndrinol 4-70," he replied. "We got downers for that kinda shit."

"Is she going to be OK?" Hooker croaked. "She's pregnant."

The medic rolled his eyes, "ain't ever heard of Kolyndrinol proscribed to moms-to-be." Painkillers wrapped Hooker in silk. He was only dimly aware of the corpsman, plucking shrapnel from his flesh and inserting an IV line. Medical equipment chirruped urgently, voices demanding updates across radio nets.

Engines screaming, the strike boat circled the Crosland Estate. Fires flickered at the Commune International's windows, figures desperately swarming down scaffolding. Leaguers capered on the plaza below, jostling prisoners towards trucks and lorries. Beyond the estate, in the shadows, columns of NatSec carriers waited. "That shit down there? Man, that reminds me of Detroit in '42," said a door-gunner, hawking over the side of the deck.

The marine next to him shook his head. "This shit just reminds me of the world."

THIRTY

"Mister Hooker? You got visitors," said the nurse, a young African-American in baby-blue scrubs. He checked a monitor, nodded approvingly and tapped something into a pad. He wore some kind of advanced body-tech Hooker had never seen before, arms covered in tiny screens. Machines whirred and hummed gently overhead.

"Visitors?" Hooker replied. Monitors beeped, tubes snaking from his arms and chest. A CCTV camera watched from the ceiling, the squelch of a personal radio audible in the corridor outside. Hooker's body tingled, bisected by post-surgery scars – thin red marks criss-crossed his tattoos, demons slashed asunder by scalpels. His arm ached, but he could flex it.

"Don't ask me, I just work here," the nurse shrugged, straightening a blanket and dabbing away an invisible spot of dust. "An' stop movin' that arm, you've broken it. It won't heal right if you keep messin' with your traction sleeve."

"Is the girl okay?"

"Sir, I don't know anythin' 'bout no girl." He tut-tutted and left, data rolling across the screens embedded in his forearm.

The first visitor was the UK Minister for Resilience and Reconstruction, Damon Rhys MP. Hooker recognised him instantly – deep tan, silvery-gold hair just-so. He wore a black Nehru jacket, a silver party badge pinned to his breast. "I hope you're well, Mister Hooker. Thanks *so* much for agreeing to meet me."

"I didn't agree to meet you."

"Quite," the second visitor replied. American, voice a smoker's growl. Like Rhys, she wore black. Little blue eyes glittered in a waxy face, hair worn in a tight bun. "I'm Elisabeth Munro. US State Department."

"You mean CIA?" Hooker sniffed. "I ain't totally stupid. Where am I?"

Munro looked slowly around the room. "RAF Topford May, the US Airforce medical facility." Topford May was tucked in a safe corner of Wessex. The aircraft that bombed North Africa and Italy flew from its windswept runways, as did the strike boats that carried commandos to Belarus and Red Kyiv.

"How long have I been here?"

"A week," the American replied.

"NatSec were holding Leah Martinez," Hooker replied. "Vassa Hyatt promised she'd get her released."

Damon Rhys held up a hand, his smile warm. An

honest broker gesture Hooker recognised from TV interviews. "Vassa was good as her word. Miss Martinez was released, just before you were rescued. She's making an excellent recovery."

"Where is she now?"

"The Green Zone – a private clinic, of course. You should also know the officer responsible for her interrogation, Chief Superintendent Bliss, has been relieved of his duties. I spoke to the Home Secretary personally when I discovered what happened…"

Hooker scowled. The monitor tracking his blood pressure bleeped. "It was an Office of Counter-Subversion operation. They're part of NatSec. Only the Home Secretary can authorise torture."

Munro wrinkled her nose at the '*T*' word.

"I'm afraid NatSec enjoys considerable influence inside London's political administration." Rhys replied. His tongue darted to the corner of his mouth, reminding Hooker of a lizard. "I agree with you entirely, but perhaps we should fight one battle at a time."

"*We?*" said Hooker.

Munro fixed Hooker with an undertaker's stare. "In times like these, Mister Hooker, you choose a side. Otherwise a side will choose you."

"I'm on a side," said Hooker. "*My* side."

Munro sighed. "I'm told you were hired to simply locate the girl, not attempt a rescue. I had to engineer a diplomatic incident to put things right."

"Lady, fuck off," Hooker replied. "It wasn't as if Bliss gave me a choice. I hope Lottie's okay – she saved my life."

"You can't talk to me like that."

"I just did."

Rhys' face hardened. "Enough – the both of you. As for my daughter, she reacted badly to the respirocite *you* gave her, Mister Hooker. Nonetheless, I'm assured she's going to recover. She's in hospital, in Wessex."

"And her baby?"

Munro and Rhys exchanged glances. "Too early to call," Munro replied carefully. "Did she say much about the pregnancy?"

"There wasn't time, one of the kidnappers mentioned it before she died. I think it was how they got to Lottie in the first place."

"I'm grateful for your interest in Charlotte's welfare," said Rhys. "She's at a difficult age. Suffice to say, any disagreements we had are now resolved. You were hired to do a job, and you did it. Given the circumstances, I cannot ask for more."

Munro gave a nod, "I'll concede you were resourceful, Hooker."

Hooker sat up, wincing at the effort. "And it was a smart move, making Lottie a US citizen."

Rhys took Munro's hand and kissed it. "Elisabeth's idea. Quite brilliant, and of course I'm deeply obliged."

Munro almost smiled. "Thank you, Damon."

Hooker took a sip of water. "Okay, what happens now?"

"After you were rescued, Lottie was unable to say much about what happened up there," said Rhys, pulling up a chair. "The respirocite interfered with her short-term memory, which is probably just as well…"

Hooker rolled the dice. "I suppose you're here about

Paolo Falcone and Operation MADRIGAL."

Munro's mouth made a thin, tight line. Finally, she spoke. "The doctors tell me your brain scan shows activity consistent with receiving a neural uplift in the past forty-eight hours. You've also got a puncture mark in the nape of your neck."

"We know *you* know," said Rhys. He rested a hand on Hooker's forearm. "What precisely was Falcone's mission? The ransom note told us virtually nothing."

Munro studied a fingernail. "Paolo Falcone's real name was Howard Glass. Before defecting to the Crimson Brigade, he was CIA-CTAG. Counter-Transhuman Activities Group."

Hooker laughed. "What a bloody web you people weave. He was one of yours?"

"He defected years ago. Had we found him, we'd have assassinated him. What was on the neural uplift?"

"I get it now," Hooker replied, smiling at Munro. "He's good cop, you're bad cop."

"This isn't helpful," said Munro.

"Paolo believed in what he was doing," Hooker replied. "He wanted people to know the truth."

"He was a dangerous fanatic."

"I'll grant you that, but you're wondering if I fobbed anything about MADRIGAL before I was rescued. I s'pose there was too much comms traffic for NatSec to intercept *everything*. And even *if* they did, would they share it with you?"

Munro sneered. "Two things, Hooker. First of all, you had your ass hauled out of there by the *United States* Marine Corps. Secondly, don't underestimate the NSA's signals intel capability."

"I don't, not for a second. But here you are, asking me anyway."

"What was on the neural uplift?"

Hooker closed his eyes. Suddenly his head ached. "I told you, details of Operation MADRIGAL."

"If you want to play tough guy, there are techniques to remove it," Munro replied.

"You mean a lobotomy?" Hooker shot Rhys a look. "We *are* on British soil, ain't we?"

"Elisabeth, there's no need for threats," Rhys said smoothly. "Mister Hooker, let's be reasonable. You saved my daughter's life, and I'm grateful…"

"I'm more interested in my deal with Vassa Hyatt," Hooker replied. "Wessex. Money. My name off the Sanctioned Persons' Index."

"We'll get to that soon," Rhys replied. "Before we do, there are decisions to be made around your knowledge of MADRIGAL. How do we move this forward?"

"*Move forward* my ass," Munro hissed. "Hooker, did you or did you not disseminate the material you received via neural uplift to any third parties prior to your extraction?"

"How old are you, Miss Munro?" Hooker replied. "Forty-five? You were a student during the Emergencies, right?"

"The past *is* the future," Munro sighed.

"Which is why you're still killing, to cover-up someone else's mistake?"

"I've only killed to stop my country falling to pieces. And occasionally yours, Hooker."

"The MADRIGAL affair opens old wounds," said Rhys. "By the time the Americans admitted MADRIGAL to us, it was too late. We couldn't *uninvent* RXP. Archangels were, and indeed are, a fact of life. The question is this – how do we best exploit their skills to rebuild what was lost?"

Munro nodded her agreement. "We've put trillions of dollars into ATLAS, helping stitch your country back together again. Hell, we made a big mistake. Now we're paying for it. We learnt that lesson in the Middle East."

"And the Archangels?" Hooker replied. "Is it true? They're coming back? You're fools if you think you can control them."

Rhys fidgeted with his cuff. "We have a miniscule group of transhumans advising us. They're the same people who helped defeat the *December 13th* plotters. Good people, Rufus. The earlier iterations of the technology were dangerous. It played with peoples' minds…"

"The first version of RXP gave many users a God-complex," said Munro. "It won't happen again. Not with the latest version. We've developed fail-safes."

Hooker closed his eyes. *Brood-mare*, that's what Paolo called Lottie. A womb of impeccable quality, carrying the next generation of the elite. Archangels who could give birth to superhumans. He slowly opened his eyes. "I made my decision on the flight out of the Goons."

Damon Rhys gripped the rail on Hooker's gurney. "What do you mean?"

"If MADRIGAL got out, will the Yanks stop sendin' Reconstruction money?"

"Yes," Rhys replied, looking queasy. "Without US

support, London would fall. The insurgents would be able to target Wessex. I imagine NatSec would try to mount a coup d'état to extend the fighting south and north. There'd be another Hate War."

"Our intel analysts broadly agree," Munro shrugged. "In fact, they believe Damon's scenario is optimistic. Our projections see the dispossessed marching on an already frail Western Europe, emboldening the NuSoviets. Eventually, our economic recovery falters. The Latin-Pacific Alliance begin arming the militias in our succession states. That's another civil war, and America's just finished her second. We don't need another."

"So why not kill me?" said Hooker, "if there's so much at stake?"

Munro nodded. "That's a darn good point. I've sent men across the Styx for less."

Damon Rhys steepled his fingers. "Decisions concerning Mister Hooker's fate are *mine* to make." For a moment, the politician looked his age, "I still believe in the values that brought me into politics."

He'd heard Rhys use similar words at the first Reconciliation Tribunal. Hooker nearly smiled. "I'm keeping my mouth shut, Mister Rhys. I was too injured to fob anything, and the neural uploads would've been destroyed in the fire. I saw a marine empty a flamethrower into the place."

"What do you mean?" said Munro.

"I'm taking what I know to the grave. Whenever that time comes, sooner or later."

Rhys stood, switching on a megawatt smile. "I'm delighted with your decision, Rufus. You don't mind if I call you Rufus, do you?"

"And that's *it*?" said Munro. "Washington expects a report. Preferably with no ambiguity…"

"There is none. Mister Hooker has chosen a side, and in this affair there are only two. Where's the ambiguity? Furthermore, I'm appointing him to my staff. He can work with Miss Hyatt – you'll find that gives him legal protection from any extradition agreements."

"Extradition?" said Hooker sharply, although an American prison was almost more tempting than taking orders from Hyatt.

"It crossed my mind," said Munro.

"Well, that's not happening. If necessary, I'll speak with President Lawlor myself," said Rhys, offering Munro his hand. "Thanks for your help, Elisabeth, especially with Lottie's passport."

The American sighed. "As you wish, Damon. I'll see Mister Hooker discharged as soon as possible."

Hooker swung his legs out of bed. "No need, I'm discharging myself. I want to see Leah."

"I'm sure you do," said Rhys easily. "I have a copter waiting, if you need a ride back to London."

Hooker grabbed his clothes, laundered but tattered, from a locker. "Thanks, *Damon*. I think I will."

THIRTY ONE

Hampshire
Wessex Secure Zone

The graveyard lay next to a medieval church, gargoyles peering from the eaves. Beatriz was christened here, nineteen years and a lifetime ago, church steps scattered with cherry blossom, Sara's parents ignoring Hooker. His father was nowhere to be seen, his mother dead. Some of the guests wore uniforms, volunteers in the military and emergency services. The War was banished for the day, to celebrate the Hookers first-born.

He'd cradled Beatriz in his arms, a tiny thing, eyes fixed on his. She never cried, even at the font. Just gurgled happily, opening and closing her pudgy fingers. Hooker walked among the headstones, moss-furred granite, names carved deep. He knelt and traced the letters with a calloused finger.

SARA ALICE HOOKER
loving daughter and mother, taken tragically from us.
Aged 36 YRS.

BEATRIZ ELIZABETH HOOKER
sleeps forever with the angels.
Aged 8 YRS.

Hooker felt like an intruder in this place of ghosts and memories, of things unseen and unsaid. Pulling the mezuzah from inside his shirt, he kissed it before pressing it into the soil next to Beatriz's headstone. Catching his breath, he placed a wreath on each grave. Peonies for Beatriz, a wreath of primrose and lilies for Sara.

The wind tore a petal from a flower, sending it to dance on the wind. "I'm sorry. You never told me they were dead," said Leah, voice a near-whisper. She wore a dark trench coat, hair dyed crow-black.

Hooker's fingers gripped Beatriz's gravestone, cold in the shadows despite the sun. "I was in prison when they died. Beatriz had a respiratory illness. Y'know, from the bomb-dust. They wouldn't release me for the funeral - said there weren't enough guards."

Leah held Hooker's hand. "How did Sara die?"

"After Beatriz's funeral she ran a hot bath, drank a bottle of vodka and cut her wrists."

"I'm sorry, Rufus."

"War. We all lost people."

"My parents just disappeared. There's no grave," Leah

replied. The wind made her good eye water. Under a patch was a newly-fitted optical implant, replacing the eye lost under torture. "Maybe it's better that way?"

"Not for me," Hooker replied, knees creaking as he stood. "I needed to see them at least once. I wanted them to be buried in London, but this is where Sara's family came from. They didn't care I wasn't allowed in Wessex."

"Are Sara's parents dead?" asked Leah hopefully.

Hooker shook his head. "They sat out the war in Canada, but Sara wouldn't go. They came from money, didn't like their daughter marrying a black ex-squaddie from Woolwich."

Leah smiled. A different smile from usual. Warm, even. "You never told me. Y'know, how you two met?"

Early autumn leaves swirled in the breeze, one perching on the gravestone for a moment. "After I left the army I worked on the knife-arch at a school. Sara was an English teacher, we caught each other's eye I suppose. When the Emergencies started, I volunteered for the Taskforces. We decided to get married and have kids - it was a wartime thing."

"My mum said that once, people were getting hitched all over the place. They thought the world would end."

"I loved Sara. And I killed her, didn't I? She was ashamed of me, Leah. She died of *shame*."

Leah went on tiptoe, fingers snaking around the back of Hooker's neck. She kissed him, lips cold. Her tongue, though, was warm. "The Emergencies killed her, Rufus. Not you."

Rufus tried not to look surprised. "That sounds like an excuse."

"The things you did, during the war. Where they that

bad?"

Hooker shrugged. "It was called the Hate War for a reason. Gordy always used to say *you can't pick up a turd from the clean end.*"

"Was that it? Making amends? You know, rescuing kids from the shops an' all that."

Hooker nodded. "When I got out of prison, me an' some other veterans decided to close down the shops. Make the No-Zone less shit, seein' as we couldn't live anywhere else." Hooker looked beyond the gravestones, over hills and fields and forests. Wessex was so *green.*

"I think Rhys is guiltier than you," Leah replied. She kissed Hooker again, this time on the cheek.

"Rhys lives where the air is clean. He always will."

Leah reached into her coat and pulled out a flask. "Here, this is the good stuff," she said.

Hooker took a sip. Cognac. "Thanks, that's good."

"No, thank you."

"Why?"

Leah took a pull from the flask, wincing her approval. "I've learnt more about you in the last five minutes than I have in the last five years."

Hooker brushed Leah's cheek with a calloused finger. "Right, let's finish what we came here to do…"

Leah looked at the graves. "D'you need more time?"

Hooker touched Beatriz's stone, tears pricking his eyes. "We've work to do. Promises to keep."

Their boots crunched on gravel as they left the church. A muddy Land Rover pulled up. "Get in," said Gordy Rice. "Was everything okay up there?"

"Did what I needed to do," Hooker replied, climbing in next to his old boss. "You've located the package?"

"This bloody ridiculous. Rufus, we could go back to London and forget the whole thing…"

"I took a job. I'm finishing it."

"Not like this," Gordy replied.

"Hey, Gordy, think of it as your good deed for the day," said Leah, tapping the patch on her face. "I mean, I lost an *eye*."

"And I paid for a new one," Gordy grumbled.

"An implant? Nah, ain't the same," Leah replied, a smile playing across her black-painted lips. "I mean, my modelling career is completely *fucked*."

"Not now, Martinez, for Christ's sake," Gordy grumbled. They drove through a forest. A curious deer watched from the trees, munching grass.

"Where are we?" said Leah.

"Hampshire," said Gordy, accepting the flask and taking a swig. "The Wessex PROTEX is eight miles due north of the next turnoff. Trashmob's on the way to the RV now."

"Okay," Hooker replied, checking his watch. "His transit pass is good?"

Gordy smiled, pleased with his skulduggery. "It's a genuine contract – Gloucester to Holyhead, fragile cargo escort. North Wales went tits-up again. This is the return leg. He'll need to check in through the Heathrow Gate, but I've got that covered."

"Must have cost you," said Leah, rubbing her fingers together.

Gordy grimaced. "Bloody fortune, pet."

"A deal's a deal," Hooker replied.

Leah finished the cognac. "Hey, Gordy, did Hyatt pay up?"

"Damon Rhys did," Gordy sighed. "Don't worry, Martinez. You'll get paid, less what it cost me to bribe the watch commander at the Heathrow Gate. That's only fair, given the bloody stupidity of what we're doing out here."

Leah scowled, and Hooker laughed. Gordy stopped the Land Rover and pulled a fob from his pocket. "I'm pinging the signal, two hundred metres east. The package is static."

"Right on time," said Hooker. Opening a bag, he pulled out a long-barrelled pistol. Satisfied it was loaded, he slid it inside his coat pocket.

Leah took the fob from Gordy. Hopping out of the Land Rover, she pulled a vintage Glock-19 from her bag. Hooker followed her along a track and over a three-bar gate. Beyond lay a bridle path, threaded through a knot of lush conifers. Leah watched a glowing icon on the pad. "Ten metres," she whispered. "Along that path."

"There's the mutt," said Hooker, pulling the pistol from his pocket.

The dog was a Jack Russell, white with black patches. It scurried towards Leah and sniffed around her feet, stumpy tail wagging. "Hello boy," she whispered, patting its head. Rolling on its back, the dog presented its pinkish belly.

Hooker moved quietly, tree-to-tree, pistol ready. The air smelt damp and clean, the only sound the rush of wind through leaves.

"Where's that bloody dog?" said a voice.

"Chasing rabbits. He'll be back soon, Jason," a young woman replied. "I won't be a moment, honest. This spot is the only place in the wood I can get a fob signal."

"No problem. It's just I know that dog…"

Hooker stepped from behind a tree, aimed, and fired. The weapon hissed, a glittering dart hitting the man in the back of the neck. He spun, hand reaching inside his jacket. Hooker fired again, a second dart hitting his arm. A third bit into his thigh, a fourth the back of his hand. The man slumped to the ground, unconscious.

"Will he be okay?" said Lottie Rhys. She wore old denim jeans and hiking boots. Her fisherman's jumper was fitted enough to show the swell of her belly.

Hooker nodded. "He'll be fine. The darts are tipped with military-grade Haloxyline. He'll sleep like a baby for twelve hours. I'll make him comfortable, then we'll go."

Lottie pulled the slumbering bodyguard's gun, unloaded it and tossed it into the trees. Her fob followed, along with its giveaway GPS signal. Reaching into some bushes, she pulled out a bulky rucksack. "I didn't think you'd come, Hooker."

"I promised."

"Rapunzel, Rapunzel, let down your hair!" said Lottie.

"Huh?"

Lottie Rhys smiled. "It doesn't matter. I've had my scan."

"How'd it go?"

"They're trying to pretend everything's normal, but *six* doctors attending a routine pregnancy scan? It's a boy, in excellent health. I heard one of the doctors whisper he's growing fifteen percent faster than normal."

"And then?"

"Dad said they'll put the baby in a special home until I'm ready to look after it. In America, naturally."

"More bullshit, right?"

Lottie nodded. "I believe what the terrorists told me, about Tristian Gramercy. It makes complete sense."

They reached Leah, the little dog tucked under her arm. "You've decided to keep the baby?" she said.

"This is Leah," said Hooker. "She's a tendency to ask direct questions."

"Charlotte Rhys," said Lottie, offering Leah her hand. "I was sorry to hear about your eye."

A shrug. "Shit happens. They bought me a new one."

Lottie tucked her hair behind an ear and made a silly face for the dog. "I'm not sure what sort of mother I'll make, but my baby isn't growing up like a laboratory rat."

Hooker thought the girl brave. He squeezed her shoulder. "It's gonna be okay, Lottie. Tough, maybe, but okay."

The dog yapped excitedly as the girl hugged it. "The three of us are going on an adventure," she said, ruffling its ears.

A tight-lipped Gordy drove them away, Lottie hidden behind privacy-glassed windows. They parked thirty minutes later, in an old farmyard. "Now we wait," he said.

Soon they heard heavy diesel engines. Three armoured PROTEX escort carriers, grey-painted monsters covered in riot mesh, liveried ECHO-SEVEN in gothic script. Old Union flags flew from whip aerials, equipment stowed on turrets. A hatch in the nearest vehicle's cab swung open. "Wessex might be green, but fuck me it's boring," said a wiry man in combat gear.

"Trashmob, good to see you," Hooker replied.

"This is the package?" he said, nodding at Lottie.

"She needs to get to the Answerer's monastery at Northwood," said Hooker. "They'll take her tomorrow night, ask for Brother Ranjit."

"Where exactly?" said Lottie, slipping a lead around the Jack Russell's neck.

"The Answerer's have a commune, up near York. They've got midwives and a nursery. You'll be safe until you decide what you want to do next." Hooker had done the deal with Brother Ranjit, the young monk intrigued and excited at the opportunity to help a woman carrying an archangel.

"These are your new ID permissions," said Gordy, passing Lottie a leather wallet. "There's now't we can do about the biometrics at the moment, so keep your bloody head down."

Lottie gave Trashmob a plastic card. "As agreed. Login, security code and crypto-key for my father's investment account. I'd empty it now, before they notice I've gone."

"Bleep's ready to do the deed, soon as you fob him," said Hooker. The OCS threatened the infomancer with torture, but Bleep simply laughed and promised to enjoy it. His lawyers were already working on a hefty settlement for false arrest.

"I'll be calling the freak soon as we hit the road," Trashmob grinned, opening the carrier's armoured side door. "Hop in, love. Mercy here will look after you."

The girl Hooker and Leah saved from the Mare Street shop lounged inside the carrier. Dressed in fighting gear, a carbine across her lap. She waved at Hooker, smiling. Hooker waved back. "How's she working out?"

"Mercy? She's a vicious little bastard with the morals of a hyena," Trashmob replied, kneading his chin. "Basically, she's perfect."

Mercy opened a panel in the carrier's hull, revealing a hidden compartment. "You must get inside when we near the checkpoint," Mercy said to Lottie. "It will not be for long."

Lottie nodded. She turned to Hooker and smiled. "Will you come and see us?"

"Er, sure. When it's safe," he replied, not expecting the question. "Now go."

"I'm going to call him Rufus," said Lottie. "The baby, not the dog."

Leah chuckled. Hooker tried to find words, but couldn't. Just took the girl's hand and squeezed. Trashmob climbed inside the cab and revved the engine. The convoy motored away in a cloud of filthy smoke. Gordy checked his watch. "Your Wessex permissions run out tomorrow, but I'd get out now. When Rhys finds out she's missing, he'll come looking."

Leah shrugged. "They'll look for her, Hooker. You know they will."

"They can't prove it was us," Hooker shrugged. "Anyhow, her kid deserves better than being brought up as an experiment. If Lottie needs me again, I'll take her somewhere else."

Gordy shook his head. "Lunacy, Rufus."

Hooker shot his old boss a look. "I did six years in prison rather than rat you out, Gordon. Now that's lunacy."

"So you keep reminding me," Gordy muttered. "I'll let you know what Rhys is up to next, and I'll get you alibis for today. But this is dangerous stuff. Bloody Archangels…"

"If we're going to have 'em breed, let them be raised like anyone else," Hooker shrugged. "Let 'em be kids. Learn about normal people."

Leah nodded, good eye locked on Gordy's. "I agree. Fuck their superman program."

"I'm glad we all see it the same way," Hooker replied, sniffing the air. It smelt of manure. "The countryside's overrated. I dunno 'bout you two, but I'm going back to work. There's a new shop near Essford needs closing."

"I dunno. Gordy's funding me to start my own company," said Leah. "Ain't you, Mister Rice?"

Gordy grimaced. "PROTEX companies are like throwing good money after bad. D'you know how much three of those escort wagons cost?"

"Four," Leah corrected. "And six technicals."

Hooker smiled. "Like I said, a deal's a deal."

Leah touched her new eye. "Mind you, it might look suspicious, me rolling in dough so soon after the girl went missing again."

"Yeah, I make you right," said Hooker.

Leah squeezed the big man's hand. "So mebbe I can help you close that shop? For old time's sake."

Hooker turned up his collar against the wind, eyes narrowed against the watery Wessex sun. "I appreciate that. Let's go to work."

Printed in Great Britain
by Amazon

74601716R00192